A Knight Two-in-One Special Edition

JILL'S GYMKHANA
A STABLE FOR JILL

Enjoy the first two adventures
in the Jill pony series

JILL'S GYMKHANA

Jill's Gymkhana

Ruby Ferguson

KNIGHT BOOKS
Hodder and Stoughton

This Jill Two-in-One Special Edition first published 1990

This edition 1994

ISBN 0 340 61940 6

Text copyright © 1949, 1993 Hodder and Stoughton Ltd.

Jill's Gymkhana

First published in a single volume by
Hodder and Stoughton, 1949

10 9 8 7 6 5 4 3 2 1

A catalogue record for this title
is available from the British Library

Printed and bound in Great Britain by
Cox & Wyman Ltd, Reading, Berkshire

Hodder and Stoughton Children's Books
A Division of Hodder Headline plc
338 Euston Road
London NW1 3BH

Contents

1 My dream

Just look at that title! You see, I am the Jill concerned, and quite honestly if anyone had told me three years ago that anything so terrific as a gymkhana would ever be associated with my name I should have thought them completely mad. Yet such was to be my destiny.

(That lovely phrase is not my own, I got it out of a library novel that Mummy is reading.)

I was only eleven, three years ago, when Mummy and I came to live at Pool Cottage, Chatton, and I quickly noticed that for all the children in that part of the world the one thing seemed to be riding. Every day I would hear the clop of many hoofs coming nearer, and I would rush to the window and see a riding school go by with a string of ponies ridden by children of all ages from six to sixteen.

So after a while I said, 'Oh, Mummy, do you think I could possibly have riding lessons? All the children here seem to ride.'

Mummy sighed, and then she said, 'Jill, I hate to have to, but you know what I'm going to say, don't you?'

'Yes,' I said. 'We can't afford it. OK.'

And that was that.

Now before we go any further I had better say that if you are blasé about ponies you had better put this book down, because you will be infuriated to find that most of it is about a beginner, namely Me. And the same thing applies if you are one of those people who was practically born in the saddle; or if you ride nothing but blood ponies; or if you happen to be the fastest woman over timber in East Woldshire; or if your father buys all his horses at Tattersall's. It will be too simple for you. You see, my pony – but I'm going miles ahead.

When my father was alive we lived in a white house that was big and rambling, at the foot of a hill in Wales. Daddy didn't ride, but he loved horses above all animals. When we went out for a walk he would never pass a field with a horse in it, but he would call the horse and somehow it would come to him, and he would stroke its nose and talk to it, and it was almost as though he and the horse knew each other's language.

One day when my father was stroking a horse's nose a farmer came by and said, 'Look-you-now!' (Which is a Welsh way of saying Gosh.) The reason was that this particular horse was supposed to be a nasty creature that its owner couldn't do anything with. But my father could, and that was why the farmer said, 'Look-you-now!'

So I naturally grew up with the idea that horses were animals to be fond of, and Daddy promised that someday I should have riding lessons. But just about then he had to go to West Africa on business for his firm, and later we got a cable to say that he had fever. And he never came back to us.

Unfortunately there was very little money for Mummy and me, so Mummy sold our house and with what money she had she bought Pool Cottage at Chatton – which is quite a decent place really – and then she only had the little that was left and what she got from writing her children's books.

We had only just come to Chatton and our cottage was actually about two miles from the shops, and we didn't know anybody and it was still the summer holidays, so apart from helping Mummy with beds and dusting and things like that I hadn't much to do. Mummy did things in the house every morning and cooked the dinner; and after dinner she got out her typewriter and settled down to work while I just went out and meandered about.

Not very far from our cottage there was a farm, and next to the farm was a paddock, and in the paddock was a piebald pony. He was sturdy but graceful, about fourteen hands, with a nice action and a very intelligent face; but his mane and tail were ragged and he looked a bit out of condition. This wasn't surprising when I discovered from observation that he spent his entire life in that paddock and nobody ever exercised him, or even worked him, or seemed to bother with him at all.

One day when I was leaning over the gate, as I got into the habit of doing, I called the pony in the way Daddy used to call. He lifted his head from cropping and looked at me, but he didn't come. However I persevered, and at last he came up to within about two yards of me, looked at me in a puzzled way, and then with rather a disappointed expression turned away.

Of course! I ought to have brought him something. I rushed home, and shouted, 'Mummy! Can I take some lump sugar for a pony up the road?'

Mummy said, 'Oh, must you! I'm right in the middle of a sentence . . . I don't think the farmers like you to give them sugar, dear, but there are some carrots in a bag in the scullery. Wash them first . . . oh, I've forgotten how that sentence was going to end now!'

I took three of the best carrots, washed them under the tap, and went charging back to the paddock on my bike. I was quite excited when I hung over the gate and called to the pony. To my surprise he came at once, at a lovely trot. When he was about two yards away he stood still, as he had done before, but this time I held out my hand with the carrot placed temptingly on my open palm. His face lighted up, as you know ponies' faces do. He looked simply thrilled, and he came and took the carrot gently while his velvety lips brushed my hand. There he stood chewing, sublimely happy, and while he chewed I stroked his nose and cheeks.

Then I gave him the other two carrots, and said goodbye, and rode off on my bike. I nearly over-balanced looking back, and he was standing at the gate looking longingly after me.

After that Mummy simply never had a carrot left; I took them all for Patchy, as I called him. Of course I told her I had more or less adopted this pony, and that now he recognised me as soon as my bike hove in sight, and he would stop cropping grass and dash to the gate to meet me and the carrots.

I asked her, too, to see if she could find out anything about Patchy and why his owner left him alone in that paddock all day; and at last the milkman told us that Farmer Clay had taken the pony in payment of a bad debt, thinking that perhaps his daughter would like to ride, but the girl didn't care about riding – can you imagine? I could just picture the stodgy thing! – so Farmer Clay being easy-going, Patchy just stayed in the paddock where he was and nobody bothered about him at all.

I went to see Patchy every day, sometimes twice, and the rest of the time, I just messed about and wished I knew somebody.

Then one day when I had reached the pony's gate I noticed that the farmer was in the paddock and was coming towards me. I thought perhaps he was angry, but he wasn't. He just said, 'Good day,' and I said, 'Good day,' and he said, 'You like the pony?' and I said, 'I should jolly well think I do.'

He said, 'I notice you've been round here a lot. That's a nice riding pony, well-mannered and plenty of spirit. Just right for you. Why don't you ask your Ma to buy him for you?'

The idea gave me such a shock that I goggled at him like a fish.

'He'd make a jumper, he would, if he was trained,' said Farmer Clay. 'A grand little pony and no mistake. You just ask your Ma what about it.'

My head was spinning round by now at the very thought of being able to own Patchy.

'How – how much would he cost?' I stuttered.

Farmer Clay thought for a minute.

'Well, shall we say five hundred pound? Five hundred pounds and that's a bargain, I can tell you. But he's on my hands, as you might say.'

Of course he might as well have said five thousand, or even twenty-five thousand.

'Thanks very much,' I said. 'I think I'd better be going home now.'

'You ask your Ma like I said.'

'Yes,' I said. 'Yes, I will.'

But as soon as I had got away I realised that I wouldn't, because I had enough sense not to worry

Mummy about something that was quite impossible. So I decided that I would never go and see Patchy again.

Four awful days went by. I didn't know what to do with the time, because I could only go to Chatton if I didn't want to pass Patchy's field, so I mooched about the house, plunged in blackest gloom. Then one night Mummy, who was very noticing, said, 'Has anything happened to your friend the pony, Jill?'

'How do you mean?' I said, turning red.

'Only that my carrot bag is quite full. You haven't been to see Patchy for days. Now there *is* something the matter! Out with it.'

So I shrugged my shoulders, and then told her all. When I had finished she said, 'Poor Jill, I wish I could buy you the pony, you know I do. But five hundred pounds! If I had that much money to spare I'd get the scullery floor relaid, or the garden dug over, and some apple trees put in, or a new roof for the hens, and the chimneys pointed, and – '

'I know, Mummy,' I said. 'It's OK. But, oh *gosh*, if I could only have had Patchy! You see, he's used to being out of doors and he could live in our orchard, and I'd look after him and everything.'

'He'd cost a lot to feed, especially in the winter.'

'I thought of that,' I said. (Actually I'd thought of everything in the silent watches of the night.) 'I thought I might lend him to one of the riding schools to use, on condition that they fed and stabled him in the winter.'

'You've never been taught to ride, Jill.'

'I could teach myself.'

'It isn't as easy as you think, and riding lessons are expensive.'

'Perhaps they would let me work at the riding

school, mucking out stables and so on, in return for riding lessons?'

Mummy shook her head.

'You know it's all impossible. Why are we talking about it? Oh dear, I wish you could have got interested in *anything* else but horses.'

2 Black Boy

I expect you have found out that life, usually so humdrum and school-dinner-ish, occasionally has magic spasms.

A few mornings later I was in the kitchen making the coffee for breakfast when I heard Mummy go to the door to meet the postman.

Suddenly she called out, 'Oh! Oh!' in an excited voice, so I went running and saw her standing at the door with a letter open in her hand.

'Oh, Jill!' she cried, 'what do you think? My agent has sold the rights of *The Little House of Smiles* and has sent me a cheque for three thousand pounds. Three thousand pounds that I never expected. And it's the very first of my stories ever to be serialised. I can hardly believe it!'

I could hardly believe it either, because frankly I always thought that *The Little House of Smiles* was quite the most revolting of Mummy's books. It was about a rather sickening little boy called Terry, who worked with his grandmother making smiles and packing them into cardboard boxes to send to people who hadn't any.

So I just said, 'Nice work, Mummy.'

While we were eating our breakfast she said, 'Three thousand pounds. I'm going to spend it on things we need. I shall get the scullery floor relaid, and the chimneys pointed, and maybe the hen house properly repaired, and I should *like* to buy a new gas cooker – '

'Yes, Mummy,' I said.

'Oh, Jill,' she said, '*you* shall have some of it for your very own, to buy what you like. I know it's extravagant and we can't afford it, but life can't be all pinching and scraping or there isn't any joy left. I'll give you – six hundred pounds for your own.'

I nearly passed out.

'Six hundred pounds! Mummy! Oh crumbs!'

And then we both had the same thought.

'Oh, Mummy!' I cried. 'Can I? Can I have Patchy?'

'I think we're a bit mad,' she said, 'but I suppose you can *if* you can feed him and care for him properly.'

So that very morning, after Mummy had been to the bank, I went along to Farmer Clay's and told him what I had never thought I should be able to tell him, that Mummy said I could buy Patchy for five hundred pounds.

'Right!' he said cheerfully. 'He'll win you a lot of prizes, that pony will. Want to take him now?'

'Oh, yes, please,' I said.

So he brought Patchy from the paddock, and he said, 'Wait a minute,' and disappeared into the stable, and the next minute he came out carrying a saddle and bridle.

'I'll throw these in,' he said. 'They're a bit shabby but they'll do till you get something better.'

I was thrilled, because until then I hadn't even thought of tack and what it would cost me to buy it.

'What about fodder?' asked Farmer Clay. 'Shall I let you have some to be going on with?'

'Oh, what does he eat?' I asked.

'You'll want oats, bran, and chaff. See this measure? Give him about one and a half of oats, the same of bran, and a double handful of chaff. Mix it well together.'

So after Farmer Clay had put on Patchy's snaffle-bridle and saddle I paid him for the pony and the fodder.

'Patchy,' I said, patting my own pony for the first time, 'Patchy darling, you're mine.'

'Do you call him Patchy?' said the farmer. 'His real name's Black Boy.'

'I like that better,' I said.

'Well, up you get,' said Farmer Clay.

I went scarlet, because I had never mounted a pony; but he didn't notice, and with a laugh he picked me up under his arm and placed me in the saddle.

The next moment I found myself riding – actually riding – down the lane. But it wasn't a bit like I thought it was going to be; I felt all wrong, and didn't know what to do with my hands and legs, and I went joggety-jog, and felt as though I was going to slip right over Black Boy's neck. And I simply prayed that he wouldn't break into a trot! But he walked along quite sedately and we got home at last.

Mummy was waiting at the gate.

'He's lovely,' she said. 'When you're tired of riding him, let's put him in the orchard and see how he likes it.'

'We'll put him in right away,' I said, 'while I find some bins for his fodder' – unfastening the bags which Farmer Clay had tied to the saddle.

But now I'm ashamed to say I was faced with a new difficulty. I didn't know how to unsaddle my pony and I didn't like to tell Mummy; so I fumbled about for ages while Black Boy looked at me in a surprised sort of way, and I'm sure I pinched him and thumped him though he was incredibly patient, and at last I got his wretched saddle off and the bridle too, though I couldn't imagine how I was ever going to get them on again.

In the afternoon I had a try, and a sorry mess I made of it. First I put the snaffle bit in his mouth, and then he spat it out, and then I tried to push his face into the cheek bands, and I simply won't go on with the sorry tale, for in the end Mummy came out to help and with her common sense and my brute force we got my pony more or less ready for me to mount.

I said mount, but it was a scramble rather than a mount. In the end even Black Boy lost his patience and walked off, with me as it were hanging between heaven and earth. I landed in the grass with a thud, and Mummy giggled like anything. So she helped me up, and caught Black Boy, and then she did what Farmer Clay had done and lifted me bodily into the saddle.

'Sit up straight,' she said.

So I rode up and down the lane outside our cottage most of the afternoon; at least when I say 'rode' I mean that my pony walked a bit and, realising that he could do anything he liked, stopped to crop grass, while I just sat there like a sack of potatoes, having no control over him whatsoever.

He started when he liked and he stopped when he liked; I was as bad as that. I pulled on the reins, as if I were trying my weight, and if Black Boy started I flattered myself that it was my doing, not realising that the poor thing was just trying to escape from this murderous woman who was jagging at his mouth. When I wanted him to stop I tugged away again, but it didn't stop him. He just arched his neck and rolled his eyes, and the next minute I was off and he was several yards away.

I am telling you this disgraceful story to show you how hopeless I was, in case anyone who reads this book is hopeless too. Of course if any hard woman to hounds has read thus far she will now be scarlet with rage and exasperation and probably trying to get me prosecuted.

But nobody could have been more disappointed than I was that first day I owned a pony. Riding had looked so easy when I saw the other children doing it. But you know how it is. I once went to Wimbledon and saw people play in the Lawn Tennis Championships, and the balls literally seemed to come right on to their rackets every time, so they couldn't have missed them if they tried. But when *you* try to do it, it doesn't work out that way at all. And it's the same with riding.

The next day, too, I was so stiff with using muscles that I didn't know I had that I just tottered about the house, and made a valiant attempt to laugh at myself as much as Mummy was laughing at me.

But inwardly I was feeling pretty low.

'Oh, gosh!' I thought. 'It isn't any use without riding lessons, and I'm never going to afford any. It will take everything I've got – and more – just to buy fodder for Black Boy, especially in the winter.'

But I wasn't going to worry about the future, when I had been so marvellously lucky as to get a pony at all; so I went jogging on, day after day, getting more used to the feel of riding, but doing everything wrong, and not knowing how to make Black Boy do the things I wanted him to do.

3 The Gymkhana

One day I saw a notice that there was to be a children's pony gymkhana the following Saturday, and I decided to go. I came away from that gymkhana sadder if not much wiser, after seeing quite small children doing the most marvellous things on ponies and riding them with a technique which left me gasping. But I'm going too far ahead.

I landed at the field on my bike a few minutes after two o'clock, and after buying an ice-cream I found a small gap at the side of the ring and worked my way in. All around me was green grass and blue sky, and wherever my eye roved it fell upon the noble Horse, which made me feel happy.

Judging was going on for the best rider under fourteen. There were twelve children in this event and they all looked frightfully good to me, as I gazed at them with the critical and envious eye of a pony-owner. They mounted and dismounted with perfect ease, ran beside their ponies, displayed a walk, trot, and canter, did a figure of eight, and unsaddled in about three swift, deft movements. I wriggled my toes inside my shoes, remembering my own awful struggles.

The first place went to a girl of about twelve on a grey pony, and I saw from my programme that she was called Susan Pyke and her pony was called Dear

Arab. The second place went to a boy and the third to another girl.

I was very interested when the stewards began to erect the jumps for the first jumping event, which was under-twelves. There were five jumps, a box-hedge, a gate, a wall, a stile, and finally a triple bar, and they all looked mountainous to me, though looking back from my present experienced state I suppose they were about seventy-five centimetres actually.

Then a voice from the amplifier said, 'All competitors for the under-twelve jumping in the ring, please,' and about fourteen children rode in on very keen-looking ponies. They rode their ponies up to each of the jumps in turn and let them see over the other side; then the ring was cleared and the first competitor came in.

She was only about ten and very nervous. Her pony refused at the first jump, and then jumped too late and brought wads of hedge down. People laughed and the girl looked hot and worried. At the second jump her pony caught his hind feet and brought everything clattering down, and at the third he refused three times and was disqualified. I felt so sorry for the girl, especially when nobody clapped as she rode off except two fat ladies with bulgy handbags who I expect were her mother and her aunt.

Then a boy of about my age rode in and took the first three jumps marvellously; but, as you know, some ponies are so surprised by their own success that they lose their heads and begin bucking and fly-catching, and that is what this one did. He had two refusals at each of the last two jumps and knocked them both down as well, and the judge said, 'Fourteen faults.'

The next was the girl called Susan Pyke who had

won first place in the riding event, and she really did jump beautifully. I was wild with envy. It was like one of those radio quizzes where they ask you who, if not yourself, you would wish to be, and at that moment I would have given anything to be Susan Pyke. How, with the general queerness of life, I came to alter my opinion this book will tell you, if you have the patience to go on with it. I expect at this moment you are saying, 'Well, of all the feeble ways to describe a gymkhana – !' Yes, it is feeble, and I was feeble, and that is why I am telling you all frightfully feeble ideas.

Everybody had to be a beginner once, even a champion show-jumper though it is hard to imagine it. What I mean to say is, however exalted and beefy a person you may be in the equestrian world, you ought to be jolly humble. Because if you are not, something usually happens to you that makes you feel lower than the worms. I am thinking of a boy I once encountered at a show who was telling everybody how demeaning it was for him to be riding in such a squalid gymkhana when he was really used to places like Richmond or even Wembley. While saying this he took a practice jump over a hurdle and his girth actually broke, and he soared through the air and landed where some of the Fat Cattle had been. And you know what Fat Cattle are like at shows.

So though now I am a person of wide experience and some knowledge of horsemanship, I try not to be superior even to people who are very young and stand round the rails in cotton frocks looking envious. I expect you think this is just an awful lot of preaching, so I will continue with my story.

The girl called Susan Pyke finished her round with only two faults, and in the end she won first prize for this event, the second and third prizes being won by boys with three and three and a half faults respectively. I was so dumb that I didn't even know how faults were reckoned.

The under-sixteen jumping which followed was much more exciting, as the jumps were raised to one metre and the competitors were more experienced. After a while, even I could tell which ponies were going to jump well, for though full of spirit they had common sense as well which showed in their lovely but steady eyes. The 'silly' ponies turned out to be no good at all, and either refused the jumps or jumped too soon or too late.

Of course, some of the faults were due to the riders' bad horsemanship; they were not in absolute harmony with their ponies. It was obvious to even an onlooker like me that rider and pony had to have complete understanding of each other and confidence in each other before their jumping could be successful.

The first prize-winner was a thin girl with a long plait, and though handicapped by wearing glasses which glittered in the sun, she had a most skilful way of holding her pony in until the split second before he had to jump, then letting him go, giving him a businesslike Hup! and putting him over like a bird.

It was interesting to hear the onlookers' comments, and I listened hard because I wanted to learn.

There was one boy who soared up into the air at every jump, which knowing no better I thought looked very distinguished. He practically stood in his stirrups in midair, and then came back into the saddle with a bang. After this had happened twice, at the third jump the pony refused, once, twice, and a third time. The boy looked very crestfallen, for he was now disqualified and had to ride off the field.

'Do you blame the pony!' exclaimed a voice near me.

I looked round, and to my amazement realised that I was being addressed by a nice-looking man with a jolly face. He wasn't really ancient either, but somewhere about Mummy's age which was thirty-five.

'Why did he refuse?' I said, too interested to be shy or to remember putting-off things like not talking to strangers. 'I thought he was doing frightfully well.'

'If you were a pony,' he said, 'how would you like to have a great lump of a boy crash down on your back every time you jumped? The pony can't say he's had enough; he can only show it by a flat refusal to jump any more. You'd wonder where and by whom some of these people were taught. I hope the lad isn't your brother, by the way!'

'Oh, no, I don't know him,' I said. 'But I thought he was riding very well, and I wished I could do it, until the pony refused.'

'Don't you ever ride yourself?' he asked.

'I've got a pony,' I said, 'but it isn't the same thing.'

After the jumping came Musical Chairs which I thought was the best game I had ever seen.

The chairs were placed in a circle in the middle of the ring, and the competitors cantered cautiously round the outside of the ring until the music stopped playing. Then they had to dismount and rush to a chair pulling their ponies with them.

Some of the ponies knew the game well, and it was an education to me to see the way those children dismounted, simply flying out of their saddles.

The final tussle was between a boy and a girl who both dashed at the last chair together and fell in a heap while everybody laughed loudly; but when the judge picked them up the girl was underneath and actually hanging on to the chair, so she was the winner and the boy was second.

'What did you mean,' asked my new friend suddenly, 'when you said that having a pony wasn't the same thing as riding?'

And then, to my own amazement, because I don't usually chatter to strangers, I found myself telling him the whole story of Black Boy. He seemed terribly interested.

'I say!' he said. 'You'll have to learn to ride.'

'Well, I've got a few ideas this afternoon,' I said, 'but I feel frightfully discouraged because when I try to do things myself it won't be half so easy as it seems to those children.'

'How would it be,' he said, 'if I came round to your place one afternoon to see your pony? I might be able to help you a bit.'

'Oh,' I said, 'do you ride?'

'I did,' he said; and then for the first time I noticed that he was actually sitting in a wheelchair and his legs were covered with a rug.

I looked embarrassed, but he gave a smile.

'My legs don't act any more,' he said. 'Isn't it a swindle? You see, I was careless enough to fall out of a plane. By the way, my name's Martin Lowe.'

'Mine's Jill Crewe,' I said, 'and I live at Pool Cottage in Pool Lane. I'd be frightfully glad if you'd come round and see me ride – or try to – and so would Mummy.'

'Then that's all arranged,' he said. 'What's the next thing? Oh, the bending.'

The bending race consisted of riding in and out of lines of poles. It was really skilful because I could see that a child had to make the pony turn or 'bend' as close to the pole as possible so as not to lose distance. I couldn't imagine how this was done, as I told my new friend.

'Watch how that boy uses his legs and reins,' said he, 'and you'll soon get the idea. As he turns to the left he presses with his right leg and heel to keep the pony's quarters from swinging too far to the right and so losing his balance.'

From this I guessed that Martin Lowe knew what he was talking about.

Susan Pyke got the first prize in the bending race, and the second was a boy who had not won before.

I could not imagine a greater thrill in life than to receive one of the coloured rosettes to fasten on my pony's browband, and then to gallop round the ring with a certificate in my teeth. It must be heaven, I thought.

'I believe you're envious,' said Martin Lowe.

'Yes, I am,' I said, 'mad with envy. But I couldn't do it in a million years.'

'Of course you could,' he said rather sharply. 'These children you see winning prizes were not born on a pony's back. Two years ago some of them had never been in a saddle. But they *learned*, and I tell you it means work. Of course you can do it, you can do anything if you're patient and obedient and willing to learn and don't get the idea that you're marvellous as soon as you can make a pony obey your aids. We'll see!'

4 Martin

A day or two later I was idling about in the lane on Black Boy when to my horror I heard the sound of approaching hoofs and along came the riding school with their master, all at a beautiful collected trot. (I didn't know then that it was a collected trot, but I knew it looked right and whatever I was doing looked wrong.) I couldn't get out of the way; and just at that moment too, Black Boy chose to ignore my feeble rein-pulling and put down his head to crop grass.

All the children stared at me as they passed, and I recognised the girl called Susan Pyke who had done so well in the gymkhana. She gave me a scornful look, and then said something to her nearest neighbour, and they both started laughing. That set the others off, and even the riding master grinned and cast me a look full of superciliousness and disdain.

I felt myself go hot and red and my hands and feet felt enormous. When they had all gone by I knew I wouldn't have any more pleasure from my pony that day. I slid off his back in my usual awkward fashion and led him home, and then I went up to my room and sat on the bed and howled like a kid for ages. Because the most shattering thing in the world is being laughed at.

And then I thought, 'Oh, Jill, you are the most awful idiot. Fancy crying because you can't ride!

When all you've got to do is to learn how, like
Martin Lowe said. If other people can, you can.'

But these thoughts only made me howl still more,
because Martin Lowe seemed to have forgotten his
promise to come and see my pony.

I suppose I should have stayed there for hours,
sniffing away in the silly way one does when one is
only eleven, but I heard Mummy calling me down,
so I washed my face and hoped she wouldn't notice
anything.

'Oh, Jill,' she said when I came down, 'I'm so
frightfully busy with my new chapter. Do you think
you could possibly make the tea today?'

So I started to cut sandwiches and spread them with
chopped lettuce and cucumber, and that made me feel
better as honest toil always does.

The very next morning, which was Saturday, as
I was finishing the dismal daily task of making my
bed, I happened to glance out of the window and
there was Martin Lowe wheeling himself in at our
gate in his chair.

I made one wild dash downstairs and met him at
the door.

'Oh, I thought you were never coming,' I said.

'Did you mind so much?' he said. 'I'm very sorry if
it seemed a long time. I caught a chill at the gymkhana
– sounds feeble, but there it is – and had to stay in bed
for a few days. But now I'm here and I want to see
that pony.'

I introduced him to Mummy, and then we all went
out to the orchard. I was feeling rather worried,
wondering whether Black Boy would deign to come
when I called him. Lately, realising that I was a pretty
hopeless person, he had begun to play me up and
would give me a cheeky look from his soft black

eye, as much as to say, 'Come and make me do it, if you can!'

So I led the way to the orchard with my fingers crossed, and wondering if I could summon up a loud commanding tone.

There was my pony, swishing his tail gently under the farthest apple tree. He looked up with surprise when he saw three of us coming, and I think it was curiosity which fetched him rather than my plaintive cry. Anyway, he came, and I felt like saying, 'Thank goodness.'

Black Boy took no notice of me, his lawful owner, but walked straight up to Martin Lowe and began to nuzzle him gently, as much as to say, 'I can tell you know something about horses, which is more than these people do.'

Martin called him a good boy, and examined his feet and his mouth, and his eyes and coat.

'He's a grand pony,' said Martin at last, 'and if he has no real faults I consider he was a bargain at five hundred pounds. Now you have to school him and bring out the best in him. I say! He's not very clean, is he? How often do you groom him?'

This was awful. I went as red as a beetroot.

'I don't know how to,' I said.

'You've got a dandy-brush, I suppose?'

'No,' I muttered. 'I don't know what it is.'

'Well, you must get one today,' was all that Martin said, 'and tomorrow I'll come and show you how to use it. You'll need a water-brush too, and a body-brush and a currycomb, and a stable-rubber for finishing off. If you go to Wilks' the saddler and say I sent you, you'll be given the right things.'

'Will they cost a lot?' I blurted out, and then shut my eyes as I caught Mummy's eye.

'Look here,' said Martin, 'there's no point in you buying those things when we've got loads of them knocking about at home. I'll bring a set round to you, and then when Black Boy gets really well-groomed you might buy him a set of his own for a birthday present. There's no actual hurry. Will that do?'

'Oh, it's frightfully good of you!' I gasped, and Mummy looked relieved and yet doubtful, as grown-ups do when they think they are being done favours to.

'Meanwhile, where are your saddle and bridle?'

'In the kitchen,' I said. 'I'll fetch them.'

I rushed and got them, and Martin said, 'Well, they could be cleaned too, couldn't they?'

This was kind, as they were actually filthy. I hadn't even noticed before. Once more I could have died.

'Never mind now,' said Martin. 'Stick them on the pony.'

'I – I don't really know how,' I muttered.

'Don't know *how!* But how have you managed – '

'Oh, just anyhow,' I growled. 'All wrong.'

'Well, show me how you've been doing it.'

Oh dear, how awful my efforts must have looked to Martin.

'Stop!' he said, and though he sat all the time in a wheelchair I assure you he could be very commanding.

'Stop, Jill, for heaven's sake. That poor pony! He must have the patience of an angel to put up with you, hurting his ears and mouth, and pinching his skin and pulling his girths too tight. I wonder he could breathe. Now we'll begin from the beginning. First speak gently to your pony and slip the reins over his head and neck. Then stand close to his head and pass your right arm round and under, taking hold of the crownpiece of the bridle with your right hand and the bit with your left. Now put his offside ear – that's the offside one, duffer – between the crownpiece and browband, and slip your left thumb into the side of his mouth. In goes the bit; now put the other ear through – there! Could anything be easier?'

'Oh!' I said.

'Now for the saddle. First run the stirrups up the leathers or they will smack your pony and annoy him. I bet you've annoyed him lots of times. Now fling your saddle on as deftly as you can and fasten the girths, but you must be able to insert three fingers, and run them down so that the flesh isn't wrinkled underneath. That's better. Now let me see you mount.'

I did my best, and Martin said, 'Oh dear! What a scramble. You look as though you're climbing a wall.'

'Well, tell me how,' I said.

'Stand with your back to Black Boy's head. Take the reins in your left hand and place it on his withers, just in front of the saddle. Now take hold of the saddle with your right hand and place your left foot in the stirrup – no, right up to the instep, please. Now spring! Spring, I said, not lumber up. Bring both feet together, over with your right leg, and sit down gently. That wasn't too bad at all. Now get down and do it all over again.'

It was like a dream, I couldn't believe it. I was having a riding lesson.

I suppose to some of you this will sound absolutely pathetic, but I told you I was going to describe things from the very beginning and the very beginning for me was when I learned to mount my pony correctly.

'I gather you're not very good at dismounting,' Martin was saying.

'Not what *you'd* call dismounting,' I murmured, wondering how much lower I was going to fall in the way of shame and abasement.

'Well, look here,' he said, 'even at gymkhanas you'll see a lot of very slack and careless dismounting. People often just free their stirrups and slither off. You can't afford to do that until you're a very experienced rider, and know when the judge's eye is on you and when you can afford to take liberties with technique. Here and now you've got to learn to do it properly every time.'

And he proceeded to tell me what your baby sister of four probably knows, about bringing the right foot over to the left foot, standing straight for a second, then freeing the left foot and jumping neatly down. He made me do this a good many times.

'Can you stand any more?' said Martin. 'Because for one thing, your stirrup leathers are the wrong length. Come here . . . there! Try that,' he added after he had directed me from his chair how to shorten my leathers.

We then had a very earnest twenty minutes while he told me how to sit in the saddle and what to do with my hands, and the right position for my feet and knees.

I expect you are bored stiff with all this, but there isn't going to be much more of it. I wasn't bored at the time, but Black Boy was and he began to show it unmistakably.

'Black Boy's looking at me with a "Save me" look in his eye,' said Mummy laughing.

'I could go on for ever,' I said.

'Mr Lowe couldn't,' said Mummy. 'He's already

getting the wild and desperate look of one who has reached the end of his tether.'

'Not a bit of it,' said Martin, quite indignantly. 'But all the same I think we'd better finish for today. Jill has got enough to practise.'

'It's awfully good of you,' said Mummy, 'to help her like this. We don't know how to thank you, do we, Jill?'

'Well, don't thank me for coming,' said Martin, 'because that's the last thing I want. I've thoroughly enjoyed myself. It's grand to think I'm doing something useful. You see, for ages I haven't been any use at all, since I couldn't walk, and it was getting me down. If I can teach somebody to ride it will buck me up no end. So if you'll let me come again, that's all I ask.'

I was wildly happy all the evening, and made such a noise about it that Mummy had to get annoyed with me, which she rarely does over simple things like making a noise.

I expect you think it was a lot of fuss about nothing, especially if you were born in the saddle and photographed with your nurse holding you up when hounds met on your ancestral lawn.

But as the weekend wore on I quietened down quite a lot, for a black day loomed before me on the following Tuesday.

5 School

The horrid truth was that the summer holidays were over and it was the first day of school. And what was worse, my first day at a new school, The Pines School for Girls, in Chatton.

At nine thirty on that grim morning I was standing in the headmistress's room, feeling very clean and stiff in my new school uniform of fawn blouse and brown tunic, and trying to stop my new shoes from squeaking.

'You are Jill Crewe?' said Miss Grange-Dudley. 'Let me see, on the results of the entrance examination we have placed you in the First Year. The average age there, I see, is eleven years and five months. How old are you?'

'Eleven years and – and – seven months,' I said, doing some violent mental arithmetic.

'Then you will have to work very hard, Jill, since you are above rather than below the average,' said Miss Grange-Dudley with a headmistressy smile.

(I had an awful time trying not to giggle, because I thought of a story of Daddy's, about a man in a hotel who said to a little bellboy, 'What is the average tip you get here?' The boy replied, 'One pound sir,' so the man said, 'Very well, here is one pound for you.' And the boy said, 'Oh, thank you, sir! You're the only gentleman who has ever come up to the average.')

Miss Grange-Dudley then pressed a bell, and a

girl of about sixteen came in, wearing glasses and a prefect's badge.

'Oh, Marguerite, this is Jill Crewe, a new girl for the First Year. Please take her along to the form room and hand her over to Miss Wright.'

So I followed Marguerite, who was in the sixth form, along a corridor and up a flight of stairs, all smelling of floor polish and chalk and blackboards; and she tapped at a door and in we went. I felt as though a thousand eyes were fixed upon me, though actually there were thirty girls and the form mistress.

'A new girl for you, Miss Wright,' said Marguerite. 'Jill Crewe.'

'Oh, good morning, Jill,' said Miss Wright, who was rather old and very thin. 'That is your desk, on the second row. Please sit quietly until we finish our *dictée*.'

Then she went on, '*Chaque jour la petite Marie et son frère –* ', and I looked round to see if there was anyone I knew. In the front row was Susan Pyke; I didn't recognise anyone else.

After the *dictée* we had books and exercise books given out, and then it was break. All the girls streamed out of the room without taking any notice of me, so I followed them into the garden. Everybody was talking in excited groups except for a few miserable new girls who like myself hung about alone, so I went and sat on a bench beside a hedge.

Presently I heard some girls talking on the other side of the hedge.

A voice said, 'Have you seen the new girl in our form? It's that awful kid who has come to live at the cottage in Pool Lane.'

'Why awful?' said somebody else.

I screwed myself round and peeped through a gap in the hedge. Susan Pyke was holding forth to several other girls who were all laughing.

'Well, the other day we passed her; she was riding on a pony, lolling all over it. Her stirrup leathers were too long and her legs stuck straight out in front of her, and she had her hands somewhere up under her chin like Fido begging for a bone.'

'Oh, Susan, you are a scream!'

'And if you'd *seen* how she was dressed! An absolute sight! Frightful old jeans, and actually *sandals*.'

'No! Not really! How awful.'

I went home at lunch-time absolutely blazing. You see, up to then I had never bothered much about what I wore, but now I wondered why I could have been so blind. All the children I had seen on their ponies had, of course, worn lovely light-coloured jodhpurs or breeches, and neat tailored riding coats and string gloves. I knew perfectly well that those clothes must have cost a lot of money, and that I could never have them. I wasn't even going to ask Mummy for them because it would only worry her. I realised that getting Black Boy was only the beginning of the expense and perhaps it was a pity I had ever bought him.

You can guess I felt pretty grim and low.

Mummy said, 'Well? How was school?'

'Oh, all right,' I said. But she must have noticed that I was rather silent during lunch because she kept looking at me in a thoughtful way.

I went back to afternoon school and got through it somehow, and came home to tea.

Then Mummy said, 'What's the matter, Jill? What's happened?'

'Oh, nothing,' I said.

We had scarcely finished tea when I saw Martin Lowe's wheelchair coming in at the gate. I felt nearly too depressed to welcome him, but when he started laying things out on the table, I got interested in spite of myself.

'What's this for?' I asked, picking up a curry-comb.

'That is actually to fetch the dirt out of the body-brush,' said Martin, 'but you're beginning at the wrong end. The first tool to get familiar with is this one, the dandy-brush. You see it is stiff, and with it you will brush Black Boy all over, working towards his tail, getting out the dirt with a circular movement but always finishing your stroke the way the hair lies. You brush his tail with that one too. Next you use the damp water-brush; then you rub him over with the body-brush, cleaning it out as you go with the currycomb. Finally you put on a shine with a wisp of hay and finish off with a clean stable-rubber. Here are all your tools; now let's go out and groom Black Boy.'

He sat in his wheelchair, and under his instructions I made the best job I could of grooming my pony for the first time. I was jolly clumsy over it, but I did try, and when I had finished Black Boy shone like patent leather, even if it was a bit patchy, and I made up my mind I would always keep him like that.

'Now let's see if you remember what we learned on Saturday,' said Martin. 'Show me how you saddle, mount, and dismount from your pony. And remember that in putting on saddle and bridle your first concern ought to be your pony's comfort. Always take time and trouble over it, and never put anything on in a slapdash way.'

Martin then praised me for the improvement I had

made, and suggested that we should go into the lane so that he could see me actually riding.

'My hands still feel wrong,' I said, thinking of the loathsome Susan Pyke.

'They're all right. Keep them low, with your elbows close to your sides.'

'How tight should I hold the reins?'

'Well, that's important. The reins are definitely *not* something to hang on to for the purpose of keeping your balance. All you have to do is to keep a light feel of your pony's mouth, and so establish contact. It's balance, balance all the time. Now show me how you walk – sit straight – straighter than that. Good! You look very nice, Jill, if you can maintain that position.'

His words of praise made me feel a bit better, after my hideous humiliation of the morning. What rankled was that it had all been true, what Susan Pyke had said, and I *had* looked awful and it had been my own fault. But at least no one should ever be able to say that I rode badly again.

However, my pride was shortly to be brought down a peg or two. Martin kept saying, 'Walk! Walk!' and I walked and walked Black Boy up and down the lane while he looked on critically.

'I'm sick of walking,' I said at last. 'Can't I do something else?'

'You can do anything you like,' said Martin.

So I used my heels on Black Boy in a way that I considered smart and horsemanlike, and off he went at a trot with me bouncing about all over the place. As I found this very uncomfortable, I pressed him to a canter, hoping for the best, and eventually finished up more or less on his neck.

'I suppose that looked pretty awful,' I said to

Martin. 'I'm really beginning to wonder if Black Boy's pace is right for me.'

'I suppose one excuse is as good as another,' he said.

'Black Boy *always* takes off on the wrong foot,' I said.

'How unfortunate,' said Martin in a maddening sort of way.

'Well, what can I do about it?' I said.

'I shouldn't trot or canter until you've learned to walk,' he said kindly. 'I'll give you some tips next time I come, and now it looks to me as though that pony has had enough, so let's go and rub him down before it gets too dark. Remember, a good rider always puts his horse's comfort before his own, and however tired and hungry you may be after a ride, Jill, your pony must be attended to and fed before you go for your own bath and grub.'

I resolved to do quite a lot of practising before Martin came again, so as not to make any more exhibitions of myself and my incompetence. Then Mummy came out and asked Martin whether he would like to stay to supper.

'It's only a scratch supper of jacket potatoes and cheese,' she said, but Martin seemed pleased to be asked.

Round the table he began to talk to us. It seemed that before he had his crash in the RAF. he had kept three riding horses and had taken many prizes with them at shows and gymkhanas. Now he was living with his parents who were rather old and fussy. His mother was always pitying him and telling him to rest and take care, which was really the worst thing for anybody like Martin, and his father was apt to say, 'I've just been looking at all the cups you won in the old days, tch, tch, tch!' Which was cruel, though not meant to be.

We tried to eat jacket potatoes politely as we had a guest, but it was difficult, and soon we were all laughing and scooping them out with spoons in our usual carefree way. Martin seemed pleased rather than horrified. Then we had baked apples, the middles stuffed with sultanas and brown sugar, and coffee made in the filter, which I always do myself.

Martin promised to come again on Saturday afternoon, and meanwhile I was to practise all I had learned. However, when I got to bed I couldn't sleep for thinking about having the wrong clothes and never being able to get the right ones. But perhaps I could do something better than jeans and sandals!

I knew jodhpurs cost the earth. I had only thirty pounds left which Black Boy would soon eat up; but after school next day I went and gazed in a few shop windows, and finally my eye lit on some quite decent-looking bluey-grey denims which were marked ten pounds.

I thought a bit, and then recklessly plunged and bought a pair. I dashed home on my bike and flew up to my room. I dug out an old white cotton shirt that was quite plain and put it on, with the grey denims. Then I put on my school tie which was fawn, brown, and green in stripes and my school hat which was plain brown felt turned up all round, and my tie-up brown shoes. I didn't look too bad at all; I was neat and sporting, anyhow, not sloppy.

I went down and had some milk and buns – Mummy was working hard that afternoon – and then I saddled Black Boy and rode him up and down the lane a bit. I felt much smarter and more of a rider. Even hating The Pines school seemed a bit less violent now; and I dashed in whistling, and made a cup of tea and took it in to Mummy who was very grateful.

6 My friend Ann

The next morning at break, to my surprise a girl came up and spoke to me. She looked rather nice, with curly red hair and a lot of freckles.

'I'm Ann Derry,' she said.

I had noticed her in the form room, of course.

'Would you like to walk round with me?' she asked, and I said I would. It was a pleasant change having somebody to talk to instead of the stony silence which is often a new girl's fate.

I wondered why Ann, who seemed quite a popular girl, had bothered with me, but she explained, 'You see, Susan Pyke seems to have her knife into you for some reason. I loathe Susan Pyke, and therefore anybody that Susan Pyke loathes, I like, if you know what I mean.'

'It's mouldy being a new girl,' I said, 'but I'll probably survive. The worst of it is, I don't know anybody in Chatton, and all the other new girls seem to know each other.'

'I'll tell you what,' said Ann, 'would you like to sit by me in class instead of where you are? I'll ask Miss Wright if you can change desks with Marjorie Miles. Marjorie won't mind, in fact she'd rather have your desk because it is next to Diana Bush whom she has rather a crush on.'

The next day Ann invited me to go home to tea with her. When we arrived, we did our hair and washed, and then Ann's mother came in and said, 'Who is this little girl, dear?' which I thought was rather a lowering thing to say, and I would have slain Mummy if she had said it to a friend of mine.

Ann went a bit red, and said, 'It's Jill Crewe, Mummy. I *told* you.'

We went down to the dining room where tea was laid with a lace cloth and silver dishes as though for a grown-up party, and there were Ann's two little sisters, Pam and Brenda, clutching dolls and being shy. I just said, 'Hullo,' and they looked as if they were going to cry. They were all right really, only much too young to bother with. We had a lovely tea, with sardine sandwiches and tarts and iced cake. Mrs Derry kept saying things like, 'You've only had *two* sandwiches, darling. You must have three before any cake. Oh dear, oh dear, Pam is hardly eating *anything*. Do you feel ill, Pam darling? Brenda, you've been running about and getting too hot, I'm sure you have! Ann, you're not chewing your food twenty times, darling, and you know what Doctor Brown said.'

However, this was over at last, and Mrs Derry said, 'Now take Jill to see your pony, dear.'

'Oh!' I said. 'I didn't know you had a pony.'

'Of course she has a pony,' said Mrs Derry. 'But she isn't a bit keen. I simply can't understand it. When I was her age I was riding and schooling my pony half the day long, and yet Ann has to be *driven* to go near Seraphine.'

'Oh, don't fuss so, Mummy,' said Ann.

'Well, we'll go to the stable,' said Mrs Derry; so off we went.

Seraphine – which I thought was rather a putting-off name anyway – was a lovely pony, grey, of about thirteen hands. She was beautifully groomed, but I learned that Mr Derry's handyman did that.

'I couldn't bother with anything like that,' said Ann.

'Actually, it's quite fun,' I said.

'Have you got a pony?' said Ann, surprised.

So I told her about Black Boy and how keen I was.

'There!' said Mrs Derry. 'I'm sure you'll do Ann a lot of good, Jill. Darling, *don't* stand so near; I'm sure she'll nip you. Why not mount and let Jill see how nicely you ride?'

'Oh, I can't be bothered,' said Ann. 'Let's go and look at the puppies instead.'

'Well, don't get your shoes muddy,' said Mrs Derry, 'and if you do, be sure to scrape them at the back door, and don't let the children handle the puppies — Ann! You've got a scratch on your hand. Oh, I hope it isn't going to turn septic like Pam's did — '

We got away at last and went to look at the West Highland puppies. I began to understand why Ann was not keen about riding or anything else.

However, Mrs Derry was very kind and told me to go again whenever I liked, and I really felt that I had found a friend at last.

When I got home Mummy said I had better invite Ann to tea the following Saturday. I had a bright idea, and I told Ann to come on her pony so that we could do a bit of schooling together. She wasn't very keen, but at last she agreed to.

I was very excitedly waiting for her when she rode up on Seraphine. She looked very nice, in buff jodhpurs and a pepper-and-salt jacket, with proper jodhpur boots. I was in my grey denims, but Ann didn't appear to notice that I was not dressed like she was, which I appreciated.

Unfortunately when we got to the orchard Black Boy let me down! I hadn't had much time for him during the week, as I had been doing homework, and he was feeling high-spirited and defiant. So when he saw me coming with the halter – it was one that Martin had brought – he gave me a wicked look, flicked his heels, and made off. Our orchard ends in quite a large field, and here Black Boy had lots of space to tease me. I simply couldn't catch him, and I felt awfully silly in front of Ann.

She said, 'Let me try,' and she took the halter and walked towards Black Boy, speaking to him in a gentle but firm voice. And to my surprise, after one little sidling prance of defiance, he let her catch him and put on the halter.

This took me down a peg, for it showed that though she didn't even pretend to be keen, Black Boy recognised that Ann had experience and was not to be played about with.

I was waiting with the bridle, but the minute I took the halter off, before I could get the bridle on, Black Boy was off like the wind and stood still about twenty yards away, mischievously cropping grass and keeping one naughty eye on me to see what I'd do.

'I say,' said Ann, 'you really ought to put the reins over his neck before you take the halter off. Then you've got something to grab hold of if he tries to run out on you.'

'I know now,' I said. 'Actually Martin did tell me that, only I forgot. Now I've learned by bitter experience.'

So Ann had to catch Black Boy for me again, and this time all went well and we both mounted and rode out into the lane. I felt very nervous, as Ann took it for granted I could ride.

Although she said she didn't care about it she certainly rode very well, and understood all the aids and everything.

'I say, how do you make Seraphine take off on the right leg for cantering?' I asked. 'Black Boy takes off on the wrong one and it makes it so jolly uncomfortable.'

'Well, it's like this,' said Ann. 'Shorten your reins – yes, that's right – and turn his head towards the left. Press with both legs, but kick with your left foot. This will put him off his balance, and he'll *have* to take off with his offside leg to save himself. That's better – now you've got it.'

'Oh, thanks!' I cried, as Black Boy responded with a perfect canter.

I could have gone on for ages, but Ann soon got bored, so we went back home and turned the ponies into the orchard, and then we went in and had tea over the fire – Mummy had made hot buttered toast and marrow-ginger – and I showed Ann my things and found she liked the same books that I liked. What was more, she told me she had a lot of very good pony books at home which she would lend me.

'I've only got one ambition,' I said, 'and that's a terrific one – to ride in a gymkhana.'

'And I've only got one ambition,' said Ann, 'and that is *not* to ride in a gymkhana. Mummy made me enter for one last year and it was awful. I was nervous and forgot everything, and Seraphine knew I was nervous and played me up, and I was last in everything except the musical chairs, in which I was first out! So in a way I was last in that too. I felt the most awful fool, and Susan Pyke won three prizes and said to me afterwards, "Ann, you'll never do any good at a gymkhana until you learn to control your pony." I could have murdered her. Ever since then Mummy has been badgering me to enter for gymkhanas, and I won't. I won't – ever again!'

'You *could* ride as well as Susan Pyke,' I said, 'and you look a jolly sight nicer.'

'Oh, don't be feeble.'

'I'm not feeble. Oh, Ann, wouldn't it be simply super if one day you and I could enter for a gymkhana and take all the Firsts and Seconds, right under Susan's nose!'

'You are feeble!' said Ann witheringly, and I was afraid she was right.

7 My little flock

One morning as I was biking to school I saw one of our small kindergarten kids standing with her mother at the gate of her home. The mother called to me, and I got off my bike.

'Oh,' she said, 'I was hoping an older girl would come along. You see, the young woman who takes Jennifer to school and brings her home is ill. Would you mind taking her with you, and collecting her again at twelve thirty?'

So I took Jennifer, who was about five; and though it was a bit of a nuisance I collected her from the kindergarten at half past twelve and took her home. Then I rode my bike home the rest of the way.

The next morning the same thing happened again, except that there were two more small children, called Jane and Elizabeth, and their mother asked if I would take them too. So I did. And the next morning there was another one called Angela, so by now I had quite a flock. Apparently this girl who usually took them all had had to go to hospital and wouldn't be back for ages.

I felt I had got let in for something, only I just couldn't be mean to these small kids who seemed quite to like me, though Ann Derry shrieked with laughter when she saw me marching off, pushing my bike out of the school drive with these four infants trotting along behind me. The kindergarten only went to school in the mornings.

After I had been doing this for exactly a week I had a truly stunning surprise. Jennifer's mother handed me three pounds, saying that was what she gave the girl who usually took Jennifer, so of course I ought to have it. Then Angela arrived and handed me an envelope from her mother holding another three pounds, and on the way home we met the mother of Jane and Elizabeth who gave me four pounds, because on two mornings I had to wait for them to finish their music lessons.

I went home in a sort of daze. Ten pounds! And as the girl in hospital was said to be worse, next week I should have another ten pounds and the week after that.

I was so excited, and at the same time relieved. You see, for ages I had been worrying terribly about money, and how I was going to feed Black Boy in the winter, let alone stable him. And now – well, I might even collect a few more children; I might even make enough to cover all my expenses! So you can imagine why I was so happy and thrilled.

I went in whistling like mad and feeling the nice round solid feel of the coins in my blazer pocket; then I washed and went down to help Mummy make tea.

She said, 'You're very cock-a-hoop, Jill. Has something nice happened?'

I hadn't intended to tell her just then, but I couldn't keep it in, so I told her the whole story, and I said, 'Oh, Mummy, isn't it marvellous? I'll be able to buy everything for Black Boy now.'

But she looked rather serious, and after a moment she said quietly, 'Jill, you'll have to give all that money back at once.'

'What – what do you mean?' I said, feeling quite shaky with the shock.

'My dear, you can't accept it. You can't take money for doing a simple act of kindness. Don't you understand?'

'Oh, Mummy!'

'You must give it back tomorrow morning, Jill.'

'But what shall I say?' I wailed.

'Say that your mother says you are to return the money, but you will be very glad to take the children to school as long as you are needed.'

'For nothing!'

'You didn't do it because you expected anything in the first case. Of course you may accept a sweet or an apple.'

'But – '

'That's enough. Now butter the toast and we'll have tea.'

After tea I went out and wept a bitter tear into Black Boy's mane, but I soon mopped it up and decided that I had better find some other way of making money.

I may add that I went on conducting those children all the term, and sometimes they asked me home to tea, and I had some very good teas and we talked about ponies, so it wasn't so bad after all.

But meanwhile I was faced with the problem of Black Boy and the approaching winter. I had simply got to stable him somewhere, and though I talked it over with Mummy we didn't seem to get any further, and of course it was really my responsibility after buying my pony so recklessly. But by now I loved him so much, and when I took him his daily carrot or apple he would talk to me with such lovely soft whiffley noises, that I felt the only thing that mattered in the world was finding him a home for the winter.

Of course, I had not mentioned this worry of mine to Martin Lowe, because Mummy had said I must definitely not accept anything more from him, he was too generous already.

So one free afternoon I groomed Black Boy with the utmost care, spending ages on brushing out his mane and tail and cleaning his feet and making him shine all over; then I dressed in my clean white shirt and the grey denims out of which I had taken some marks with Thawpit, and I brushed my shoes and put on my school mac and hat, and I rode feeling very nervous to a nearby riding school – not the one that Susan Pyke went to, but another kept by a lady called Mrs Darcy.

When I got to the gate I saw that several ponies and horses were in the paddock, and a girl groom was crossing the yard carrying a bucket.

I said, 'Oh – good afternoon.'

'Have you come about lessons?' she said, looking at Black Boy unrecognisingly.

'Er – no,' I said. 'Please could I speak to Mrs Darcy?'

'Just a moment,' she said. 'I'll fetch Mrs Darcy.'

Mrs Darcy proved to be a lady with grey hair, wearing a khaki shirt and breeches and some very neat riding boots.

She looked at me, and said, 'Is it about riding lessons?'

'Well, no, it isn't – I'm afraid,' I said. 'It's just that – well, Mrs Darcy, I'm Jill Crewe and this is my pony Black Boy. I haven't anywhere to stable him for the winter and I wondered if – '

'I'm afraid I don't stable ponies,' she said quite pleasantly; 'I haven't the accommodation.'

I felt myself going red.

'What I wondered was whether – whether you would care to use Black Boy in your riding school in return for stabling him,' I said, all in a rush.

'Oh.' She looked hard at Black Boy. 'Do you groom him yourself? He looks very nice.'

'Yes, I do.'

'Is he well schooled and trained?' she asked next.

'I – I'm really only just beginning to school him now,' I said.

She smiled kindly.

'I'm afraid he wouldn't be any use to me. You see, I can only use thoroughly well-trained and schooled ponies who understand my teaching routine. And I couldn't offer an untrained pony even as a hack.'

'Yes, I see,' I said, my face falling.

I thought for a moment and then said, 'Oh, Mrs Darcy, is there anything at all I could do, for Black Boy's stabling? I'd clean tack or do grooming or feeding or anything. I could come before school in the mornings, and at weekends when you're busy.'

'I'm sorry,' she said. 'I have all the help I need.'

I knew then it wasn't any use, and I just said, 'Thank you,' and rode away.

8   The stable

'Now we have got to get down to some serious schooling,' said Martin. 'Our job is to mark out a riding school in that so-called field of yours. By the way, I wonder what happened to the hay from it?'

'Hay?' I said.

'Yes, hay. Somebody cut it and took it away before you came here, obviously. I'll bet it was Farmer Grimes, and that he's been doing it all the time the cottage was empty. There should be enough hay here to keep your pony supplied all winter. I'll see Grimes about it.'

'Hay!' I said again, looking quite pole-axed, because hay was one of the things I had had on my mind for ages.

'Haven't you ever heard of the stuff?' said Martin. 'You look as if you'd just had a load of it tipped over you. Now if you'll look on the floor of the chair, round my feet, you'll find, one – a tin of lime-wash, two – a brush, three – some pegs, four – yards and yards of twine. Do you know how to mark out a circle? Well, I'll tell you.'

Martin wheeled his chair into the middle of our field, and sat there while he instructed me how to measure out a wide ring with the pegs and mark it with the lime-wash. This took us till tea-time, when Mummy appeared in the orchard to call us. We went in as hungry as could be and even Martin who usually hadn't much appetite ate a huge tea. Then while I washed up and Mummy put the china away he told us funny stories until we were helpless with laughing.

Then we went to inspect the newly made riding school.

I saddled Black Boy, and Martin made me ride round and round, walking, trotting, and cantering at his orders; and sometimes he would call me into the ring and make me turn and stand on the spot he told me to. I suppose I made rather a feeble show, because he made me do it over and over again.

'It isn't a case of will it do, Jill,' he said. 'It has got to be perfect.'

He then made me dismount and mount again several times. He was particularly fussy about dismounting, and reminded me that I must not swing off the pony or merely jump down, but do it the proper way; namely, to lift my right leg over and bring the foot close to the one in the stirrup; then to pause for an instant while I put my weight on my two hands; release the left foot from the stirrup and then spring from my hands to the ground. At last I was able to do this to satisfy him.

'Now spend a week in practising what I've shown you today,' he said, as it began to grow dusk.

'Thank you, I will,' I said; for I had realised by now that to be a good rider means endless patience and hard work, and it is no use thinking you have finished with the early stages and ought to go on to something more spectacular.

'You have forgotten something,' said Martin, as I dismounted and began to take off Black Boy's saddle.

'What?' I said.

'You've forgotten to pat your pony and thank him for what he has done. That's awfully important, Jill; you must never forget it. Whatever your horse does for you, always pat him, speak to him, and tell him he has done well. He understands, and your sympathy will help him next time. When you go to big shows and gymkhanas you will see how the best riders always pat and speak to their horses after – say – a jumping round.'

'Jumping?' I said. 'Oh gee!'

'Yes, jumping,' said Martin, 'and it isn't so far off from you as you think.'

I patted Black Boy and rubbed his cheeks, saying good night to him while I took off his bridle.

'Isn't it about time you put him in at nights?' said Martin casually.

My legs went all rocky.

'I – i – n?' I stammered.

'In the stable.'

'But – oh Martin, I can't find anybody who'll stable him, and Mummy said I wasn't to worry you about it and I haven't, have I? – but honestly I don't know what to do. I want a stable for Black Boy more than anything in the world.'

'Well, what's the matter with the one you've got?' said Martin.

'The – the what?'

'That!' said Martin, pointing at what we called the garden shed which was really a rather tumbledown-looking building with a steep gable in which Mummy had stacked our trunks and boxes when we came to the cottage.

'Do you mean the shed?' I said. 'But – '

'Shed? It's a stable – at least it was when I used to come here and play with Tom Jarvis, years ago.

Tom kept his pony there. Let's go and see, shall we?'

I didn't need inviting twice. I rushed round to the shed and pulled out the padlock, releasing the hasp. The door opened, and revealed a medley of trunks and wooden boxes, piled up high.

I began to pull at the nearest, and when two or three had come out there was revealed a cobbled floor with a gutter running along it.

'Oh!' I yelled in my excitement.

I pulled away like mad at those boxes, and presently with a crash the whole lot descended; I fell flat on my back; Martin shouted, 'Look out!' and Mummy came running out of the house crying, 'What on earth has happened?'

'Mummy!' I shrieked, 'It's a stable! Look! I can see the manger. A proper stable. Oh, gosh, I'm going mad.'

I jumped up and began to whizz round in circles, letting out whoops of joy.

'And what are you going to do with all my boxes?' said Mummy.

'Leave them to me,' said Martin. 'We've got loads of room at our place and I'll store them for you. Yes, there's a nice stall here for Black Boy, and a place for keeping tack and fodder too.'

'Thank goodness,' said Mummy. 'Now I shan't find corn and cleaning rags all over the kitchen.'

Martin ran his chair backwards a little way and peered upwards.

'In that gable there there's a small door, and I'm sure you'll find a useful hayloft there. It will do for your hay when I get it from Farmer Grimes.'

'What's this about hay?' said Mummy.

'Oh, Mummy, don't ask me questions yet!' I

gasped. 'Such marvellous things are happening today I'm nearly crackers with joy.'

'You'll have a bit of work here,' said Martin. 'This stable is filthy and you can't put Black Boy in yet. I'll tell you what, I'll send a man round to clean it out and give it a coat of whitewash – '

'Certainly not,' said Mummy. 'Jill can do everything herself, except for the whitewashing, and I'll help her with that. She is so thrilled about the stable that she will find the cleaning of it part of the fun.'

'But – ' began Martin.

'Yes, I'd love to clean it out,' I said. 'It's all right. Mummy and I will do it in no time.'

'Do what?' said a voice, and I looked round to see Ann Derry standing there with her bicycle.

'Oh, look, Ann,' I cried. 'We've found a stable that we didn't know we had. It's for Black Boy, and we're going to clean it out and whitewash it.'

'Goody,' said Ann. 'I'll come home with you after school on Monday afternoon, and help. Can I?'

'Rather!' I said.

Actually Ann turned out to be just as excited about cleaning out the stable as I was; and on Monday school seemed to drag terribly.

Directly we were released at four o'clock we flew back home and could hardly wait to eat the tea which Mummy had ready for us.

We got ourselves up in ghastly-looking overalls and tied dusters over our hair, and then we set to work.

It was fun. And soon the reason for Ann's excitement emerged. At home her mother would not allow her to do anything that was messy, but told the handyman to do it, or got a man in, whereas all sensible people know that really messy manual labour is one of the jolliest things in the world, when you are dressed for it and it doesn't matter how filthy you get.

We worked and worked until it got too dark to see properly, but still we went on, working by feel. We had taken it in turns to slap on the whitewash, which as you might say was the cream of the job in hand, and the inside of the stable looked splendid. We had swilled and brushed, and scrubbed the woodwork of the stall, and Ann had even brought some tile-polish for the cobbles! As they were originally grey, the red polish made them look as though somebody had spilled a sunset over them and the general effect was very chic.

At last it was all finished, and straightening our aching backs we went in for supper. Mummy melted down some cheese and Ann and I made hot toast, and we poured the cheese on the toast and added some grilled mushrooms which Mummy had found in the field that morning. (I don't mean they were grilled when she found them.) We had milky coffee to drink, and consumed this gorgeous meal sitting round the kitchen fire with our feet in the fender. I don't think even the Queen had such a good supper that night.

A few days later – when Black Boy had begun to get used to his stable – along came a farm cart with a load of hay. It was just as Martin had thought; Farmer Grimes had cut the hay in June and taken it away, though in justice to him it must be said that the cottage had been empty for a long time and he hadn't known that we were coming or that we should keep a pony.

So he generously sent an awful lot of hay, quite enough for my pony for the whole winter, and the man who brought it very kindly forked it up into the loft above my stable (which Mummy and I had cleaned up in hopes).

Meanwhile Mummy took rather a dim view of all her trunks and boxes and things lying about the garden, until Martin reminded her that they had loads of outhouses at his home where they should be stored and sent a cart to fetch them away. Of course this involved more gratitude and burdens of obligation towards Martin, but we really didn't see what we could do about it.

9 Jumping

One day I had a letter which proved to be from Miss Eileen Harvey, a friend of Martin's.

It said:

'Dear Jill,

'My mother and I are arranging a few days' riding holiday at the half term and would be so pleased if you would join our party. There will be about seven of us. We are going to make our headquarters at a farm on the Downs and go long rides each day, taking picnic lunches and teas. Perhaps you would like to tell your mother that the four days will cost under one hundred pounds for yourself and your pony. I do hope you will be able to come.

'Yours sincerely,
'Eileen Harvey.'

Well, actually I just put this letter in my pocket and never told Mummy anything about it. It wasn't only the hundred pounds – though I wouldn't have thought of asking Mummy for that sum since she hadn't had a holiday herself for ages – but it was the old, old question of not having anything to wear. I couldn't go away for four days with seven riding people in my grey denims, one cotton shirt, and a school mac. So I wrote a letter to Eileen Harvey saying that I was very sorry but I wouldn't be able to get away at half term but it was frightfully nice of her to have asked me. I hoped she wouldn't tell Martin in case he thought that I hadn't wanted to go with his friends.

One day at school I said to Ann, 'I wish you'd come and bring Seraphine some Saturday afternoon. Martin wouldn't mind, and we could have a little gymkhana, just the two of us.'

At the hated word Ann's eyes goggled and she swallowed hard.

'All right then,' I said hastily. 'You needn't do a thing, but you can watch me and see if you can give me a hint or two. And do bring Seraphine, she would be such nice company for Black Boy.'

So in the end I persuaded her to come, and Martin gave her quite a welcome and the ponies seemed frightfully glad to see each other. I rode round the 'school', and after a bit I noticed that Ann was following me, which was a good sign. Before the afternoon was over she was getting quite interested.

Martin said, 'Do you jump, Ann?'

She said, 'Well, I did do, but I couldn't be bothered.'

'Jill is ready to begin jumping,' he said. 'It would be a tremendous help to her if you would do it with her. We'll have some easy jumps set up, and then you and Seraphine can take the lead.'

'Oh, do, Ann!' I cried. 'Oh, please do! I'm dying to jump, and I know I'll do it better if you're there to show me.'

'Oh, all right,' she said.

After that we set to work making jumps, and this being lovely messy work and manual labour of the hardest kind it appealed to Ann, just as cleaning the stable had done.

Martin got us a lot of wood, bars, hurdles, and nails, and showed us how to fix them together. We constructed a triple bar with wings which looked marvellous until Ann accidentally leaned against it, when it fell apart and she sat down heavily on the ground.

We next made a gate of sorts, and also a box which we filled with heather. These things took ages to make and we had lots of fun over them. Ann said her father had bought her a set of jumps, and she hadn't realised that making them was a labour of such pleasantness.

All these jumps looked terrifically high to me, but they were actually about seventy-five centimetres. Martin said that they must be made easy to knock down at a touch of the pony's foot, and ours were easy all right – too easy, as they usually fell down the minute the wind blew.

When the jumps were made, the next thing was to paint them, and the wings, white. We had a great time over this; Ann and I looked like snowmen when we had finished and there were dabs of white all over Martin's chair. I don't know how they got there! Mummy was concerned and said we must get turpentine and take them out, but Martin just laughed and said he looked upon them as worthy decorations.

The night before my first jumping lesson I couldn't go to sleep; and when at last I did I dreamed I was jumping six-metre walls with the greatest ease and Susan Pyke was watching me in speechless admiration.

When Martin arrived next day the first thing he did was to give Ann instructions to set up a pole across two bricks about thirty centimetres off the ground. This was to be my first jump.

'I feel weird,' I said.

'Nonsense,' said Martin. 'The jump is so low that you'll hardly notice it at all. The great thing to do is to grip with your knees and to keep your balance and go *with* the pony. Above all, you must *not* hang on to your reins to maintain your balance, or you will jag your pony's mouth and he will dislike jumping and refuse, quite rightly, to do it. Keep your legs still and firm, and slightly lean forward as you approach the jump, for he will swing back as you cross the obstacle and that has to be counteracted. Remember, *you* are not jumping; let the pony do the work, and I do *not* want to see daylight between you and the saddle, Jill. Now tighten your girths a little, and mount. Ann, take the lead and show Jill how easy it is.'

Ann walked, and then cantered easily up to the pole; in a split second and quite effortlessly Seraphine was over.

'Good!' cried Martin.

Now it was my turn. I put Black Boy at the jump and hoped for the best. I hardly felt him rise, and then realised that we were over!

'Jolly good!' said Martin. 'Easy, wasn't it? And Black Boy is going to love jumping. I can see it in his happy face. Do it again, two or three times, and then we'll raise the pole.'

To make a long story short, we jumped the pole several times, and also a low hurdle, and then Ann jumped by herself, a one-metre jump, and looked quite pleased with herself.

'Oh, Ann!' I said. 'How beautifully you did it.'

'I quite enjoyed it,' she confessed. 'Riding here with you is much more fun than in the paddock at home with Mummy watching all the time and telling me how to do it.'

I felt as though I should never be tired of jumping, and on I went, over the low jumps, until to my surprise Black Boy presented me with my first refusal.

'It's no good, Jill,' said Martin laughing. 'He isn't having any more.'

'Why do horses refuse at jumps?' asked Ann. 'I've always wondered that at gymkhanas, because obviously the horse wouldn't be there if he wasn't a jumper.'

'Well, Ann, when a horse refuses at a jump the rider should first ask himself, is it *his* fault? Very often it is. The horse is not presented at the jump properly, or is held back too long or urged forward too late, or his stride is not quite right. The horse wants to jump well in most cases – though you will always see horses which are just being nappy on purpose. Even that may originally be the rider's fault. You must never, on any provocation, punish your horse for a refusal, however disappointed you may be. Give him another try; take him back calmly, pat him and speak encouragingly to him. Ten to one he will respond with every bit of his gallant nature and take you over the fence.'

'He could refuse because his tack was uncomfortable, couldn't he?' asked Ann.

'He certainly could. One of the most fidgety horses I ever saw in a show actually had a sore mouth from a too sharp bit. I can't tell you too often to take extra time and trouble to make sure that saddle, bridle, bit, and all tack is perfectly comfortable to your horse.'

'May I ask another question?' asked Ann.

'Ask fifty. That's what I'm here for.'

'Well, why do they have wings on jumps at all? Is it just to look well?'

'Or to make rocky jumps like ours stand up properly?' I said.

'Certainly not. The main use of wings is to make the horse go straight at the jump.'

'Oh, yes, I see that,' said Ann. 'Thank you.'

'Now spend the week practising low jumps,' said Martin, 'and don't make that pony go on when he's sick of the game. You wouldn't like people to make you go on when you were sick of a thing. Next week I am going to test your balance by making you do the jumps with your arms folded before you. And later you will do the same with your stirrups up in front of the saddle.'

'Gosh!' I said. 'Circus tricks already. And last night I hadn't even jumped.'

'Not circus tricks at all,' said Martin calmly. 'Jumping is a matter of balance and gripping with the knees, as I said before. So if you can't do it without hanging on with toes and hands, then you aren't fit to jump at all.'

'Let's practise, Ann,' I said eagerly. 'Let's practise like mad and surprise him.'

'All right,' she said, unexpectedly. 'I'm game.'

10   Christmas

I woke up on Christmas morning at peace with all the world. The day before Martin had set me a test of changing legs at the canter, getting my pony on the wrong leg and putting him back, and by good luck and with a bit of good management too I had done it perfectly and felt frightfully bucked.

He had praised my collected trot too, and that was something from Martin who never flattered and could be very sarky if you didn't appear to be trying, or showed impatience, or thought you knew everything.

It was still dark, and I lay there thinking how frightfully cosy it was and what marvellous institutions holidays were, when you didn't have to get up at practically midnight to muck out the stables before going to school.

Then it occurred to me that after all it *was* Christmas morning, and something *might* have happened during the night, so I sat up in bed and lighted my candle – because our cottage hasn't got electric light and only gas downstairs – and sure enough there were several interesting things on the table beside my bed.

At first I thought I would wait until it was light, but I hadn't got the strength of character, so I picked up the first thing, which was a registered envelope from my godmother who lives at a place called Witten-le-Wold.

The envelope contained a ten pound note, and a card with a verse on it which said: 'The auld auld wish in the auld auld way, frae a freend baith kind and true.' I wonder why so many Christmas cards go all Scottish like this? I was awfully pleased about the ten pounds, which of course I intended to spend on something for Black Boy.

The next thing I picked out was from Mummy, small and narrow and wrapped in tissue paper tied with green ribbon, and with a little tag tied on, saying, 'Merry Christmas, darling.'

This parcel contained a fountain pen which I had always wanted. However, to show to what a depth my squalid nature had descended, I admit that it promptly occurred to me that the pen must have cost at least fifteen pounds, and could have been jodhpurs. But I put this unworthy thought from me, because the pen was jolly decent of Mummy.

I then inspected three quite interesting parcels, I mean interesting from their shape. I do think the shape of parcels tells you a lot. These three were from my cousin Cecilia, who was then about fifteen, and my two aunts, Olive and Dorothy.

Cecilia's parcel contained a book called *The Madcap of the School*, and she had written in it, 'To Jill with best Xmas wishes from Cecilia' and then for some unknown reason, five xs. I must state that Cecilia had no intention of being patronising, as books like *The Madcap of the School* are the ones she likes herself.

Aunt Olive's parcel contained a card of a coach drawing up outside an inn, and a manicure set of some little tools with ivory handles; unfortunately people who muck out stables and groom ponies have not the sort of hands that manicure sets can do anything for.

Aunt Dorothy's card was of a bulldog dressed up in a blouse and bell-bottomed trousers, and her present was a thin flat box of handkerchiefs with 'J' in the corner, which were quite useful only not very exciting.

There was still a parcel left, and I wondered if it could be from Martin. However, it proved to be from Ann, and was a pair of yellow string gloves. I was quite overcome by this splendid present, which had a little card inside, quite plain except for 'Love from Ann' written on it; and then I was plunged into deepest gloom as I realised that I hadn't even thought of getting anything for Ann.

I couldn't stay in bed any longer, and a sickly dawn was now breaking, so I put my dressing gown on and went into Mummy's room. She had lighted her candle too, and was sitting up in bed opening her presents. She said the one she liked best was the blue linen nightdress case I had made for her, with her initials worked on it.

I had a sudden thought and said, 'Stay where you are, Mummy, till I come back?'

Then I flew downstairs and put the kettle on the new gas cooker we had got, and when it boiled I made her a cup of tea in the fluted green cup and saucer that she likes, and carried it up.

She said, 'Oh, what a treat! This is real luxury, tea in bed on Christmas morning.'

Then we got dressed and went down and had breakfast, and I took Black Boy an extra feed of oats for his present, and mucked out the stable.

When this whirl of toil was ended and we breathed again, I told Mummy about the lovely yellow string gloves and how awful it was not having sent anything to Ann.

'Oh, that's all right,' said Mummy. 'Ann brought the parcel last night when you were in the stable, and I told her to come this afternoon and get her own present off our tree. Martin is coming too.'

'That was quite a brain wave,' I said, 'but we haven't anything to give her, have we?'

'Oh, yes,' said Mummy. 'As a matter of fact I've got a spare copy of *Winnie Wish-Too-Much* and I'll autograph it. I'm sure Ann will like that.'

My lips said, 'Oh, that's marvellous,' but I gave a hollow inward groan. *Winnie Wish-Too-Much* was one of Mummy's least attractive efforts, about a girl who was always wanting things she hadn't got, until her fairy godmother sent her to live in the Town of Lost Happiness until she found the Key of Contentment. The way Winnie kept nearly finding the key and then just missing it made me, for one, feel seasick.

Anyway, Mummy autographed this book, and I wrote in it, 'Ann from Jill with love' and wrapped it in blue tissue paper and tied it on the little tree we always have at Christmas.

Then Mummy said it would be nice to go to church on Christmas Day and sing carols; so we did, and there were quite a lot of girls from school there, and afterwards we all said Hello, and some of their mothers said Hello to Mummy, which she liked as she didn't know many people in Chatton.

After dinner we cleared away and I washed up while Mummy wrote one or two thank-you letters, because if you don't do these in the first flush of enthusiasm you can't think what to say and even forget what the person sent you.

I had hardly finished when Ann arrived. To my surprise she was quite thrilled with the 'Winnie' book, and couldn't get over the fact that Mummy had written it. She said she would start reading it as soon as she got home and was sure she would love it as it would be a nice change from pony books.

About ten minutes later Martin arrived. First he handed me a parcel which contained a beautiful riding stick, just what I wanted, and then he handed Mummy a large bunch of purple grapes, the very luscious expensive kind that you usually have to be nearly dying to get.

Next I gave him my present off the tree, which was a rather nice and quite plain navy-blue tie, and he liked it very much, and Mummy gave him one of those calendars in a glass frame, where you take out cards and stick them in again and it goes on for ever.

'And now,' said Martin, 'for Black Boy's present. I thought he would rather have food than anything, so you will shortly be receiving enough corn to set him up for the rest of the winter. I hope it will be useful.'

I was so overcome that I stood there opening and shutting my mouth like a goldfish.

'What's up with you?' said Martin.

'Oh, Martin!' I gasped. 'You have taken such a frightful burden off my mind.'

But Mummy said at once, 'It's too much. We can't accept it, Martin. Feeding Black Boy is Jill's own responsibility and she must stand the expense. You give us too much and we can't repay you.'

Martin looked very serious.

'Repay?' he said slowly. 'There is only one thing that can't be repaid, and that is what I owe to you. You don't know what you and Jill have done for me, I don't think I'll ever make you understand. When I come here I feel I'm not only useful but happy. This is the only place where I forget – yes, actually forget – what's wrong with me.'

'Oh, but you must have so many friends,' said Mummy, while I stood wondering.

'Yes, many friends. But – oh, can't you understand – when I'm with them it's awful. They knew me as I used to be. They try and adapt themselves to me as I am now. They try not to say or do anything that would make me realise what I've missed. And all the time I can see in their eyes, "Poor old Martin, how rotten for him." Perhaps it's because you and Jill didn't know me before. Whatever it is, this is the one place I look forward to coming to, the place where I have fun. And you talk of owing me anything. It's I who owe you everything.'

After making this long speech Martin went red and looked very awkward, and I was tongue-tied too, but Mummy rose to the occasion and said, 'Thanks, Martin, that's very nice of you and I understand. We won't talk about obligations any more; we'll just say thank you.'

After that we all had tea, and everything looked rosy to me, and we had iced buns and a proper Christmas cake that an old friend of Mummy's had made and sent to her. But the delights of this day were not over. While we were having tea there was a knock at the door, and when I went to answer it a boy handed me a very large soft parcel, saying, 'This is for Miss Jill Crewe.'

'Gosh! Thanks!' I said, and carried it in.

'It's for me,' I said, holding it out to let Mummy see. 'Is this something to do with you, Martin?'

'No,' he said. 'Cross my heart, I know nothing about it.'

'Who on earth can it be from?' I said.

'Do open it and see,' said Mummy.

The magnificent thing was soon revealed, a lovely

dark-blue pony rug bound round with scarlet. I was speechless. It was Mummy who picked up the card and read aloud, 'To Jill Crewe, with many thanks from the mothers of Jennifer, Angela, Jane and Elizabeth.'

'I don't know how they knew,' I said. 'Honestly I didn't say anything to them, Mummy. I can't guess how they knew.'

(Afterwards I found out that they had asked Ann what I would like and she had suggested the rug.)

Of course the first thing I did was to rush off to try the rug on Black Boy. He looked wonderful with it on, and exactly like a blood pony, and he arched his neck and bucked a bit, just showing off because he knew how nice he looked; so I walked him up and down in front of the cottage windows and Mummy and Ann and Martin waved approval.

After getting all these wonderful presents, especially the horsy ones that I hadn't expected, I think you will agree with me that it was a very nice Christmas.

11 Cecilia's visit

A few days later I took Black Boy to the forge, and while Mr Blankett the smith was engaged in shoeing him he happened to say, 'If you haven't got a double bridle, I've got a nice one here for sale. It belongs to a gentleman who's going abroad and selling off all his used tack before he goes. I'll fetch it in a minute.'

So when he had finished Black Boy he went and fetched the bridle which really was a very nice one, and though well-used had been well-cared-for, with the leather supple and clean and the bits and curb chain shining.

I said, 'I expect it's rather expensive.'

'Oh, no,' said Mr Blankett. 'He wants to get the stuff sold. He's asking ten pounds for this, but I think he'd take nine.'

So of course I just dived into my pocket for my godmother's ten pound note, and the change went towards the shoeing. I thought I had done very well indeed. I felt that my stable was getting well-equipped; and it was such a thrilling thought after my weeks of making do and using makeshifts, that on the way back I let Black Boy buck and prance and do all the things he shouldn't do, just for sheer joy.

It was a lovely winter day, with a pale blue sky and sunlight brightening the red berries in the hedgerows and making the puddles glitter along the road.

When I got home the post had arrived, and Mummy

said, 'There's a letter from Cecilia's mother. She has to go to Ireland next week on business and she wonders whether Cecilia could come here for a few days. Of course we'll be glad to have her, won't we, Jill?'

'OK,' I said.

'I'll write out a telegram and you can bike down to the post office and send it at once. And, Jill, you'll have to sleep with me and let Cecilia have your room.'

'Oh blow!' I said. But I knew this would have to be as we only have two bedrooms at the cottage.

'Of course,' said Mummy, 'if you'd rather sleep with Cecilia in my room and let me go in yours – '

'Oh, no, she can have my room,' I said, but I began to feel very unenthusiastic about Cecilia's visit. I don't know how it is, but having to give up your room to a guest always seems to arouse murderous feelings in the breast.

The following week, on the Tuesday, Mummy and I went down to Chatton to meet Cecilia's train. I was actually feeling more than a bit scared, as fifteen is just on the verge of being grown up and I didn't know how Cecilia would react to me being not quite twelve. However, when she got off the train I saw that she wasn't any taller than I and didn't look at all grown up, not so much so as our prefects at The Pines School. She had plaits, and was wearing a brown school mac and a school hat right at the back of her head.

'Hello, Aunt Catherine!' she said. 'Hello, Jill!' And she kissed us both in a very friendly way, which struck me, as I am not very good at kissing myself.

On the way home in the bus, Cecilia said, 'And what are you doing with yourself these days, Jill?'

I said, 'Well, actually, I'm learning to ride.'

'What, still?' she said. 'I thought you learnt weeks and weeks ago.'

'I'm only just beginning,' I said.

'Good gracious!' said Cecilia. 'It's not so difficult, surely. Isn't it just a matter of learning to hang on?'

I shuddered slightly, and said, 'As a matter of fact, you can spend a lifetime learning to ride. If you are a really good horseman you know there's always something new to learn.'

'Good gracious!' said Cecilia.

However, when we got home she went into ecstasies over the cottage and said that the garden reminded her of that 'God Wot' poem and she would send Mummy a copy to hang up; and then I took her to my bedroom and she said she had always wanted to sleep in a bedroom with a sloping roof and she thought it was all simply wonderful.

She then went to my bookshelf to look at my books and I knew she would be looking for the one she had sent me for Christmas so I had put it rather towards the middle.

Cecilia said, 'Oh, there's the one I sent you, *The Madcap of the School*. Didn't you love it? I've got all Sallie T. Scott's books and I've read them over and over again until I nearly know them off by heart. There's *A Fourth Form Secret*, and *Prefect Patsy*, and *Sonia's First Term*. Don't you adore school stories? I never read anything else.'

'As a matter of fact,' I said, 'I get enough school in term time not to want to read about it in the hols, but,' I added, so as not to look disobliging, 'I know a lot of people read those books and I expect they're frightfully good if you're keen on that kind of thing.'

Cecilia looked at the rest of my books in a rather

bleak sort of way; and then I said, 'Shall we go down and see my pony before tea?' and she said she'd like to.

So we went down to the orchard and I called Black Boy and for once he came. Cecilia patted his nose, and said, 'You don't hunt, or anything, do you?'

I looked a bit blank, and said, no I didn't hunt or anything.

Cecilia said, 'Where do you ride?' so I showed her my riding school in the field, and then I saddled and bridled Black Boy and rode him round the ring a few times and he behaved beautifully.

'Good gracious!' said Cecilia. 'Is that all you do? I mean, just sitting on the pony and holding it in?'

'What I was doing,' I said, 'was a collected trot. I'll show you a collected canter, if you like, and a figure of eight with Black Boy changing legs in the middle, only I'm not frightfully certain of it yet.'

'Don't you ever do proper riding?' said Cecilia.

I felt myself boiling inside and thought how I should have swooned with shame if Martin had heard this remark. I had been going to invite Ann to tea on Saturday, but thought I had better not. It looked as though Cecilia was going to turn out to be the stain on the family escutcheon, as it says in books.

The next day Cecilia looked on with horror while I mucked out and fed Black Boy, but she thought it was fun to put down fresh straw, and she got quite enthusiastic over the hens and thought them 'sweet'. As it happened, Mummy had a cold, so I had offered to do the hens for once. It looked as though Cecilia was a henny rather than a horsy person. She said, wasn't it cruel to take their eggs away from them? And when I replied that all hens thought about was food and they were incapable of any sublimer feelings, I could tell she thought I was a callous and hardbitten woman.

She looked very disapproving when I said, 'Get off it!' to Maria Marten, who was a dopey type of fowl, and gave her a push out of the box.

When we went in to breakfast Cecilia said she didn't like porridge and could she have some cornflakes? We hadn'. got any cornflakes, so she said she would just have a lightly boiled egg. Mummy said that after breakfast I had better go down to Chatton on my bike and get some cornflakes for Cecilia, which I did. Cecilia said she didn't want to come, as she always read after breakfast in the holidays.

When I got back with the wretched cornflakes I found that Mummy had washed up and made the beds, while Cecilia was still reading. Then she said she would like to write to her mother, which took her about an hour, and I showed her where the box was in the lane to post her letter, but that didn't suit her at all, as she said that somebody she knew had once posted a letter in a box in a country lane and it hadn't got to where it was going for about a week, so she wanted her letter to be posted at a proper post office.

Mummy said I had better get my bike out again and go back to Chatton and post Cecilia's letter, so I did this, and so the dreary morning was spent.

The next morning at breakfast Mummy put out the cornflakes for which I had made my toilsome journey, but Cecilia only took one mouthful and then put her spoon down with a kind of patient-under-suffering look.

'Is there anything the matter with the cornflakes?' asked Mummy.

'Oh, no, Aunt Catherine,' said Cecilia. 'They're awfully nice really, only they're just not a bit like the ones I have at home, so if you don't mind I'll just have a lightly boiled egg.'

As you know, January is not what you'd call a lavish month for eggs, so Cecilia was pretty well appropriating our whole production.

I said I simply must give Black Boy some exercise today, so we went out. Cecilia rode my bike, and we went as far as Neshbury Common. Cecilia didn't think anything at all of my riding and she didn't think I would ever make a rider until I let myself go and wasn't afraid to give my pony his head. She said that a lot of her friends were marvellous riders, and their ponies were full of spirit and showed it and they galloped about and looked simply terrific.

I thought I would show Cecilia the kind of thing she evidently liked, so I sat well back in the saddle and thumped Black Boy with my heels, and he must have thought I had gone mad. However he rose to the occasion and bucked and side-stepped, and then went off at a mad uncontrolled pace and threw his head about, and I bounced up and down in the saddle, and when we got back Cecilia clapped her hands and said, 'Oh, jolly good! That was marvellous. You see, you can ride after all when you try.'

I was mopping my brow with relief at having got through that fearsome exhibition without being seen by anybody who knew me.

'Could I have a try?' said Cecilia.

'Well, actually, Black Boy's had enough for today,' I said doubtfully.

'Oh, you are mean,' she said.

So I had to say all right. Getting Cecilia into the saddle was like getting a sack of potatoes on to a lorry, but at last she was up. She stuck her feet straight out in front of her, leaned well back, pulled at the reins with a sprightly jerk, and said, 'Come up, now. Come up!'

It was too much for Black Boy. For the first and only time in his life he actually reared and stood straight up on his hind legs. Cecilia gave a scream and slid off, making a wild grab at his tail and fortunately missing it. She sat down with a thud on the grass, and to my relief Black Boy promptly came back to earth, and with a look at me, as much as to say, 'No more of this, if you please,' stood still in offended dignity.

'Oh!' said Cecilia. 'What an ill-bred horse! No well-bred horse *ever* rears. A man who knows all about horses told me that. You'll have to get rid of him. He's what they call a confirmed rearer.'

'He's nothing of the kind,' I said. 'He's never done it before and he'll never do it again. He's not used to having his mouth jerked like that.'

'Well, what on earth are the reins for?' said Cecilia getting up and brushing bits off her skirt, and smiling the slow superior smile of one who knows.

After this I started counting the hours to Cecilia's departure. I had to endure one final insult, when on the morning before she left she said innocently, 'Do you always ride in a mac and jeans? Shouldn't you have breeches and a jacket, or don't they bother round here?'

I honestly don't think she meant this maliciously, but I had my arms full of hay at the moment, and I could easily have smothered her with it.

However the darkest hour of human suffering comes to an end (Mummy's library book) and at last we were standing on Chatton station waving goodbye as Cecilia's train disappeared into the tunnel.

Mummy said, 'I don't think you liked Cecilia very much, did you, dear?'

'I thought she was awful,' I said frankly.

'You mean, she didn't like the same things that you liked. As grown-ups say, she didn't speak your language. But Jill, you mustn't be intolerant. You must make allowances for the other person's point of view, and look for a common ground of interest instead of emphasising your differences. It's the only way to live happily in a world where there are so many, many kinds of people.'

'Did you like her, Mummy?' I said.

'Yes, I did. She has charming manners and listens to what her elders have to say without interrupting.'

I gave a contented sigh. Cecilia was gone, so it wasn't worth starting an argument with Mummy.

12 Jodhpurs

I could now clear one-metre jumps easily, and wished
I had something better to practise on than my home-
made affairs.

It was a great piece of luck for me that Black Boy
liked jumping and was never reluctant to try, but all
the same Martin said that I must learn the proper way
to aid a pony who *was* nervous or reluctant. So he
invited me to go over to his home, The Grange, one
Saturday in March and try a pony he had there.

I was very bucked at the invitation but more than a
bit scared also. The night before, I scrubbed my mac
with Mummy's nail brush and took all the spots off
my jeans, and I washed and ironed my socks, shirt
and tie, and brushed my hat and shoes.

I set my alarm for six thirty next morning so that
I should have lots of time to give Black Boy a special
grooming. I crept downstairs in the chilly dawn, lit
the fire, and put a kettle on the gas ring. Then I
fed and groomed my pony, keeping one eye on the
kettle because I know what kettles are if you don't
do this.

When it boiled I climbed on a chair and got Mummy's soap-flakes out of the corner cupboard where
she thinks she has hidden them, and made a lovely
lather and washed Black Boy's tail, and while it was
drying I crawled about the kitchen floor, taking up
the tell-tale bits of soap-flake with my handkerchief.

I suppose you think this was very wicked of me, but I am surprised if you haven't done such deeds yourself, and everyone knows that the best quality soap-flakes are the nicest thing for washing a horse's tail.

Then I brought all the tack into the kitchen and cleaned it in front of the fire. I worked like a Trojan for about two hours altogether, and by then I was so ravenous that breakfast tasted specially good.

After breakfast I did my room and then began to dress. I stood in front of the mirror, wondering how I could make myself look more than twelve. In the end I combed my hair well and fastened it behind my ears with some of Mummy's grips. The new hair style made me look quite a bit sophisticated, though I didn't look in the least how I wanted to look which was like a girl who worked in a stable.

When I got to The Grange, Martin's father saw me and came out and shook hands with me in a very grown-up way. He said he had heard a lot about me from Martin, and I didn't know what to say because you never do when anybody says that kind of thing to you, so I just sort of smirked and said, 'Oh.'

Then he took me inside and introduced me to Martin's mother, who was rather old-fashioned and grandmother-ish and was sitting in an easy chair reading *The Times*.

I tried to look nonchalant and horsy, as I could tell this had been a horsy household from all the photographs and cups and horse brasses and whips that were hanging on the walls and strewn about, but it was rather spoilt when Mr Lowe said, 'This is the little girl that Martin is teaching to ride.'

And Mrs Lowe said, 'And what did you say your name was, my pet?'

So I just said, 'How do you do? I'm Jill Crewe,'

and I pushed in one of the grips, drawing attention to my sophisticated hairstyle.

Just then Martin came bowling in in his chair, and said, 'Hurrah, you've come. Now we'll cut the cackle and get to the 'osses.'

We went right through the house and out at the back, and it all looked like a most beautiful dream to me when I saw the long, low stable buildings and horses' heads looking over half-doors. The Lowes, unlike other people who had pulled down their stables or converted them into garages and flats for their friends, could not bear to live without horses, and Mr Lowe – who had won heaps of driving and hackney classes in his time – still kept a high-stepping hackney for his own use, and Mrs Lowe had a pair of matched greys and went to visit her friends in a carriage in the old-fashioned way. Mr Lowe was fond of buying and selling horses too, and so the stables at The Grange were always happily filled. I thought it must be a heavenly place to live.

There was a nice smiling groom there who led out a roan pony of about fourteen hands for me to try.

'This is Silvio,' said Martin. 'It will be very good for you to ride him, because you will find that he does not read your mind and anticipate your wants like Black Boy does, and he will wait for direction from you.'

It was funny to see the look on Black Boy's face when he saw me mount Silvio. It was fun riding Silvio, but I had to be on my mettle because he didn't do a thing except when I gave him the right aid. I felt I was making a mess of it, but Martin actually said, 'Jolly good.' This didn't elate me as it would have done six months before, because by now I had learned the true humility of a rider.

Then two boys came out and erected three jumps for me to try. I was so used to Black Boy's enthusiasm at the very sight of jumps, that I felt queer when I noticed that Silvio sort of sneered in a distasteful way, as much as to say, 'Oh bother! Jumping again.'

Therefore I was prepared when he refused the first jump, a rare experience for me. I patted him and spoke to him, took him back and put him at it again, but again he refused. So I tried all over again, and all I got was a third refusal.

'Oh gosh!' I said to Martin.

He roared with laughter.

'It's up to you, Jill,' he said.

I took Silvio back, and whispered in his ear, 'Oh, Silvio, dear Silvio, for heaven's sake jump it or you'll cover me with disgrace for ever.'

We tried again, and this time he made a very bored effort and down came the whole gate.

'Oh, help!' I said, looking back disgustedly.

'Jill,' said Martin, 'I warned you to expect no assistance from that horse.'

'No assistance!' I said. 'That's putting it mildly.'

'If you want to know,' said Martin, 'Silvio's stride was not right for the jump – which you ought to have seen to – and you said "Hup" just about one-twentieth of a second too soon.'

'If he's going to be as fussy as that about details – ' I began.

'He's a born obeyer, is Silvio. He likes to obey, and he puts the whole of the burden of *thinking* on to his rider. Now try jumping the bush. He is used to being held in until the exact second when he must go right for the jump. It is for you to learn what is that exact second and give him his aids. Off you go!'

By now I didn't expect much from Silvio, but I

tried frightfully hard and soon I did begin to get better results. Before the morning was over I felt that I really had learned something about jumping. Then, because Black Boy had been watching Silvio enviously for so long, I changed on to my own pony and put him over the jumps twice and it seemed so easy and effortless that I fairly sighed with relief.

But I quite realised that I could never call myself a horsewoman until I could cope with horses like Silvio, and far, far worse.

I thanked Martin very much for giving me the chance, and he said, 'That's all right. I hope you'll come again often, in fact you'll have to before the gymkhana season begins.'

'Why? What has that to do with me?' I said.

His eyes widened.

'I hope you're going to do me credit,' he said. 'Surely you want to ride in gymkhanas?'

'*Want to!*' I cried. 'I can't imagine anything more marvellous. But I never thought I'd be able to for years and years. I'm not nearly good enough. I'll make an awful fool of myself.'

'I shouldn't enter you if I thought that,' said Martin.

'To ride in a gymkhana!' I said. 'Oh crumbs!'

'Don't look so awed,' he said, laughing.

'But it's the dream of my life. I mean, to ride round the ring with a rosette at my pony's ear and a certificate in my teeth.'

'Is that why you want to enter for a gymkhana?' said Martin. 'If I thought it was I wouldn't be so keen on entering you.'

'Why?' I said. 'Don't you want me to win?'

'Of course I do. But I say that the type of rider who enters a gymkhana simply with the idea of winning cups and rosettes has no business to be there at all. I should hate you to be that kind of person, Jill, but I'm quite sure that you won't be. What do you suppose gymkhanas are for?'

'I suppose, to give people a chance to show that they can ride and compete with others,' I said.

'Partly,' said Martin. 'But the real purpose of any gymkhana is simply to raise the standard of horsemanship and to bring out the best in horses and riders. Remember that. And now we'll go in and have some coffee and cakes.'

So we went indoors and had lovely elevenses – only it was twelve o'clock by then – and Mrs Lowe told me about her greys and how long she had had them, and I listened very intelligently and I'm sure she thought I was about fifteen.

All the way home I was singing, 'Gymkhana! Gymkhana! Gymkhana!'

As usual Mummy had a few things to say about my having gone mad.

It was a few days after this that one afternoon she gave me ten pounds to call for my shoes which had been soled and heeled; so after school I set out for the cobbler's shop which is in the main street at Chatton, and in case anyone is interested, his name is Mr Price and he does the shoes really well.

On the way I passed the auctioneer's place, and the doors were open and a crowd of people inside. I couldn't resist stopping to listen, though it turned out he was selling frightfully dull things like sets of wine-glasses and rugs.

I wormed my way through the crowd, right up to the edge of the table where the various rather scruffy-looking lots were set out, and all of a sudden my eye fell upon something that looked cordy and fawn-coloured. I thought at first it must be a bit of a rug, but with my usual curiosity I pushed my way up to this object and poked it open with my fingers.

Then my jaws fell apart and I'm sure my eyes stood right out. 'It' was a rolled up parcel consisting of a pair of jodhpurs and a little check jacket, and at a glance I could see that they would just fit me.

I simply couldn't believe it; it was like a fairy tale. When I came more or less to my senses I noticed that the jodhpurs had a ticket on with Lot 233 printed on it in red.

The auctioneer was just shouting out, 'Lot 225,' which was a marble clock with brass angels on the top. The next few minutes went by in a kind of daze; I wanted those jodhpurs and that jacket so terribly, and I knew that in a minute they were going to be auctioned and I should see them knocked down to some awful undeserving person and I couldn't bear it.

How much would they fetch? Probably pounds and pounds. That marble clock had just been sold for the fabulous sum of fifty-five pounds.

I looked at Mummy's money in my hand, which was to pay for my shoes being soled and heeled and leave some change over.

'Lot 233,' said the auctioneer. 'Pair of girl's jodhpurs and riding jacket. Now here's a lovely lot, one of the finest lots I've had through my hands for many a long day. Buy this fine outfit for your daughter and there's nothing to stop her being England's premier lady jockey. See her win the Grand National. Now, ladies and gentlemen, what am I bid for this really magnificent outfit of the finest quality. Somebody give me a start, please.'

There was silence. My heart turned over. Actually

I might have known that in a place like Chatton people who bought riding outfits didn't have to buy them secondhand, and that this was a set that some child had outgrown and there wouldn't be much demand for it.

'Give me a start, ladies and gentlemen, *please!*' said the auctioneer in a very pained voice.

'Three pounds,' said a voice at the back, fairly reluctantly.

The auctioneer looked round in patient suffering.

'Very well, very well. We'll start at three, though that is simply a joke for this fine riding outfit which is worth ten pounds of anybody's money. Three I'm offered, three pounds I'm bid. Now . . . four pounds. Four, *please!*.

There was quite a silence.

I gave a little gasp, and the next minute the auctioneer had looked at me and said, 'Thank you, madam. I'm bid four by the young lady. Now five pounds . . . five pounds, please.'

This time the silence was awfully long. My excitement was crawling all up me and getting into my throat. At last the man at the back must have given a nod because the auctioneer, looked straight at me and said, 'Now, madam, there's five pounds bid against you. Make it six? Six pounds for this magnificent riding outfit which I can see will just fit you. Six pounds, madam, *please*.'

'All right,' I said with a dry throat.

'Any advance on six pounds?' said the auctioneer, looking round, but nobody said anything, and the next minute his hammer came down with a crack.

'Sold to the young lady in the school uniform. Next Lot 234.'

Still I couldn't believe it. I pushed my way up to

a man who was writing in a book and said, 'Please can I pay and take my things away?'

'Certainly, madam,' he said, very politely, and he looked at his book and said, 'Six pounds please,' and I gave him a ten pound note – Mummy's – and he gave me four pounds, and a receipted bill, and I went up to the table and took beautiful Lot 233 in my arms and walked out into the street with it, feeling all shot up and weak.

I had just enough money left to go and collect my shoes, and I biked home wondering what Mummy would say. Of course I knew I had no business to spend her money on things for myself, but somehow it all seemed to have been meant, as though the fairies had done it. Surely Mummy would see this.

Still money was money, and I did know very well that Mummy was going through a tough time. There hadn't been any cheques for a long time, and Mummy simply never bought anything for herself. She hadn't had anything new to wear for longer than I could remember, and I had had all that new school uniform. She had been what she called 'budgeting for every penny' and here was I gaily flinging six pounds into the maw of an auctioneer in return for jodhpurs.

Oh, but I hugged my parcel. It was just a dream come true.

I took my bike round to the back of the cottage, and walked into the kitchen with my parcel in my arms, and stood wondering what to say.

'Hullo, Jill,' said Mummy. 'You're a bit late, aren't you? Did you go to Ann's? Oh, of course, you had to fetch your shoes. How much were they?'

Then she looked at me, and said, 'What have you got there?'

'Oh, Mummy,' I said, all in a burst. 'It's jodhpurs.

Look. I – I – ' and out came the whole story, though it was a bit jumbled up, what with excitement and guilty conscience.

'Oh,' said Mummy when I'd finished, and looked a bit blank. Then she said, 'You know you shouldn't spend money on yourself that I'd given you for something else.'

'Yes, I know,' I mumbled, going very red, 'but – but I'd been simply dreaming about jodhpurs for ages and ages, and it – it seemed like magic.'

Mummy sighed.

'I know,' she said. 'I – I ought to have guessed. It's all right, Jill, only don't buy anything else without asking me, will you? I mean, money is money.'

I rushed at her and enveloped her in a bear hug.

'Oh, thank you, Mummy!' I said in a heartfelt way. 'And I won't do it again because I know I oughtn't to, with no cheques, and you never have anything yourself, and I do feel a pig about it honestly, only just to *see* them lying there – '

'That horse!' said Mummy. 'I knew what it would be.'

'Oh golly!' I said. 'I must go and feed him.'

'And as for these things,' said Mummy looking with strange distaste at my beautiful jodhpurs, 'goodness know where they've come from.'

'Oh, that doesn't worry me,' I said. 'Only nice people have jodhpurs, anyway.'

'I'm not sure,' said Mummy. 'Anyway, they're dirty and so is the jacket, and I suppose you've noticed – but of course you wouldn't – that one elbow is out and there are three moth holes in the collar – '

'Oh, that's nothing,' I said hastily.

'Well, you must take them to the cleaner's. You'd

better do it tomorrow, and that'll be about *another* five pounds!'

This thought made me feel awful and just put the lid on all my pleasure. I couldn't even tell Mummy to take it out of my pocket money because I actually owed her quite a bit already that I'd had in advance the week before.

I was plunged into blackest gloom as I went out to the orchard to catch Black Boy, and when he didn't come at once I spoke to him crossly, which I think was the first time I had ever done so, so it shows how my nature was becoming depraved.

I felt more awful still when next morning I found that Mummy had done the things up in a nice neat parcel for me to take to the cleaner's; but I didn't say anything, and took them on my way to school, and the woman gave me two tickets.

A week later Mummy gave me the money and I went to collect the things. When I opened them out in the kitchen they looked so nice that I had to give a gulp, and just then Mummy came in and said, in an understanding way, 'Don't look so blue, Jill. We're not ruined yet.'

13 The bring and buy sale

It was amazing how my riding improved after I got my jodhpurs. I began to feel I was really getting on and could nearly call myself a rider, though Mummy said this feeling was psychological.

Funnily enough, I don't think Martin even noticed my lovely new rig-out, and if he did he didn't say a word about it, but Mummy said men are like that.

When I went round to Ann's on the Saturday afternoon, she said at once, 'Gee whizz! You do look smashing.'

I said, 'Let's go for a ride somewhere,' and for once she was quite enthusiastic.

One day during eleven o'clock break at school, Ann said to me, 'What are you grunting and sighing about?'

'I was just thinking,' I said.

'What about? That awful Latin?'

'No. I say, Ann, you don't by any chance know any ways of raising money, do you?'

'Of course,' she said surprisingly. 'It's easy.'

'*Easy!* What on earth do you mean?'

'It's easy,' she repeated. 'Mummy's always raising money. You just have a Bring and Buy Sale. They had one last week at Mrs Fairedge's and raised about eight hundred pounds.'

'Eight hundred pounds!' I gasped. 'Easy! What on earth's a Bring and Buy Sale? How do you do it?'

'Well, you have it at somebody's house,' said Ann. 'You have a table in the garden, or in the dining room if it's wet, and you stand behind the table and say, "Hello, Mrs Derry. Frightfully nice of you to come along," and heaps of people come, and they all bring something to sell and put it on the table, and then they all buy something and go home. And at the end you have heaps of money.'

'But doesn't it cost you anything?' I asked.

'Of course not, silly. People bring something and then they buy something and go away. It sort of balances out, and you get the money.'

'I never heard of it,' I said, overwhelmed by the brilliance of this simple scheme. 'It sounds terrific. I say, Ann, do you think you and I could have one?'

'A what?'

'A Bring and Buy Sale, or whatever you call it.'

She gave a whoop.

'Oh, I say, what fun! Oh, yes, Jill, lets. Do you mean at your house? When?'

I began to think furiously. I wanted to do this Bring and Buy Sale thing all by myself, and I thought it would be as well to have it when Mummy wasn't there as she might fuss and worry about having things just right. As it happened, she had talked about going to see an old school friend of hers the following Saturday; and as this old friend lived about twenty miles away, it would mean that Mummy would have to leave our cottage about ten o'clock to catch the bus in Chatton, and she couldn't possibly be back here before about six, so that would leave us heaps of time for a Bring and Buy Sale. What a thrill it would be when she came back if I could tell her, quite casually, that I had raised eight hundred pounds very, very easily! It *must* be all right to have a Bring and Buy

Sale if Ann's mother did it, because Mrs Derry was such a very particular person.

So I said to Ann, 'Look here. Mummy's going away for the day on Saturday. Let's have the Bring and Buy Sale then, in our garden. It will be fun. You know all about it, so you can come round early and help me with the arranging.'

Ann was jumping about with excitement by now, and I was pretty well topped-up myself. We could hardly wait for Saturday to come, and then my heart sank into my shoes on Friday night when Mummy said, 'If it's a wet day tomorrow I shan't go.'

So about five o'clock on Saturday morning I was leaping out of bed and rushing to the window to see what sort of day it was going to be. Everything looked dry and sort of hopeful, even at that early hour which is usually so depressing, and it turned out to be a lovely, bright, sunshiny spring day.

Of course Mummy fussed a lot about leaving me alone, even when I told her that Ann was coming to spend the day with me. I nearly told her about the Bring and Buy Sale, only I didn't want to raise her hopes until I actually knew how much money we had got.

At last she was ready, and I went with her to the bus stop and saw her on to the bus, and waved until she was out of sight. Then I went back to the cottage, and it had that funny silent feeling that houses have when you are in them alone. I can never understand this, because even if there is a person in another room where you can't see them, you don't get that funny hushed feeling.

However, about five minutes later Ann arrived and we started writing notices on sheets of paper torn out of our map books, which are rather large, using red crayon to write with.

BRING AND BUY SALE
AT
POOL COTTAGE, POOL LANE
THIS AFTERNOON AT 2 UNTIL ABOUT 4.30

We thought we had better stop about four thirty so as to clear up and have our tea before Mummy got back, only if business was brisk we could always go on a bit longer.

We fastened one of the notices on our garden gate with drawing pins, because actually a lot of people go along Pool Lane, and then we biked to the end of the lane where it joins Greenwood Road, and we fastened another notice to the hedge there with safety pins.

Then we went back home and began to make our preparations. Actually it didn't take long, as all we had to do was to carry out the kitchen table and put it inside the little garden shed, after we had taken the garden tools out to make more room. It looked a bit bare, so I brought down the Paisley shawl off Mummy's bed and we covered the table with it.

Then we wrote another notice which said, THIS WAY TO THE BRING AND BUY SALE, and then a lovely arrow pointing, and we pinned it up just inside the gate, showing the way to the garden shed.

Ann said we should want something to put the money in, so she fetched a Pyrex dish and put it on the table on the Paisley shawl, and the Bring and Buy Sale was ready and it looked really elegant.

By now we were starving, so we went inside and ate the cold lunch that Mummy had left and washed up the plates and things, and then there was still about an hour, so we practised Musical Chairs a bit with Black Boy in the orchard. We both had our jodhpurs on, and clean shirts.

At ten minutes to two we washed our hands and brushed our hair and went and stood behind the table in the shed, most frightfully excited to see what would happen and if anybody would come.

'I'll die if nobody comes,' said Ann.

'Oh!' I said. 'Do they sometimes have a Bring and Buy Sale and nobody comes?'

'Oh, no,' said Ann reassuringly. 'Heaps of people come always. Only I suppose I just got the needle because this is our own affair.'

'Help!' I said. 'I believe somebody's coming.'

'It's old Miss Acheson,' said Ann. 'She's frightfully benevolent and always goes to all the Bring and Buy Sales.'

Miss Acheson was about eighty and very short-sighted. She peered at Ann, and said, 'Good afternoon, my dear. I came early because I have to go on to the Girl Guides' display. I've brought you this – ' and she laid a brown paper parcel on the table.

She looked a bit surprised when she saw the table was bare.

'Oh dear!' she said. 'It is a Sale, isn't it?'

'You're the first,' said Ann. 'We haven't got anything to sell yet.'

'Oh, what a pity,' said Miss Acheson. 'Still, it can't be helped. Good afternoon.' And away she went.

'That's a bit awkward,' said Ann. 'Anyway, now we've got something to sell, if anybody else comes'; and she opened Miss Acheson's parcel which contained a home-made wool scarf knitted in a rather poisonous shade of green.

We laid this out on the table.

Just then I saw another lady come in at the gate.

'It's Mrs Newton,' said Ann.

'Hello, Ann,' said Mrs Newton, looking rather surprised. 'I didn't know this was one of your mother's efforts?'

'Well, it isn't exactly,' said Ann.

'I've brought you a bottle of my home-made chutney,' said Mrs Newton. 'I suppose I'll have to buy something. What have you got?'

'Well, it's a bit early,' said Ann. 'We've only got this scarf.'

'Oh, I don't want that,' said Mrs Newton. 'Perhaps I'll come back later, if I have time.'

So she said goodbye and went.

'Now we've got two things to sell,' said Ann.

'But we haven't taken any money yet,' I pointed out.

'I say!' said Ann, unscrewing the top of the bottle of chutney. 'This chutney smells pretty awful. I hope it hasn't gone bad.'

'Well, screw it up tight,' I said, 'and let's hope that somebody will buy it without smelling it.'

Presently an elderly gentleman and lady came in. I didn't know them and neither did Ann.

The lady said, 'We always believe in supporting all the local efforts.'

She put down a parcel on the table, and picked up the chutney and said, 'How much is this?'

Ann looked blank, because actually we had forgotten to talk about prices.

'One pound,' I said wildly.

'All right, I'll have it,' said the elderly lady. 'You don't seem to have much to sell yet, do you?'

I put the proceeds in the Pyrex dish, feeling frightfully bucked that we were actually raising money at last. Ann opened the parcel and disclosed a bag of rather greasy-looking buns and a shaving mug with A PRESENT FROM BOURNEMOUTH on it. We put the mug next to the green scarf and arranged the buns round. The table began to look pretty good.

Then there was a lull and for ages nobody came at all. We both felt very low. Then about three o'clock, five people arrived all at once. Actually they had brought rather nice things, like gardening gloves and quarter-pounds of tea, so they all bought each other's things, and when they had gone away there was eight pounds sixty in the Pyrex dish, and we still had the buns and the shaving mug and the green scarf.

'Gosh!' I said. 'It's getting exciting.'

Then something even more exciting happened. A car drew up at the gate and a chauffeur got out and came walking up the path carrying something in his hand.

He said, 'Mrs Sullivan sends her compliments and is very sorry she can't attend the Bring and Buy Sale as she has a previous engagement, but she asked me to bring you this.'

'This', was a little straw punnet filled with paper shavings, and on the shavings there sat six lovely brown eggs.

Then for about half an hour we were most frightfully busy, and when the smoke, as you might say, cleared from the battlefield I found that Ann had sold the eggs for one pound fifty, the buns for one pound and the green scarf for eighty pence, and I had sold the shaving mug for forty pence, and there was somehow or other thirty-three pounds and sixty-nine pence in the Pyrex dish, and on the table was a bundle of rhubarb and a dog collar and a book called *What to Do till the Doctor Comes*.

Then a small girl of about seven came in and said her mummy had sent her to buy something, so we sold her the book for fifty pence and the dog collar for two pounds, and as her Mummy had given her three pounds to spend we said she could have the rhubarb for forty pence.

That cleared us out, and made the money in the Pyrex dish up to thirty-seven pounds fifty-nine pence.

Nobody else seemed to be coming and I was nearly dying of thirst, so I went into the house for a drink of water, and as Ann said she wasn't thirsty she stayed outside in case any more customers came.

Unfortunately, I managed to break the glass I was drinking out of, and it took me a long time to sweep up all the pieces. When I went outside again, Ann said, 'I say, I hope you don't mind but I've sold the Paisley shawl.'

'Oh,' I said, feeling a bit taken back.

'I got an awful lot for it,' said Ann. 'Ten pounds. A man came with a little cart, and I said, "I'm afraid we haven't got anything left to sell," and he said, "Well, what about this?" and I said, 'Well, actually it belongs to Jill's mother," and he said, "I'll give you ten pounds for it," so I thought you'd be pleased, and I said OK. Oh, and he gave me fifty pence for the Pyrex dish, so that more or less clears us out, and we've made forty seven pounds – no, forty-eight pounds and ninepence. I've counted it.'

'I hope to goodness you haven't sold the kitchen table,' I said, 'as we haven't got another.'

'Oh, no,' said Ann. 'It's still here.'

So actually there was very little clearing up to do after the Bring and Buy Sale. We just carried the kitchen table in, and put the tools back in the shed, and took the notices down; and then we made a plate of jam sandwiches and had tea.

Ann said, another time we'd arrange tea for the customers, as her mother said that always made a lot of money.

Talking of money made me realise that after all we hadn't made eight hundred pounds and that anything we had made, namely forty-eight pounds nine pence, would have to be shared with Ann, as it had been her idea and she had done quite half the work. So I said we had better share fifty-fifty, but Ann said no, the sale had been at our house and therefore I ought to have the most, so she would just take five pounds towards the cassette deck she was saving up for, which left me with forty-three pounds nine pence.

After she had gone home, which was at half past five, I began to feel a bit funny about this, as such a lot of it had come from Mummy's Paisley shawl and our Pyrex dish, and I began to think that perhaps Bring and Buy Sales were not so profitable after all as a means of raising money.

When Mummy did get home I was quite glad to pour out the whole story to her, only I will now draw a veil, as the storm burst. It was awful, because though in a way I had been quite innocent, Mummy pointed out to me that Bring and Buy Sales are always in aid of some charitable object such as orphans or missionaries, and never, never in aid of Yourself.

She said I would have to make a list of all the people who had been to our sale, and what they had spent and go and give it back to them, and see that Ann did too. And when I told her about the Paisley shawl she went quite white, because it had belonged to her great-grandmother, and though it was worth a great deal more than ten pounds it was what they call the sentimental value which counted most.

To make a long story short, Ann and I did give the money back, though some people were very decent and laughed and wouldn't take it, as they said they had enjoyed our Bring and Buy Sale so much it was worth whatever it was they had spent.

Next day Mummy went to the police, and they found the man with the cart and made him take the ten pounds fifty back and give up the Paisley shawl and the Pyrex dish.

Thus ended our Bring and Buy Sale and my efforts to raise money. In the end, of course, it was Martin who came to the rescue once again. He had heard the story somewhere, and he said, 'Surely you didn't think I would enter you for a gymkhana and not turn you out properly? Our stables are full of saddles and what not, and I'd have offered you a better saddle for Black Boy long ago, only you're so proud and always talking about silly things like obligations that don't exist.'

So his groom brought the saddle, and Mummy said it was a lot more than I deserved.

14 Camp Pegasus

Will you believe me? – in less than a week I was in trouble again. Mummy came in one day with that tight, saving-it-up look on her face, and at lunch-time out it came.

'Jill, I hear that you refused an invitation from Mrs Harvey some time ago, without consulting me? How was that?'

I thought furiously for a minute, and then remembered how in the autumn Mrs Harvey had invited me to go for a riding weekend to a farm and I had refused without telling Mummy because it cost one hundred pounds.

So I just said rather cautiously, 'Oh.'

'I don't know what "oh" means,' said Mummy crossly. 'But I think you were vey rude. You know how I detest casualness. It was most ungrateful to Martin too. Why on earth didn't you tell me about it at the time?'

'I don't know,' I mumbled.

'And that is no answer,' said Mummy. 'Really, Jill, you get worse and worse.'

'OK,' I said, and got up from the table shrugging my shoulders in a pretty awful sort of way, only I didn't mean it a bit like that. I went up to my room and stood staring out of the window, feeling like those noble people in history, Joan of Arc and others, who were misunderstood. They may have got a kick out of it but I didn't.

Mummy didn't come near me and the afternoon dragged along. It was awful. At four o'clock I couldn't bear it any longer; besides, I was jolly hungry, so I went down and said, 'I didn't tell you about it because it cost one hundred pounds and I'm sick of being noble. In future I'm going to be an adventuress.' And I grabbed Black Boy's tin off the sink and went out of the back door.

Mummy came after me and we had a reconciliation, and went back for tea.

'The fact is,' said Mummy, 'that Mrs Harvey and Eileen have sent you another invitation of the same kind. They are getting up a party to spend a week at a farm in Warwickshire, and they wondered if you would like to go and take two friends. I want you to go, Jill, so if you like the idea we'll call it settled.'

'Oh, how marvellous!' I fairly shouted. 'How absolutely wonderful, super, and smashing.'

'I thought you'd like it,' said Mummy. 'You'd better go round and tell Ann, because I presume she'll be one of the two you want to ask.'

Black Boy was ready for some exercise, so I changed, saddled him, and went charging off to the Derrys' house. Mrs Derry said that Ann could go, though she fussed a lot about whether the farm would have proper sanitation, and I said I didn't know but I was sure that Mrs Harvey would be most frightfully sanitary wherever she went.

Then Ann and I started discussing who else we would ask, and after going through practically the whole school we finally decided to ask Diana Bush from our form, who was a very decent sort of person and rode quite well too.

At last the great day came, and at tea-time our party arrived at Applegate Farm. The very look of it was exciting. The house was very old, Tudor in fact, and had gables and twisty chimneys, and odd little windows with ivy framing them, and a romantic appearance which made you think of highwaymen and lovelocks and things.

The stableyard, however, was far from antique, it was most beautifully modern and clean and spacious, and there were loose boxes for the horses who were as excited as we were and all snorting and whiffling with pleasure at being in such a nice place and in each other's company, for horses like being in parties as well as people do.

Mr and Mrs Cave who kept the farm were most welcoming, and knew Mrs Harvey well, in fact Mrs Cave had been Eileen's nurse. We all sat down to tea, which consisted of ham and eggs and stewed rhubarb and real cream and very fruity fruit cake; and then Mrs Harvey said, 'Now all to saddle, girls! Let's go and explore.'

Our first ride was one I shall never forget; everything looked and smelt so fresh and lovely. I don't know what sort of holidays are taken by people who read this book, but actually there is no holiday on earth to compare with a riding holiday, and I speak from a wide experience as I have been to Torquay and to the Lake District and other so-called popular places.

Our party consisted of Mrs Harvey, who was about forty but not too old to enjoy life, and a friend of hers about the same age called Mrs Mason who was the best person at telling campfire stories I ever heard. Then there was Eileen Harvey, and a friend of hers – also nineteen – called Gail Dunham; and Eileen's two cousins, Jean and Peta Graham who were fifteen and thirteen, and Ann and Diana and me. Nine in all.

Our sleeping arrangements were great fun, for we slept in two enormous attics which went right across the farmhouse. One had four beds and the other had five. The four older people slept in one, and we five younger ones in the other, which was just like a school dorm, with iron beds covered with patchwork quilts. The roof of our bedroom sloped down nearly to the floor, and every time you sat up in bed there was a slight crack as your skull hit the roof. After a bit we got used to this. There was a funny dormer window, too, that you had to stand on tiptoe to look out of.

The first night, though we were tired out, none of us could sleep for toffee, and we kept bouncing up in bed and saying, 'Oh!' as our heads cracked on the roof, and then saying, 'Help! I *can't* go to sleep!' This seemed to go on for hours, but at last one by one we all fell asleep from sheer exhaustion. I only seemed to have been asleep a minute when I woke to find Ann shaking me, and it was six o'clock and the sun was simply pouring in at the dormer window, and we all got up and did a war dance at the prospect of a lovely day.

In about ten minutes we were all dressed, though we had to queue up to wash at the one big china wash-bowl with red roses on it, and then out we dashed to do our ponies. We then ate an enormous breakfast, and by nine o'clock were on the road for an all-day ride.

When we got back at night we were all full of fresh air and sunshine and nearly dropping asleep in our saddles, but Mrs Harvey put us through the full routine of rubbing down and feeding our ponies before we ourselves collapsed gratefully in the Caves' hospitable kitchen. Though Mrs Harvey was the greatest fun, she never allowed one minute's slackness or laziness in the jobs we had to do, which was quite right, because if you are slack you will never make a rider, nor will your pony do you credit, and that won't be the pony's fault.

At night we had great fun. It was lovely warm weather, and down at the bottom of the orchard we made a campfire and all sat round it, roasting potatoes and telling stories, mostly about horses, but some about dogs and about children of other countries.

Mrs Harvey produced a scarlet pennon which she fastened to a staff and fixed up beside our campfire, and on the pennon Eileen had embroidered the words Camp Pegasus in white because that was what the Harveys always called their camps, Pegasus being the loveliest horse in any story that has ever been written.

On the fourth day of our holiday Mrs Harvey, Mrs Mason, Eileen, and Gail went to spend the day with some friends, and the rest of us decided to go for a ride by ourselves to visit a ruined castle. However, we didn't get as far as the castle, because we had just clattered through a rushing stream when Ann called out, 'Wait! I've dropped my watch in the stream.'

'Oh, how did you do that?' said Jean, who was given to making pointless remarks.

'The strap was loose. I felt it drop off,' said Ann, giving Jean an exasperated look.

'You ought to have got a new strap,' said Jean infuriatingly.

'Well, I'm going back to look for it,' said Ann,

plunging Seraphine back into the stream which wasn't very deep and had a gravelly bottom. We all went in too, to help Ann, but unfortunately the ponies stirred up the bottom and the water went all pink and sandy so we couldn't see anything.

'If you'd all get out,' said Ann, 'I might have a chance.'

Just then Peta Graham who was on the bank a little farther downstream called out, 'There's something bright here. Perhaps the current's carried it down.'

'Right-ho,' said Ann, 'I'm coming.'

She turned Seraphine to the place where Peta was pointing, but the stream was much wider here and also much deeper, and what was worse it had a mud bottom, and the next minute Seraphine was stuck and floundering madly about trying to pull her feet out and going deeper and deeper in. The mud was all churned up, and the more Seraphine struggled the worse she was caught.

'Can't you keep her still?' said Jean.

'Don't be an idiot,' said Ann. 'It's as much as I can do to stick on her. Can't one of you get in and lead her out?'

'I will,' said Diana, 'but I'll have to take off my jodhpurs.'

So she took off her jodhpurs and she was wearing her gym briefs underneath, and she got down into the stream which came well above her knees, and got hold of Seraphine's bridle and pulled like mad, but it wasn't the slightest use. The next minute Diana was stuck too, and she let go of Seraphine's bridle and sat down with a plop. Then she scrambled out to the bank, oozing mud all over the place and spitting it out of her mouth.

'Goodness, you are a help!' said Ann to the rest of

us. 'Jean, yours is the strongest pony. Bring him close
to the bank and give me hold of his reins. That's right.
Now start him forward quickly!'

With Ann holding on to his reins, Jean gave Bullet,
her pony, a hard thwack, and off he went with a will.
The next minute Ann came right over Seraphine's
head, slap into the water, while Bullet went loping
away into the distance.

We started to shriek with laughter.

'Well, of all the mutts!' said Ann witheringly,
dragging her dripping form up the bank.

'It's all your own fault,' said Jean. 'You ought to
have hung on to Seraphine. I took it for granted you'd
do that. Mutt yourself!'

'Look, there's a farm over there,' I said. 'Let's
go and see if they'll lend us a strong horse to pull
Seraphine out.'

The rest thought this was a good idea, so Peta and
I set off to the farm while Jean stayed with the soaking
Ann and Diana to keep their morale up.

'And hurry up!' shouted Ann. 'I'm freezing to
death!'

The only person we could find at the farm was
a deaf old man of about ninety, and it took us ten
minutes' shouting at the top of our voices to make
him understand what we wanted. When he finally
understood he told us that all the men were out
working in the fields, but we could borrow old
Bingo if we liked. He pointed to where old Bingo
was standing beside the horse trough with his eyes
shut, apparently sound asleep.

Old Bingo was an enormous Suffolk Punch who
looked about thirty years old and had a large white
moustache and beard.

'Could we have him harnessed?' said Peta.

'He ain't no use for no fancy ridin',' said the old man.

'No, no!' we yelled. 'We want him *harnessed*, with long *traces*, to pull a pony out of the stream.'

'He ain't much good at pullin', ain't Bingo,' said the old man. However, he eventually found a set of harness, mostly tied together with string, and we got it on Bingo, and we knotted up the traces. We had to keep waking Bingo up, as he fell asleep again as soon as he was left alone for a minute.

We led him out of the farmyard at last, while the old man stood looking after us and shaking his head as though he thought we were all going to our doom.

When we got back to our friends, they were standing in a row, looking very blue and regarding Seraphine who was also standing, shivering, with the muddy water swirling round her hocks.

'What's that you've got?' said Diana. 'I bet it was in the Ark.'

'You wait,' I said. 'Here, Ann and Diana, you're wet already, so you'd better get in and tie these traces to Seraphine's girths. And tie them tight, for goodness sake.'

'It'll be a scream if Seraphine pulls Bingo in,' said Peta.

'You really do think of the funniest things!' I said witheringly.

It took Ann and Diana about ten minutes to get Bingo's traces tied with reef knots to Seraphine's girths, and they used all the bits of string we could lay our hands on in the process. Meanwhile Bingo went calmly off to sleep again.

'Now!' said Ann at last. 'You three get at Bingo's head, and Diana and I will get behind Seraphine.

When I say Go! you give Bingo a good slosh on the flank, Jean, while Jill and Peta pull at his bridle. That ought to get him started. And, Diana, when I say Shove! you shove like mad. Got it?'

'OK,' we said.

'Right,' said Ann. 'Now – Go! Shove!'

So we all did our part, but Bingo's enormous hoofs only churned about madly as he failed to get a grip on the bank.

'Oh, stop!' I shouted, 'or we'll all be in the stream. We'll have to pad his hoofs with something.'

'What with?' said Jean.

'Our jackets,' said Diana. 'It's all we've got. Wrap them round his feet and button them up his legs.'

So we all took off our jackets, except Jean who was wearing a knitted cardigan, and muffled them round Bingo's feet while he looked on, now fully awake, in a very worried way.

Then we all took action stations again.

'Right!' said Ann. 'Now off you go. Go! Shove!'

Bingo's mighty heave astonished us all. The jackets gripped well, and the next minute we all fell flat on our backs while our equine giant went staggering up the bank with Seraphine plunging after.

'She's out,' said Jean.

'You're telling me!' said Ann. 'Gosh, look at our jackets.'

Our jackets were by now just clots of mud, while Peta's and Ann's were very badly torn by Bingo's hind hoofs.

A quarter of an hour later, looking a very sorry crew, we headed back home, wondering what on earth Mrs Harvey would say. But our farmer's wife, Mrs Cave, proved to be a real sport. She didn't go into hysterics or anything when she saw us. She just said, 'Well, we'll have to get you girls straight before Mrs Harvey comes back.' Which was our own idea.

'Just look at our awful jackets!' said Ann.

'That's all right,' said Mrs Cave. 'I'll have those sponged and pressed in no time, and run up the tears on my sewing machine. Now get out of those wet clothes, girls, and in front of my big fire.'

So we all sat in a row with our feet in a kind of pig trough full of steaming hot water and mustard, and drank cups of boiling Bovril. And Mrs Cave was a real fairy, I do believe, because by the time Mrs Harvey and the others got back we were all clean and clothed again as though nothing had happened.

Mrs Harvey said, 'Have you had a nice day, girls?'

'Oh, marvellous!' said Ann with great presence of mind. 'My pony stuck in a stream but we pulled her out.'

The next day Ann and I went back and found her watch lying quite peacefully in the gravelly part of the stream, and it didn't seem much the worse either. Then we went along to the farm and took a handful of carrots that Mrs Cave had given us for Bingo.

'Bingo's a dear,' said Ann to the farmer. 'You will let him stay here and have a peaceful old age, won't you?'

'That I will,' said the farmer. 'No old horse that has worked for me shall ever go to them nasty knackers to be made into cat's meat.'

'If I were a millionaire,' I said, 'I'd buy acres and acres of parkland, and fill it with old horses, so that nobody could be cruel to them or sell them.'

'You're a couple of grand little horsewomen,' said the farmer.

'Not so little,' growled Ann as we rode away.

So at last Camp Pegasus broke up, though we all agreed we would have liked to stay for ever.

15   A job for Jill

One day when I was exercising Black Boy, cantering happily along the grass verge of a lane and singing to myself in my own peculiar style, I heard someone say, 'Hello there!' and looked round to see Mrs Darcy who owned the riding school overtaking me astride a raking chestnut of about seventeen hands.

'Grand morning!' she said, and I agreed that it was. Mrs Darcy was the sort of person who always seemed to have an exclamation mark after everything she said; that is why I have put one.

'I've seen you about quite a lot,' she went on. 'You're Jill Crewe, aren't you? That's a good pony, and you've got quite a decent style! *Quite* a decent style!'

'Oh. Thanks,' I said, rather taken back.

'I hope you're spending plenty of time on schooling,' she went on. 'Riding isn't just cantering about the lanes, you know! It's easy, but it isn't equitation!'

'Oh, I know,' I said. 'I put in as much schooling as I can find time for.'

'Soon be gymkhana season!' said Mrs Darcy; and I nodded, feeling a thrill at the magic word, and also at Mrs Darcy's assumption that I should be interested in gymkhanas this season.

'You once came to see me about a job, didn't you?' said Mrs Darcy. 'Let me see, how old are you?'

'Twelve,' I said.

'And you've got sense?'

'I hope so,' I said.

'You groomed your pony yourself this morning?'
I laughed. 'Well, if I didn't, nobody else would.'

'Right! I'm in a bit of a fix. My young groom has
broken her arm and will be off work for several
weeks, and we're very busy at the stables. If you're
in the same mind about doing a job of work, I wonder
if you'd care to come and help for an hour or two
each day, between school hours? If you're keen on
horses, as I think you are, it will be good for you
to get stable practice, and hard work never hurt any
rider! My father stabled eighteen hunters when I was
a kid, and I tell you I put in some honest toil! So what
about it?'

The idea of working in the stable fascinated me.

'When would you want me to come?' I asked.

'Well, if you could manage an hour before school
in the morning, and an hour or more after – '

'Oh, I think I could do that.'

'I'll pay you two pounds an hour, but I mean an
hour of work! No leaning against doors chatting!'

We finally arranged that I should be at Mrs Darcy's
every morning from seven to eight o'clock, and every
afternoon from five to six-thirty, provided of course
that Mummy said I might do it.

I didn't know how Mummy would cotton on to
the idea, but I was pretty full of enthusiasm when I
put it to her.

'Well,' she said, 'I'm rather keen on initiative, and
I don't think a job of work ever hurt anybody.
But you'll find it stiff going, Jill. It's easy to start
something in the first rush of enthusiasm, but it isn't
so easy to keep it up – especially when it involves

getting up early every single morning for several weeks. I doubt if you'll stick it.'

'I'll stick it,' I said. 'Only please, Mummy, *say* I can start. I do want to. It will be so marvellous working in a real stable with a lot of horses.'

'If,' said Mummy, 'I find that this is interfering with your school work I shall stop it at once. I shall soon find out if you are dreaming about stables all day instead of thinking about your arithmetic.'

'I won't let it interfere,' I promised.

So the next morning I turned up at Mrs Darcy's in my jeans and an ancient sweater, and my oldest shoes, and I did mucking out while the girl groom, Angela, who was about twenty, did the feeds. Angela was awfully nice, though Mrs Darcy didn't allow talking and there was too much to do in any case.

I went back after afternoon school and cleaned tack on a large scale. Actually the whole time I was working at Mrs Darcy's was just an orgy of mucking out, feeds, grooming, and cleaning tack, and of course I did most of the dirtier work as that was what I was there for. Mrs Darcy was frightfully strict and had an eye like a hawk. She always looked first at all the parts you might have missed if you didn't want to bother. You never stood still a minute, either; she kept you whizzing round.

Mummy was right, it was tough going, especially after the first thrill of realising that I was actually working in a stable wore off.

I jolly well had to make myself stick it, but my pride was such that I wouldn't slacken off, and after about the first fortnight I got my second wind and felt as though I could go on for ever. I did enjoy the work, and I learned stable practice as it should be learned and how to do things for horses in the professional way.

It made me much quicker and defter with my hands. I also picked up lots of new ideas about equitation and schooling. And the money each Saturday came in jolly useful too.

My days were now quite crowded. I set my alarm for half-past-five, and at six I was at work in my own stable. Meanwhile my porridge and egg were on the gas cooker, and I ate my breakfast and biked up the hill to work by seven o'clock. At 8.15 I was home again for a hasty wash and change into my school uniform, and I was at school at ten-to-nine. Afternoon school finished at four; I was home at 4.15, had tea, changed into my working clothes, and was at Mrs Darcy's at five. Home again at 6.45; attended to my own pony; then homework from 7.15 to 8.15; then supper, and I was in bed and asleep by nine. Mummy insisted on this, if I was to get up at 5.30.

You will see that this didn't leave me any time for riding and schooling Black Boy except at weekends; but to my surprise and pleasure Ann suddenly said that she would come round each afternoon after school to exercise Black Boy and give him a bit of schooling, and this she did, and I thought it very decent of her. Besides, it had a good effect in making Ann much keener on horses generally. The horse is like that; the more you have to do with it, the more you want to.

On Saturdays I did my two and a half hours at the stable and spent the rest of the day working at my own pony, partly under Martin's instruction. Ann came round every Saturday afternoon, and we had terrific times. We were both getting pretty good now.

Sunday afternoon was a very busy time at the riding school, so I used to go up there from eight to nine in the morning, and then go to church with Mummy;

and go back for grooming and cleaning tack in the evening. But I did this latter because I liked it, for Mummy would not allow me to take money for working on Sunday.

One Saturday, just as I was finishing work, Mrs Darcy called, 'Come here, Jill.'

She was out in the yard, holding a black mare called Inez, the one horse in the stable I did not like, for she had an uncertain temper and rather a grudging nature, but Mrs Darcy frequently rode her and hired her out as a hack to friends.

'Come along. Let me see you mount,' said Mrs Darcy. 'No use working in a stable if you can't ride the horses!'

I went up to Inez rather reluctantly. For one thing, she was much too big for me, being fifteen-two. The stirrup iron was high, and I had to make two attempts before I could get my foot in it; then I kept hopping and springing, but I couldn't get up, and the more I tried the worse it was.

'Oh, get down!' said Mrs Darcy. 'You're awful. If you messed about like that at a gymkhana they'd disqualify you!'

'Inez is miles too big for me,' I said sulkily.

'Nonsense,' said Mrs Darcy. 'I've seen a child a head shorter than you mount a horse of sixteen hands like a fairy. You don't know everything about riding yet, you see!'

I turned away, rather angry, and was walking back to the stable when she called me.

'Now don't go away in a huff. Come here, and let me see what I can do with you.'

Then to my surprise she spent about half-an-hour on improving my mounting and dismounting, and general style. I was very grateful to her. Mrs Darcy was like that, her bark was worse than her bite. Before I left her, I could ride any horse in her stable. What was more, when my half-term holiday arrived and I had a free Monday and Tuesday, she let me take out a party of children, and also arranged a jolly evening ride for myself and Angela and a few more.

Though my days were long and packed and I hardly had time to breathe, and no time at all for my own affairs, and though Mummy watched me like a lynx to see that my school work didn't suffer from my horsy occupations, I was really quite sorry when Sheila came back and it was time for me to leave Mrs Darcy's. I had learned so much and it had been such fun.

I stayed on for a week after Sheila came back, so that she could work her arm in gently, and all the talk was about gymkhanas, and the horses that Angela was going to ride and the novice-jumping events that she hoped to win on Mrs Darcy's horses. It was simply thrilling.

The last evening I was there, they all came to the gate to say goodbye to me, and Mrs Darcy clapped her hand on my shoulder and said, 'Well, I didn't think you'd stick it! But you're welcome here any time! Thanks!' Which was such high praise for her that I nearly collapsed.

16 La Blonde

It was early summer now, and sunbeams, green leaves, little birds, and gymkhanas were in the air.

At school you heard nothing else, and three girls in my form were sent to the headmistress for reading gymkhana schedules inside their history books.

'What are we going to enter for?' said Ann one morning at break, waving the schedules of Lentham Park children's pony gymkhana at me. Ann was by now nearly as keen as I was, thanks to Martin's influence and the great friendship between our ponies, Black Boy and Seraphine.

'Well, I haven't got an earthly in the riding classes,' I said. 'And the very thought of the jumping – well, I'm sure people don't enter for the jumping in their very first gymkhana. That only leaves things like Bending and Musical Chairs and Egg-and-Spoon.

'There's the cleanest pony,' said Ann, not too hopefully.

'I expect some people will take their ponies in travelling boxes and groom them all over again when they get there,' I said. 'By the time you and I have hacked to Lentham Park, our ponies will look like something out of the farmyard.'

'It's under their saddles and in their ears where the judges look,' said Ann. 'You'll see. Now what *are* we going to enter for?'

'They all scare me stiff,' I said, 'down on paper.' Just

then Susan Pyke came by, and for once she stopped and gave us a patronising smile.

'Is that the Lentham Park schedule?' she said. 'I know just how you feel. I was the same when I began, feebly reading over all the events I daren't go in for.'

We went on seething for ages after she had gone, and Ann said her only ambition in life was to be about thirty and a famous showjumper and to beat Susan Pyke.

However about two days later Susan came up to us and said, would we go home to tea with her that afternoon, and out of sheer curiosity – and after obtaining our mothers' permission at lunch-time – we said we would.

Susan Pyke's house was a rather glassy-looking place with wood floors and antique furniture, and bowls of spiky, uncomfortable hothouse flowers. Susan's mother was majestic and had a deep voice and kept calling us 'children' as if we were six.

'Come in to tea, children! . . . Wipe your shoes, children!'

The other two people there were twin sisters from our form called Valeria and Jacqueline Horrington-Hobday-Heath. That really and actually was their name, though at school they were called Val and Jack Heath, and they were quite decent sort of people.

'I hear that all you children are learning to ride,' said Mrs Pyke while we were having tea.

Nobody said anything, there isn't much you can say to a remark like that, except yes.

'Well, you must all work very hard at your riding,' said Mrs Pyke, 'and then one day you may be as good as Susan. Even Susan had to begin once!'

'Golly!' said Ann under her breath, and Mrs Pyke

said, 'A little choke, dear? Take a drink – not too quickly.'

'When I was a child,' said Mrs Pyke, 'I was the youngest rider to hounds in the county. I remember the Master of Fox Hounds once lifted me on to my pony himself, and there I sat in my little habit with my long fair curls hanging down to my waist. Children had the loveliest hair in those days.'

Personally I thought *(a)* it was impossible to picture Mrs Pyke as a child at all, and *(b)* that curls down to your waist must have looked pretty awful all waving in the breeze like floating corkscrews. I'm sure Mrs Darcy would have had something to say about it. I mean, there are always plaits.

After tea we found out that the object of our visit was to see Susan's cups. They were all set out on the sideboard and they really did look terrific, gleaming and flashing with Goddard's Plate Powder.

'A very nice array,' said Mrs Pyke, and we just said yes. At least Val Heath – who had frightfully good manners – said yes, and then Jack said yes, and then Ann and I said yes too, as the others had said it.

'And now perhaps you'd like to see Susan's certificates,' said Mrs Pyke. 'Get them out, Susan dear.'

I will say to Susan's credit that she went a bit red, but she opened a drawer in the sideboard and there they were. A great big thick pile of red, blue and yellow certificates – mostly red and blue – and not a green one to be seen. Either Susan never condescended to be highly commended, or else she just threw her green ones into the wastepaper basket.

Susan was still a bit red, and when she had closed the drawer she said, 'Let's go down to the stables. I've got something to show you. That's why I asked you to come.'

So we all went down to the stables – which I can't describe because they made me so envious, being just the kind of stables I always dreamed of possessing when I was grown up – and Susan opened a door, and there it was.

It was a new pony, and when we saw it we all gave a gasp. It was the showiest Show pony I ever beheld in all my long and varied experience. It was fourteen hands, and it had the most beautiful flowing lines, and it held its head like an Arab steed. In colour it was pale biscuit, gleaming like satin, and its mane and tail though long were perfectly groomed and a sort of soft gold colour.

'Daddy found her for me,' said Susan simply. 'She's called La Blonde.'

'Can't you just *see* Susan on her!' said Mrs Pyke. 'Let's take her in the paddock, children. You must see her action.'

So Susan saddled La Blonde – and all the tack was new – and rode her round the paddock, and did a few perfect figures-of-eight, and changed legs with nonchalant efficiency (excuse those big words, but I have had them written down on a bit of paper for ages waiting until I got a chance to use them. You can look them up in the dictionary). We stood round and watched.

'I got a First in the riding class at Pillton last August,' said Val suddenly. 'Under-fourteens.'

I suppose she couldn't bear this 'beginners watching the expert' feeling any longer.

But nobody took any notice, and I don't think Mrs Pyke heard.

On our way home Val said, 'I bet that pony fairly hypnotises the judges at Lentham Park.'

'It's nothing but a circus pony,' said Jack.

'Oh, no, it isn't,' said Ann. 'It really is something special, and I'm sure it's half Arab. I expect Susan's father bought it from a sheik for about fifty thousand pounds.'

'You don't buy things from sheiks,' I pointed out. 'They give you horses for saving their lives.'

'I wouldn't mind saving a sheik's life,' said Val. 'I've done First Aid at the Guides.'

'Well, I don't see any of us getting to Arabia before Lentham Park,' said Ann, 'so we might as well make the best of the ponies we've got, as they're all we'll have. La Blonde! Golly!'

So then we all started giggling and playing a game, and Ann was La Blonde, and I was Susan, and Val was Mrs Pyke-as-a-child, and Jack was the MFH. who put her up on her pony; and in the end we were all sitting in a row in the ditch shrieking with laughter.

Next day Martin told us that he had entered Ann and me for all the events at Lentham Park, and it made us feel as though we were going to the dentist's.

For my birthday Mummy had bought me a pair of jodhpur boots and a blue shirt, and Martin's mother had given me a riding hat, and I got everything cleaned and ready in time – for once.

Well, I don't want to go into details about my first gymkhana, because I certainly did not cover myself with glory. I was frightfully nervous, and that ruined everything; and what was worse I communicated my nervousness to my pony – which always happens – so that he didn't behave a bit well, and it was my fault really. So far as I was concerned things went from bad to worse. Ann was much better than me, and got a Third in the riding class under fourteen, and a Second in the bending race under sixteen. My only comfort was that lots of other children were as bad as I was.

It was Susan Pyke's day. When she rode into the ring on La Blonde everybody gave a gasp. She looked marvellous. She had a perfect black jacket and cream cord breeches, and black boots, and a white shirt and yellow tie, and a new hat and cream string gloves.

Just as Val had said, the judges were hypnotised. I don't think they were very good judges at Lentham Park, because usually judges are the most fair and sporting of people and look for fine points in equitation rather than a showy appearance, but these judges were taken by surprise, and Susan was called in within two minutes and got First in all the showing classes, *and* in the equitation, though even I could see that she had lost her head and was over-riding La Blonde and sawing at her mouth and letting her over-bend. This turned the feeling of the spectators against Susan; and now that I have a long and varied experience of gymkhanas, I do think the feeling of the crowd towards you can either help or hinder very much.

Whatever La Blonde looked like she certainly couldn't jump. She just shoved her way through everything, and soon people were laughing, and then there was a roar and Susan went scarlet with rage and began beating La Blonde about the head with her whip, and the next moment the judge had ordered her off the field. Ann and I looked at one another unbelievingly.

However, Susan turned up again in the Musical Chairs, and won the First in the under-fourteens and the Third in the under-sixteens. I think this was partly luck and partly that La Blonde seemed to have a natural gift for Musical Chairs.

When it was over I joined Mummy and Martin and a few of our friends who had been watching, and said, 'I say, I'm sorry I was such a wash-out.'

'Not a bit,' said Martin. 'Whoever heard of anybody doing anything at their first gymkhana? You didn't do a thing wrong, Jill, and you looked very nice and I was proud of you.'

Then Ann came riding up with her rosettes, and quite honestly I was as pleased as if they'd been mine.

When we were on the way home Mummy said, 'I don't believe in giving you a swelled head, Jill, but in case you may be feeling a bit low, I'll tell you that as you rode past I overheard two people behind me say, "I'm surprised that girl in the blue shirt hasn't won anything; I'd say she was the most promising rider of the lot."'

'Oh, you're making it up,' I cried.

But Mummy assured me that this was true.

17 I go on a visit

Of course at school on Monday we had the inquest on the gymkhana. Nobody could talk about anything else but just where they went wrong and what bad luck they had.

Susan Pyke said, 'What do you think? Daddy is going to sell La Blonde. He was simply furious at the way she let me down in the jumping. He says he can't have my chances ruined by a pony like that!'

'I thought your chances were ruined when you started bashing her on the head and the judge ordered you off the field,' Ann could not resist saying.

'Oh, Ann Derry you are a beast,' said Susan, and to our surprise burst into tears, whereupon several of Susan's friends rallied round her and we stood exchanging sarky remarks and insults until the bell went.

It happened to be two days before the exams, and having had a heart-to-heart talk from Mummy I did try very hard to give my mind to such squalid matters as the dissolution of the monasteries, and Thomas Cromwell and Oliver Cromwell being two different persons which was something that always bothered me, particularly as I could never remember which was which even when I got them apart.

I biked home from school intending to swot like anything that night, but somehow my nobler intentions are always frustrated and this was no exception.

Mummy was making tea and looking rather blue when I arrived, and presently she said, 'I've just been to the dentist's and I'm afraid I'm going to have to go into the Dental Hospital at Rychester for a few days for a dental operation.'

'Oh, I'm sorry,' I said. 'When?'

'About Thursday.' Mummy gave a watery smile, and added, 'I don't know how it is, but dental operations always sound so sordid. In books, people's mother's have such romantic things the matter with them, in pink bed-jackets. I'm sorry I couldn't oblige with anything but teeth. But the point is, Jill, something has to be done about you.'

'Oh, that's all right,' I said. 'I can manage here perfectly well by myself.'

'I wouldn't think of leaving you here by yourself,' said Mummy.

(I don't know where parents get the idea that people over ten years old can't manage the house as well as they can, but they are all like this.)

I argued a bit, but it wasn't any use. Then Mummy said something that sent an icy chill through my bones. She said, 'I'm glad that we had Cecilia to stay in the Christmas holidays because I don't feel any compunction now in asking them to take you. In fact I rang up this afternoon when I was in Chatton, and they'll be very glad to see you at White Ferry' – which was the misleading name of Cecilia's house, as it wasn't white and there wasn't a ferry within miles of it – 'and I'm sure that Farmer Clay will put your pony up while you're away. So that'll be all right,' concluded Mummy, in a deathly silence through which nothing could be heard but my madly beating heart.

'Oh, Mummy!' I cried, and my voice went all

up and down and wobbled. 'Don't make me go
to Cecilia's. I couldn't! I should die! I'd go into a
decline or have a stroke or something. Not Cecilia's!
Couldn't I go to the Derrys'? I'm sure Ann – '

'No, you can't,' said my hard-hearted parent. 'I
don't know Mrs Derry well enough to be under such
an obligation to her. You must go to your cousin's,
so don't be so silly. It's the obvious thing.'

'Oh, Mummy!' I wailed. 'Let me go to Mrs Darcy's.
I could sleep in the hayloft. She wouldn't mind.
Please!'

'Go and wash your face, darling,' said Mummy.
'It's all settled, and anyway it's only for five days or
so.'

'People can die in five days,' I said grimly, 'when
they're in durance vile.'

Tea was a very damp sort of meal, and when it
was over I put my mac on and went for a walk. I
wandered stonily along the lanes, feeling as though
the end of the world had come, I was so miserable.
I think now that I must have been pretty selfish,
too, not to have been thinking of Mummy and
her beastly dental operation, than which I cannot
imagine anything worse happening to a person. It
makes me go cold all over when I am just going
to have a tooth filled. But I wasn't thinking of poor
Mummy at all, only of myself and what I should
suffer at Cecilia's.

And then as I kicked a stone along the road before
me, there suddenly came the most beautiful thought.
The exams began on Wednesday! And with Mummy
so keen on the exams, how could I possibly be
away at Cecilia's? I couldn't! It was just like Hetty
Sorrel in Adam Bede when the rider comes dashing
through the crowd crying, 'A reprieve! A reprieve!'

I jumped right up in the air, and yelled, 'Yippee! Yoicks! Tally-ho!'

'Dear, dear!' said a voice behind me. 'The girl has gone quite mad.'

I looked round, and there in her carriage with the matched greys was Martin's mother, Mrs Lowe.

'I thought it was you, Jill,' she said. 'Whatever has happened?'

So I poured the whole story into her sympathetic ear, and when I had finished she said, 'But of course you must come and stay with us while your mother is away. And bring your pony too, there's lots of room. Tell your mother I won't take a refusal, and I'll see that you go to school every day at the proper time.'

I was so relieved and happy that I rushed home and poured this all out to Mummy in a breathless jumble, and though of course she wanted to say a lot about obligations and so on, she saw my point about the exams, and actually she was in what is known as a cleft stick.

I was thrilled at the prospect of going to stay at Martin's home, though I must say that when the actual moment came and the taxi was at the door to take Mummy to the hospital I did feel perfectly awful. I mean, it is a most shattering feeling to see your beloved home being locked up and your dearly loved mother being dragged away to a squalid hospital while you yourself are turned out into the cold world, and I hope nobody who reads this book will ever have this experience.

When the taxi was out of sight and there wasn't anything left to wave to, I felt like leaning my face up against my pony and having a good howl, but I managed to strangle this feeling and, without a backward glance at the locked and desolate cottage, I mounted and rode towards my new home.

Gradually my spirits rose as I thought of the good time I was going to have at The Grange. It would be fun staying with the Lowes, and being made much of, and riding all those horses.

When I came in sight of the drive gates, there was Martin waiting for me.

'I thought I'd be on the look-out,' he said. 'Welcome, Jill. I hope you'll treat us as if you belonged here for the next few days. And cheer up, it won't be for long.'

'Thanks very much,' I said.

I led Black Boy up the drive beside Martin as he propelled himself along in his chair.

'There's one treat in store for you,' he went on, 'you'll have some good company of near your own age. Two young cousins of mine, Pierce and Mary Lowe, have come to stay. They're twins of sixteen, and their schools have broken up a bit in advance of yours – in fact Mary goes to school in Paris. They're both grand riders and will be able to show you a lot.'

All the way up the drive he went on talking about Pierce and Mary, telling me what marvellous people they were, so consequently by the time we arrived at the front door I was certain I was going to hate them, and all the pleasant anticipation of my visit had oozed out of my shoes. It is a funny thing, but whenever your friends tell you how much you are going to like some wonderful people they know, you always start hating them on the spot.

Martin showed me into the dining room and at once my worst fears were realised.

Pierce and Mary, who were standing by the window looking at some snapshots of the Lowe horses, were very tall and grown up. Mary, who had just come in from a ride, was a typical hard woman to hounds, while Pierce had the supercilious look worn by boys who are nearly men.

'Meet Mary and Pierce!' cried Martin. 'This is Jill whom I told you about – another doughty horse-woman.'

Both the twins said, 'How do you do'; then Pierce gave me a bored glance and looked away, closing his eyes as though he couldn't bear the sight; while Mary just looked at me and then at Martin, as much as to say, 'Need we be bothered with the infant class?'

'Just take Jill up to her room, Mary, that's a good chap,' said Martin; and Mary said, 'Certainly. Please come this way.'

So I followed her up the stairs, and she marched on without saying anything, finally opening the door of a pretty white-panelled bedroom.

'This is yours,' she said. 'Tea is at four. Don't be late, please.'

With this she left me alone, and I sat down on the end of the bed feeling like one of those unfortunate people whose relatives put them into a Home. I looked at my watch, which said half past three, and wondered if I was supposed to stay in my bedroom until tea. Apparently I was. For something to do I unpacked my suitcase, and put into the drawers my dreary and dejected-looking garments which, in addition to my riding clothes, consisted of two clean school blouses, my best shoes, a navy-blue dress with a white collar wich made me look about ten, and some underwear.

At last a silvery gong sounded and I went down to

tea, which took place in the drawing room. Mr and Mrs Lowe were there and gave me a very nice welcome, except that they would talk about mummy in that prepare-for-the-worst way that some grown-ups do when anyone is ill. Then the conversation became all about people I didn't know and Pierce and Mary did, so I felt rather like that feeble game where people throw a tennis ball back and forth above your head and you have to jump and try to catch it as it whizzes over you, which is practically impossible and very maddening.

I thought somebody might suggest a ride after tea, but nobody did, so I wandered out to the loose boxes and saw that Black Boy was being most beautifully looked after, and he gave me a smug look as if to say, 'Home was never like this.'

Then Mrs Lowe called me in and reminded me that she had promised Mummy I should do my homework, so I sat down in a little morning room which she said I could have all to myself, and began to swot up geometry, as it was the geometry exam next day.

Dinner was as bad as tea, except that they all talked in a very magazine-ish way about Paris, and my only hope was that any moment somebody would say *Pas devant l'enfant*, in which case I was going to say something very sophisticated and crushing, but the opportunity never came.

After dinner Mary said to Mrs Lowe, 'Do you mind very much if Pierce and I dash off to catch the bus? There's rather a good film in Chatton.'

But instead of saying, 'Yes, of course, and take Jill with you,' Mrs Lowe made the humiliating remark, 'Well, don't be too late, dears; and Jill must go straight to bed now, because I promised her Mummy that school work should come first.'

All I could think of in that moment was that it served me right for not going to Cecilia's.

But worse was to follow.

The sun shining on my face woke me at seven next morning, and I bounded out of bed, dragged on my faded old dressing gown – which I had when I was nine and which by now only came to my knees with the sleeves halfway up my arms – and dashed to the bathroom. But I arrived at the same moment as Mary, who was wearing a very smart tailored dressing gown of brown satin with white spots, and we both grabbed hold of the door handle together.

Feeling conscious of my awful appearance, I gasped in what I hoped was a nonchalant way, 'Oh, you have it; I won't bother about a bath.' She raised her eyebrows and gave me a very superior look, and as I rushed back to my room I realised that she must be thinking I was a grubby little kid who was glad of an excuse not to have a bath.

This sickening thought pursued me all the time I was dressing, and at last, though I had done my hair and got my blouse and tunic on, I was mad enough to take everything off again and get back into my pyjamas and dressing gown. Then I seized my towels and marched along to the bathroom, and in order to show Mary that I wasn't in the least afraid of her, I banged heartily on the bathroom door and shouted, 'Hurry up, you! This is Jill, and I want a bath when you've done.'

To my horror Mr Lowe's voice replied, 'Don't be in such a hurry, young lady. You must learn to wait for your elders.'

I just choked, tore back to my room and flung my clothes on anyhow. At breakfast I couldn't say a word, and my misery was added to by Mrs Lowe making such kind but misguided remarks as, 'Do you always eat so little breakfast, Jill dear? If it isn't what you have at home you've only to ask. Don't worry about Mummy, dear, she'll soon be better.'

Martin just looked awkward, and the twins ate and ate and ignored me. I got to school and made an awful mess of the geometry exam, making such howlers as 'A right-angled triangle is one in which all the angles are right angles' – which was read out to the class later by Miss Greaves.

During exam time we did not have afternoon school, so I went back to the Lowes' in time for lunch.

During lunch Mary and Pierce kept saying what a grand day it was for a ride, so my spirits lifted a bit, and when we had finished eating I followed them to the loose boxes in time to see them leading out two magnificent hunters, just the sort of horses they *would* own. Mary – who was beautifully turned out in full hunting kit – had a shining bay mare of about fifteen-two, while Pierce's horse was a light roan with black mane and tail, very tall, lean, and long-legged.

I said nothing, but led out Black Boy who had been groomed to perfection by Martin's man, Bob, and looked a dear.

'Oh, what a sweet little pony!' said Mary, trying to be nice, and making me feel as if I were five and about to be lifted on to my first Shetland.

'OK,' I said, shrugging my shoulders, and then mounting with what I hoped was a sophisticated air.

'I say,' said Pierce, 'you're not expecting to go with us by any chance? I mean, we're going over some pretty fierce country. I mean, you'd find the going much too much.'

'Oh, I don't want to go,' I said carelessly. 'I've got lots of schooling to do.'

So they rode off, and I went and lowered all the jumps in the field and then put Black Boy round them rather dispiritedly and we made an awful mess of it, so that Mr Lowe who happened to be watching from a window banged on the glass and put his head out and shouted, 'No, no! All wrong!'

Though it was only three days from the day I arrived until Saturday it seemed like a year. Mary and Pierce ignored me, and Martin seemed so dense, as though he thought I was actually having a good time with them. I hated them so much that I almost loved Susan Pyke by comparison, and I hated the way they obviously pitied Martin. Mary was always saying things like, 'Let me help you round the corner,' in the way that he had told us he loathed.

Saturday dawned with a pouring wet morning, and we all had to stay indoors. Pierce read a pile of copies of *Horse and Hound*, and Mary chatted to Mr Lowe in a very affected way about bloodstock sales. Nobody bothered about me, so at last I slipped out to the stables to have a word with Black Boy. I would have enjoyed cleaning tack, or anything homely and squalid, but it had all been expertly done by Bob. Even then I couldn't get away from Mrs Lowe who came to fetch me in out of the wet.

The one bright spot was that I was going to see Mummy in the afternoon, so directly lunch was over I dashed off to get the bus to Rychester, which is about twenty miles away. When I got to Rychester, I found I had three pounds as well as my return bus fare, so I bought some flowers to take to Mummy.

When I eventually got to the hospital I collapsed thankfully on Mummy's bed like a desert traveller at an oasis. She looked a bit pallid and her voice was croaky, but it was Mummy all right.

'Oh, when are you coming home?' I gasped. 'It's been like a hundred years.'

She looked surprised.

'But aren't you having a marvellous time at the Lowes'?'

'Oh, Mummy, it's truly awful,' I said. And then I told her about Pierce and Mary.

'They just ignore me,' I said, 'and everybody treats me as though I was about six – even Martin. They're so superior, and the Lowes treat them as if they were grown-up, and I hate them – I loathe them!'

'Jill,' said Mummy, 'I think you're very feeble.'

'Feeble?' I gasped.

'Yes, feeble to let yourself get an inferiority complex just because two people a bit older than yourself manage to gain some of the attention which you think ought to be exclusively yours,' croaked Mummy. 'Why don't you buck up and be yourself?'

'But they're beastly,' I said. 'Oh, Mummy, are you coming home on Monday? I don't like it a bit at the Lowes'.'

Mummy looked grave.

'Jill dear, you make it very difficult for me to say this. I have to tell you that they couldn't complete the operation last Thursday. I have to have another one on Monday, so it will be about Friday before I can go home.'

I looked at her, dumb with horror.

She went on, 'As soon as I knew this, I asked the doctor to phone Mrs Lowe for me, and to say that if it was imposing too much on her kindness to keep you I would make arrangements for you to go on to Cecilia's. Mrs Lowe replied that she would be delighted to have you stay longer, and that you were having a lovely time.'

'Lovely time!' I interrupted. 'Gosh! *Lovely time!*'

'I asked Mrs Lowe not to tell you what had happened,' went on Mummy calmly, 'as I preferred to tell you myself today. I thought you would have been pleased to stay.'

'Of course, if you *want* me to go into a decline!' I said bitterly.

'Self-pity *is* painful,' said Mummy, 'and I'm sorry for Mrs Lowe for having had to cope with you. You can't have been very cheery company. You had better arrange to go to Cecilia's tomorrow.'

'That's even worse,' I said with a groan.

'If anyone had asked me,' said Mummy, 'I should have said you were a nice, natural, friendly person who could fit in anywhere. If Pierce and Mary really are nasty, all the more reason for you to be the same Jill that the Lowes have always liked, instead of smouldering in the background. But if you can't take it, then you'll just *have* to go away and miss the rest of the exams. It's my fault for landing in this silly hospital.'

'OK,' I grumbled. 'I can take it. I'll stay at the Lowes'.'

'That's a relief,' said Mummy with a sigh.

'I do think you might sympathise with me a bit,' I said.

'People with inferiority complexes need bracing, not sympathy,' said Mummy briskly. 'Poor old Jill! Friday will soon come. How's Black Boy? Tell me you've had some riding.'

'A bit,' I said grudgingly. 'By the way, I brought these flowers for you.'

'Oh, how lovely!'

Just then the nurse came in and said it was time for me to go, so I kissed Mummy and went out again into the cold world. It was raining. I felt awful. And then suddenly I realised that I was probably the most awful beast that had ever existed since the beginning of the world. I hadn't asked Mummy how she was, or said how sorry I was about her having to have another operation, or done anything but grouse about myself. I rushed back to the hospital, but the door was shut. I banged on it, and when a nurse came and opened it I said, 'I want to come in again, I've forgotten something.'

She only said coldly, 'I'm sorry, visiting hours are over. The wards are closed now.'

Weary, worn, and sad, I caught the bus and crawled back to my inhospitable lodging.

I expect by now you are saying, 'Well, of all the soppy, feeble little beasts – !' and you are quite right. I was in that silly mood of self-pity in which I should have been quite glad if they had forgotten to keep me any tea. Instead of that I found a huge fire – in spite of it being so-called summer – and Mrs Lowe made me sit right in front of it and brought me a tray with smoking hot buttered toast in a silver dish, and strawberry jam, and cake with marzipan on top, and *Mary* poured my tea out and put heaps of sugar in it, and they said things like, 'You poor woman! You must be drowned!' and other self-respecting remarks. It was like a dream and I was quite dazed.

In the evening Mrs Lowe and Mary went out to visit friends, and by some chance I found myself alone with Pierce. He looked at me very self-consciously, and I thought I would remove my revolting self from his presence, but suddenly he said, 'I say – do you think this is any good?' And he handed me a painting of a pony. It was a grey with a tossing mane, standing on a hilltop against a windy blue sky with racing clouds.

'It's super, isn't it? Who did it?' I asked.

He blushed.

'Well, as a matter of fact, I did. That's why I asked you. I wanted to try it on somebody impartial. I mean, Mary or Martin would have tried to be polite about it whether they meant it or not.'

'I think it's absolutely wonderful,' I said, because it really was. 'It's as good as Morland or any of those people.'

'Oh, I say, come off it!' he said. 'What do you know about Morland anyway, at your age?'

'Why, how old do you think I am?' I said.

'Oh, about ten – eleven perhaps,' he added hastily, seeing my look of indignation.

'I'm practically thirteen,' I said. 'Gosh, it's not much younger than you. I bet you can remember being thirteen.'

'Yes, I can,' he said, quite humbly. 'I want to be a painter of horses, only I'm so nervous about my work. I keep thinking I'm no good.'

'*You* think you're no good?' I said in amazement. 'I thought you were so frightfully clever and conceited you knew everything!'

'*Me* clever and conceited!' he said opening his eyes. 'Gosh, no.'

'Then Mary is,' I said, flinging discretion to the winds. 'She's so frightfully superior that she makes me feel as if I could crawl under a blade of grass. I'm terrified of you both, if you want to know; and even if you are sixteen you're not all that marvellous. I know some people of nineteen who are much cleverer than you and Mary, and fifty million times nicer.'

'Oh, I say!' said Pierce. 'You've got us all wrong. I mean, Mary's terrified of *you*! She told me so. She says she feels all stiff and weird when you give her those icy looks. We'd both heard so much about you before we came – that you were one of these Wonder Girl Riders, and full of promise and a future queen of Wembley and all that, it quite put us off and we decided to squash you – '

'But I'm not!' I cried. 'I can't really ride for toffee, and when I saw your marvellous horses, and Mary said my pony was a sweet little thing – '

'Look here!' said Pierce. 'If you like, you can have a try on my horse tomorrow. Would you like to?'

'Rather!' I said.

'And can I try Black Boy? I think he's got a lovely action, and I'm not too heavy for him, and I don't think my feet will quite touch the ground. Mary will be relieved that you've come unstuck. It's given her a pain in the neck trying to hold her own with you.'

To make a long story short, before the next day was over Mary, Pierce, and I were quite good friends.

18 Chatton Show

'I'm looking forward to Saturday,' said Ann, as we rode happily homewards after a gallop on Neshbury Common. 'Up to yesterday I was scared stiff, and now I've changed right over and I'm dying for it. Isn't that weird?'

'It's the biggest thing we've ever entered for,' I said. 'Chatton Show.'

It was a year later than all the other events I have recorded in this book, and Ann and I were now thirteen and a half and experienced riders. We had several gymkhanas behind us, and both had certificates in a drawer at home, though I had never won a First.

The event we were talking about was the Chatton Show gymkhana which was to be held the following Saturday and was *the* event of the year. Not only were there classes for children but also for grown-ups, and the Open Jumping at Chatton attracted some of the most famous riders in England so we were longing to see it, apart from anything else.

Ann and I had both entered for everything.

'It was Susan Pyke's birthday yesterday,' said Ann, 'and she was fourteen. So that puts her out of the under-fourteens. All the better for us.'

'I'm sorry,' I said. 'I'd rather compete with her. If I could beat her in just one event I'd pass out with joy.'

'There's the under-sixteens events,' said Ann. 'She'll be in those.'

'Fat chance I have of winning anything in the under-sixteens,' I said, 'with people like Maureen Chase and Frank Stabley who ride at Richmond!'

'Maureen Chase is one of these fast women over timber,' said Ann, 'and they nearly always lose their heads and use their whips too much. One of the judges is Major Parkinson, and he simply hates whips and deducts marks for using them. I'm not even going to carry a riding stick; then I can't be tempted. If Seraphine doesn't know my hand and foot aids she jolly well ought to by now.'

'Black Boy's jumping pretty well,' I said. 'He's taken two Seconds for jumping, though one was at Ashbrow Farm which was only a small affair. And the other time I was competing against kids of about ten. I hadn't the slightest excuse for not getting a First.'

'Do you remember our first gymkhana together?' said Ann with a giggle. 'It was at Lentham Park, and La Blonde – '

'Goodness, yes!' I said. 'I got twenty-three faults in the jumping. It seems an age ago.'

'I *am* looking forward to Saturday,' said Ann enthusiastically, and I agreed, 'Same here.'

When we got to our cottage we found Martin there with the gymkhana schedule and we rushed to examine it.

'Oh!' I yelled. 'The riding class isn't under fourteen, it's fourteen and under, so we'll have Susan in it after all. I'm jolly glad, though of course I haven't a hope.'

'There's a sixteen-and-under riding class too,' said Ann. 'Bending, fourteen and under – ditto sixteen and under. Ditto, ditto, musical chairs. Open egg-and-spoon race! Gosh! Open? How weird! Do you suppose there'll be *men* riding in an egg-and-spoon race?'

'If there are,' said Martin, 'I pity them. I back you children every time for balancing eggs.'

'Look!' I said. 'There's only one children's jumping class. Sixteen and under. Clear round for Maureen Chase, obviously.'

But I was laughing when I said this, because I really had a happy feeling about the whole gymkhana. I didn't expect anything, and therefore I was going to enjoy the riding and have the time of my life, and Martin said that this was the ideal spirit for a gymkhana.

'I have got *just* a hope in the bending,' said Ann. 'Seraphine's developed a passion for it. I think she practises by herself when I'm not there, she's got so good lately.'

We shrieked with laughter at the thought of Seraphine solemnly practising bending by herself, in and out of the trees, and Martin said, 'Well, above all, don't go through the last two poles so quickly that you over-run and lose ground. Keep your head, and leave the bend to Seraphine; she knows her stuff. I must say, I've never seen a pony turn with such economy of space at the last pole. Let's hope she'll do it on the day.'

It was now getting late and Mummy had to come in and drive Ann and Martin off to their respective homes or we should have been discussing the gymkhana programme all night.

Ann was round at our cottage early on the day, and we spent the morning in an orgy of grooming, washing tails, and cleaning tack. It was a glorious day with a high blue sky and big white billowy clouds like feather beds, and a lively little wind blowing Black Boy's tail about. He looked lovely when I had finished him; his coat was like black satin and he arched his neck as though he knew how beautiful he was. I hugged him and gave him oats in my hand.

When we got to the Showground the band was playing, flags were flying, and large fat cattle were parading round and round. We rode in through the competitor's entrance, and made our way to the shade of the trees where the other children, looking so efficient, were leading their shining ponies up and down and putting finishing touches to what looked more perfect grooming than ours. I don't know how it is at gymkhanas, but however nice you think you look when you leave home everybody else seems to look so much better.

However, we joined the others, and presently a steward came along and gave us our numbers. Ann was twenty-two and I was twenty-five. We fastened them on our backs, and then in rode Susan Pyke on another striking pony! This one was described as a roan, but quite honestly it was nearer rose-pink, and it was hogged and docked and had very long legs and looked as if it could win the Grand National.

'Hello!' said Susan in a very friendly way. 'Hello, Jill. Hello, Ann. How do you like my Jupiter? He's a show jumper. Daddy said he wasn't going to make any mistake about my winning the jumping this time.'

'Well, his legs are most awfully long,' said Ann. 'I should think he'll just stride over the jumps.'

'I suppose you two have entered for everything,' said Susan. 'Well, I hope you'll have better luck than you had last season. Of course it's rather tough for you as beginners being up against anybody like Frank Stabley. He always takes the Firsts in the two riding classes.'

'Which is he?' I asked.

'Over there, on the chestnut. Number fourteen. Well, good luck.'

'Good luck,' we echoed.

Everybody was moving now to the collecting ring. The gymkhana was on a much bigger scale than anything I had ever entered for before, the ring, the grandstand, the judges, and many grown-up riders, but still I didn't have the needle. I just thought what a wonderful sight it was and how lucky I was to be part of it and to have a heavenly pony like Black Boy to ride. I wouldn't have changed him for any pony I saw on the field.

Presently the first class was called, and we were all riding quietly round the ring in the fourteen-and-under. It was a lovely feeling. Then the judges told us to trot and then to canter, and off we all went. I noticed how beautifully Black Boy was holding his head, and I had never known him pace so smoothly. Then I saw that Frank Stabley had been called in. The judge was calling another number, but I didn't take much notice until Ann, who was riding behind me, said in an excited voice, 'Go on in, Jill, you idiot! Twenty-five – that's you!'

I couldn't believe it. As though in a dream I rode in and took second place, next to Frank Stabley. A girl I didn't know was third, and Susan Pyke fourth. Then the others lined up beyond.

Frank did a beautiful figure of eight. He dismounted and mounted, unsaddled and saddled again, walked and ran with his pony. It looked perfect to me. I did what was told me in a daze, thinking that every minute I should be sent down; but I wasn't. And five minutes later the judge was handing me a blue rosette and I was fastening it at Black Boy's ear. Second in the riding class!

I think it was the biggest thrill of my life as I galloped madly round the ring with a blue certificate in my teeth, and from the tail of my eye caught sight of Mummy and Mrs Derry and the small Derry children and Martin and his father and mother, all sitting together and clapping like mad.

'Oh, jolly good!' shouted Ann enthusiastically as I joined her in the collecting ring. 'And did you see what happened? Susan lost her fourth place because that pink horse of hers dug his heels in and showed his teeth at the judge. Now you've got your ambition!'

So we all rode into the ring again for the sixteen-and-under, and this time we were up against some competition, including the famous Maureen Chase in full hunting kit. I don't know what kind of pony Maureen usually rode, but this time she had foolishly chosen a wild-eyed bay that she could hardly hold in. At first she looked very striking, but after Comet — as he was called according to the programme — had run backwards into three other ponies, and given an exhibition of fly-catching, she was certainly 'out' so far as the judges were concerned.

A girl called Peach Morrison who was in our sixth form at school was first, I — to my amazement — was second again, Frank Stabley was third, and Ann was fourth and got the green 'highly commended'.

By now I was so happy that I didn't mind what else happened.

'I think the judges must be cockeyed,' I said to Ann.

'I've never seen you ride so well, Jill,' she said. 'There's something magic about you today.'

'I never enjoyed myself so much,' I said. 'Oh dear, I do hope Martin won't think I'm pot-hunting, because I'm not. He hates anything like that.'

The next event was the bending race. In my heat I

was lucky enough to get the outside position, which gives you more room, provided your pony doesn't mind the crowd. Black Boy didn't; he seemed to be chuckling as he threaded the poles and came thundering home to win me my heat. To my delight Ann won her heat also, and we raced in the final side by side. We thought Frank Stabley was a certain winner, but he got over-excited and missed out the third pole without realising it, so he was disqualified, and I was first and Ann was second.

Then came the sixteen-and-under bending, and Ann actually was first in this and I was third, with a sixteen-year-old boy called Tom Jobling second.

By the time the Musical Chairs began we knew we were going to have fun. Black Boy always did love Musical Chairs and never had to be dragged into the ring, but fairly galloped up to a chair with me loping along beside him. Susan Pyke and I were left in together at the end, and finished up a dead heat by crashing down on the chair and breaking two legs off, so everybody roared and we had to do it again. Again we crashed into each other simultaneously, and had to run it off a third time. By now I was utterly breathless, so I left it to Black Boy who, defying the rose-pink roan, got me home just one second before Susan. So I got the first and she got the second. I went straight in for the senior event, but was out early. To my delight, Ann won third place in that.

The egg-and-spoon was lovely; grown-ups and children all in together. I won my heat, and was in the final with Maureen Chase, and a strange man, and my old friend, Mrs Darcy!

Maureen kept her egg on the spoon, but her nappy pony ran out and disappeared into the far distance, and that was the end of her.

I dropped my egg and thought I was finished, but when I went back for it I saw that Mrs Darcy had also dropped hers, and the man was nearly home. I thought it was a foregone conclusion, then there came a yell from the crowd. In handing the egg on the spoon to the judge, the man rider had dropped it!

Mrs Darcy and I were both up again by now; it was a neck-and-neck race between us, and she won by half a head. I was glad she was first; and I was second.

Next came the tea interval and I went to join Mummy and our friends who greeted me and Ann with slaps on the back.

'Nice work,' said Martin as we came up, and we both glowed a bit.

'Mine was just luck,' said Ann, 'but Jill's riding like a cyclops.'

'You mean, if she had two eyes she'd be riding like a centaur,' said Martin, and we all laughed as we munched our sandwiches and put away a lot of ice cream. Then we went to have a look at the ponies and made a fuss of them for doing so well, and we found them resting quietly in the shade of the trees and making soft little nickering noises of pleasure when they heard us speaking to them, and saw the handfuls of oats we held out to them.

19 'Jill's Gymkhana'

'What lovely jumps!' said Ann.

'They look like precipices to me,' I remarked. 'But they are lovely, all the same.'

We were leaning over the railings to watch the first event after the interval which was the Open Jumping. I always think this event is the most wonderful thing in the world to watch; there is something utterly splendid about it, to see the tall, magnificent horses soar into the air under their skilful riders' touch, all in such harmony and effortless control. Everything around is beautiful too; the white painted jumps and the bright green field, the eager faces round the ring and the grandstand packed with people ready to cheer. And to think that there are actually people who never go to gymkhanas!

When number thirty-one was called we saw Mrs Darcy ride into the ring on a lovely lean grey called Martha, who I knew from my own experience was capable of anything if she could keep her temperament in control. This was one of Martha's good days, and she jumped a beautifully collected round, finishing with only one and a half faults.

'I think she's got a chance,' I said excitedly.

However, a strange man on a black hunter won first place with no faults, and a boy of twenty who we were told had won Firsts all over the country was second with one fault. To my joy, Mrs Darcy got third place, which was pretty good considering the competition, as there were nineteen entries.

The open event over, the stewards began to lower the jumps for the novice jumping. In this event I had the thrill of seeing my friend Angela jump a clear round on Inez, and everybody cheered like mad. In the end she tied for first place with a hunting man called Markham, who kept a lot of horses, and they jumped it off and Angela won! It was a great honour to have won a First in the novice-jumping at Chatton Show.

Then the jumps were lowered again, and this time it was US. So Ann and I rode round to the collecting ring, and we both had the feeling that our hearts were jumping about inside and doing gymkhanas on their own. In any case they say that if you don't have this feeling you are not much good.

There were twenty-six children competing, of all ages from twelve to sixteen; and there was the famous Maureen Chase looking cool and distant, and the famous Frank Stabley who I thought looked an awfully nice boy, and Susan Pyke, backing her pink horse into the others and getting black looks from everybody.

She kept saying, 'I can't help it. He's so full of spirit. You see, he's a show-jumper, not just an *ordinary* pony' – and she gave all our 'ordinary' ponies very scornful glances.

'Well, you're *in*,' said Ann to Susan, as a boy called Peters came riding back to the ring and the megaphone called out 'Thirteen faults.' 'So you can let your charger charge!'

All eyes were on Susan as she made a spectacular entrance; but I didn't like the way the roan pawed the ground, or the look in his eye. He had a silly, wild look, not the sensible clever look of a pony who is going to do any good at jumping.

He went straight at the first jump, which was the bush, before Susan was ready, and nearly unseated her; however he cleared the jump with inches to spare, and a girl next to me said, 'Some show-jumper!'

Susan was now obviously trying to collect her pony, but he refused to be collected. He went full tilt at the next jump, which was the gate, soared into the air, bucked in midair, got his feet in a knot, and sent Susan flying six metres. She landed with a thud, and the pink horse, having done his stuff, ran right out of the ring neighing at the top of his voice.

Susan sat there on the ground, quite openly weeping for all to see. Two stewards went and helped her up, and there was obviously nothing the matter with her, so presently she landed back among us looking very low.

'Serves her jolly well right!' said a girl next to me. 'She always ruins every gymkhana for everybody else. They ought to disqualify her permanently.'

Susan could not help hearing this remark, and Ann who was soft-hearted went across to her and said kindly, 'It was jolly hard luck, Susan.'

'Oh, thank you, Ann,' said Susan, in a very humble and heartfelt tone, quite different from the usual bragging one.

Meanwhile Maureen Chase had gone in and done an efficient but uninspiring round, to finish up with two faults, and a boy called Michael Grant was making the crowd roar by sending everything flying.

Then it was Ann's turn, and I knew she would enjoy herself because she didn't expect much from Seraphine. To my surprise – and hers – Seraphine jumped the round of her life, finishing with only four faults, and she and Ann looked so pretty and graceful jumping that the crowd clapped and cheered like mad, and the judges all smiled with pleasure at Ann as she rode so neatly and nicely off.

Frank Stabley had very bad luck. He took four jumps pefectly, but as he approached the triple bar a dog fight broke out in the crowd only about five yards away. Frank's pony reared, and then being quite upset gave him three refusals. I was awfully sorry about this as Frank certainly was an excellent jumper.

Then my number was called. As I rode into the ring I had the strangest feeling of being most awfully happy, and I could tell that Black Boy was feeling the same way. I whispered into his ear, 'Now, angel, don't bother about all those people. We're just jumping for fun, like we do at home, and it's going to be heavenly.'

He arched his neck, and looked both proud and serious, and so at a collected canter we approached the first jump. I only had to whisper, 'Hup!' and the next minute we were over, so smoothly that I had hardly felt him rise. I knew then that he was going to do it! I knew that he and I were just like one single person. So we took the gate, and then the wall, and then – with only the slightest pause – the tricky in-and-out. We were coming up to the triple bar now. I stroked his neck, and whispered, 'Don't rush, boy. Do just as I tell you.' I had forgotten the crowd and everything except those three white bars ahead, sparkling in the sunshine.

'Now!' I said suddenly. 'Hup!'

And then I did feel him soar. I felt him gather his legs up in that lovely careful way of his, and I felt the rush of the wind on my face, and then I could hardly believe it for we were on the ground again and everybody was clapping and I wasn't quite conscious as I patted him and couldn't say a word as he carried me out of the ring and the megaphones blared, 'Clear round.'

Was this really me, or was I dreaming? Surely jumping a clear round in the under-sixteens at Chatton Show was the sort of thing that *could* only happen in a dream? But I came round when some of my friends began to thump me on the back until my tie nearly flew off, and I gasped, 'Well, it's nothing really. About six other people are sure to jump clear rounds.'

But strangely enough nobody else did, and presently three of us were called in. I was first, a boy called Lloyd was second with one fault, and Maureen Chase was third with two. After I had received my red rosette I was told that I must also go up to the grandstand to receive the Hopley Challenge Cup, to be held for a year. So with a scarlet face and hands that felt like hams I took this large silver cup in my arms, and muttered something like 'Oh, thanks!' to somebody in tweeds who I afterwards found out was Lord Hopley. And then my at-no-times-particularly-graceful exit was completely ruined when I dropped the black ebony base of the thing, which fell on the ground with a resounding thud and had to be rescued by a steward, while howls of derision mingled with the cheers of the populace.

One place where I simply dared not look was the front row of the stand where Mummy and my own friends were sitting. I let myself go in the usual wild gallop round the ring; and when I came to the exit, there they all were.

'Good kid,' was all that Martin said. And Mummy added, 'Not bad at all, Jill, but why on earth did you have to drop that thing?'

'There's nothing left now but the Grand Parade,' said Martin. 'Hand Black Boy over to Bob here, who'll give him a rub down and you scoot off and have a wash and brush-up.'

'Jill Crewe,' said Ann solemnly, coming up to me, 'do you realise that you've taken three Firsts, three Seconds, and a Third!'

'You mean Black Boy has,' I said. 'I wish I was as nice a person as he is a pony.'

So with my cap, boots, and jodhpurs brushed, and my tie retied, I rejoined Black Boy who under Bob's skilful hand looked as if he was made of patent leather. Then headed by the local band we joined in the Grand Parade – in which everything that has won Firsts in the Show marches slowly round and round the ring – and Black Boy gave me quite a look when he found he had to do a collected walk behind a lot of fat cows and dairy turnouts.

At last it was all over. As I rode out I passed Frank Stabley and his father, and they smiled at me and I heard Frank say, 'Look, Dad, that's the girl who won everything. Pretty good, eh?'

And Mr Stabley said, 'They say that Martin Lowe trained her, so you'd *expect* something.'

I was frightfully happy, but I didn't feel the least bit cocky or conceited, because I knew that I'd had a lot of luck and that this was the sort of day which only comes to a person once in a lifetime. And I have written this book to show what a quite ordinary person can do with a quite ordinary pony, if he or she really cares about riding.

As we all left the Showground together, there stood Mrs Darcy and gave me an enthusiastic salute.

'Well, well, well!' she said in her loud, hearty way. 'It certainly has been Jill's gymkhana!'

And with those magic words ringing in my ears, I turned my pony happily towards home.

But the wonders of this great day were not quite ended. Mummy, of course, had gone on ahead in the Derrys' car, and when I reached our gate I saw her standing at the door waiting for me, and looking very excited.

'Oh, Jill,' she cried. 'What do you think?'

'If anything else nice happens I shall burst,' I said.

'Well, prepare to burst,' said Mummy. 'When I got home there was a letter on the mat to say that a firm of American publishers want to buy the American rights of *all* my books, and they're going to pay me a simply stunning sum for them. We'll have money to spare, Jill, so if you'd like it, we can move into a much bigger house and buy new furniture and things.'

'Jolly good!' I said. 'Congrats, Mummy.'

I went upstairs, picturing all the cute little American children simply wallowing in the squalid adventures of Winnie and Terry and the Fairy-of-Little-Duties-Daily-Done and the rest. I went into my room and pushed everything off the chest of drawers and put the three red rosettes and the three blue rosettes and the yellow one, and the certificates that went with them, and the cup and the ebony base that I'd dropped, and the prize money that was all going to be spent on Black Boy, all down on the white runner. And the weirdest choky feeling came in my throat. I went and looked out of my funny little window, and there was the lane and Black Boy standing patiently where I had left him with his reins hitched over the fence waiting for me to go and feed him and turn him into his nice orchard.

Gosh, how choky I felt!

I threw my riding hat on the bed and went charging downstairs.

'Mummy,' I said. 'I don't want to go away from the cottage and live in another house. We don't have to, do we? It's been such fun here, and all the *nicest* things have happened.'

And suddenly a kind of light broke all over her face.

'I don't want to leave either, Jill,' she said. 'Let's stay!'

'Oh, wonderful!' I said.

Then I had an idea.

'I say, Mummy,' I said, 'if you really do want to spend some money, what about enlarging the stable? I mean, I hate to think of it, but soon Black Boy is going to be too small for me, and I shall need something about fifteen-two. And' – I added as an afterthought, my plans soaring into the region of the grand and spacious – 'if we could run to about three loose boxes, you could have a horse and learn to ride too. Think it over while I go and mix the oats.'

A STABLE FOR JILL

A Stable for Jill

Ruby Ferguson

KNIGHT BOOKS
Hodder and Stoughton

Printed and bound in Great Britain by
Cox & Wyman Ltd, Reading, Berkshire

Hodder and Stoughton Children's Books
A Division of Hodder Headline plc
338 Euston Road
London NW1 3BH

Contents

1 The cold world for me

'Hello!' I said to my friend Ann Derry as we met after school one afternoon. 'How's the Best Dressed Child feeling today?'

For answer she pulled the hair ribbon off my plait and threw it into the road where it was squashed flat by a passing car.

'You asked for it,' she said.

We were referring to an event which had just taken place in the village of Chatton where we live and where everybody rides and there are lots of pony shows and other horsy events such as I have described in my other book *Jill's Gymkhana*.

A woman called Mrs Beverley had had the bright idea of offering a special prize for the best dressed child rider, the idea being to add a bit of interest to the Rectory garden party in aid of mending the church steeple which it badly needed. Actually it was a frightfully silly sort of prize, but everybody seemed to get very excited over it. I decided not to compete myself, as the clothes I wear are adequate for the kind of riding I do but far from showy, but some of the girls at school and their mothers went simply crackers. For days people were talking about what they were going to wear, or else telling you it was a grim secret, and some girls' mothers rushed them off to London to exclusive tailors who usually only make for the nobility. I should think the amount of money that was spent on those tailors would have built fourteen new steeples for the church, never mind repairing the old one.

There was a girl in our school called Susan Pyke, about whom I have told you in my other book, who said she was absolutely certain of getting the prize, which was distinctly putting-off for all the others if they had believed her, but nobody did.

My friend Ann told me rather apologetically that her mother was making her enter for this Best Dressed event, and knowing Mrs Derry I wasn't really surprised. Thank goodness my mother is much more sensible. I said to Ann, 'Well, for heaven's sake don't let her get you up as Bonnie Prince Charlie or anything like that.'

Ann said no, she was simply having new cord breeches and boots and a covert coat and a new white shirt and string gloves, and she wasn't even trying because she thought the whole thing was absolutely potty and just the sort of thing that Mrs Beverley – who turned out to be Susan Pyke's aunt – would think of.

Well, when the competitors rode into the ring on the day it was terrific and more like a fancy dress parade than just child riders.

There was one girl got up in a Charles the Second huntswoman outfit, all flowing green velvet with ostrich feathers in her hat, which fell off the second time round the ring and the pony behind trod on it; and there was another wearing scarlet jodhpurs with a sort of white Hussar tunic, and then all this extra special hunting kit from the exclusive London tailors.

Everybody was gasping, and I was thoroughly enjoying myself and having a good laugh as I leaned over the rails, when Susan Pyke rode in.

She did look marvellous, all in black and with silver epaulettes and a silver stripe down her breeches, and her boots were actually patent leather and the whole thing was crowned with a woman's hunting topper and she had gloves with enormous gauntlets like a Guardsman's. She was riding her father's black horse, Punch, which was seventeen hands and much too big for her, and unfortunately she got on his neck and couldn't get back again and then she lost her stirrups and after that she didn't look so good and the judges lost interest in her.

I will say for the judges, they had good sense. In spite of it being such a silly prize they didn't lose their heads and they weren't impressed by all the glamour that people had put on. When my friend Ann Derry rode into the ring I couldn't help feeling proud for she actually was without question the best dressed child rider that you could hope to see in the whole of England, and the judges knew it. Her pony,

Seraphine, a grey, was beautifully groomed and Ann rode her with the utmost confidence. From head to foot she was perfectly and unobtrusively dressed, just right, and just as I should want to be dressed if I ever rode at Wembley or with the Quorn, which I never expect I shall do.

She so obviously deserved the prize that everybody clapped, and the judges gave it to her, and it was fifty pounds and a certificate. But after that I used to rag her by calling her the Best Dressed Child, which always got her goat.

It was the end of the summer term and we were having exams, which are always revolting but in this case were more revolting than usual as they had been devised by some fiend in human shape.

'What was your paper like?' yelled Ann as we whizzed down Orchard Road on our bikes.

'Sickening,' I said. 'History. What *was* the Treaty of Utrecht?'

'Search me!' shouted Ann.

Then she turned off for her home and I went on to our cottage and burst into the kitchen and threw my school case on the floor. There was just time to saddle up and have a ride before supper.

Just then Mummy came into the kitchen with a letter in her hand and a strange look on her face. I knew at once that something was up though I do not claim to be physical, or whatever they call it.

'Gosh!' I said. 'Is it good or bad?'

'I don't know whether you'd call it good or bad, Jill,' she said. 'But it's rather terrific.'

My mother is very well-known as a writer of children's books, and I suppose some children must buy her books and read them – or else their aunts buy them for them for birthday presents to go in the bookcase – because simply huge numbers of them are sold and keep Mummy and me and the cottage and Black Boy, my pony, going; but the fact is I can't get on with them at all, they are so whimsical, and the children in them, though considered sweet, are I think perfectly revolting.

'It's books,' I said. 'It's another publisher wants another serial.'

'Oh, no,' she said. 'It's much more than that. They want me to go to America for two months, to visit summer camps and tell stories to the children. They'll pay all my expenses and give me a lot of money as well. What am I to say, Jill?'

'Why, you'll go, of course,' I said promptly. 'It'll be marvellous for you, and I'll be all right. It'll be the summer holidays anyway, and I'll make my meals when I feel like it and ride most of the day and dust every morning. It'll be fun.'

'But you can't possibly stay here by yourself,' said Mummy.

I knew that was coming. And I knew that however much I argued, Mummy wouldn't change her mind.

'Oh,' I said coldly. 'What happens then?'

'That's just the trouble. I hate to leave you, Jill, because I know you won't like – '

'Not Cecilia's!' I said. 'Oh Mummy! How perfectly foul!'

Cecilia is my cousin and an absolute blot.

'I think I'd better not go to America,' said Mummy.

'OK,' I said, and went to the orchard where Black Boy, my pony, was waiting for me. He came to me at once and nuzzled my shoulder, making lovely snuffling noises from sheer pleasure. I stroked his neck and pretended to chew his forelock, and he said as plainly as anything, '*Are we going to ride today?*'

I knew I was being a beast, and I knew that it wouldn't be a bit of good going on being a beast because I am not the kind of person that can be a beast and be happy at the same time.

So I went back to the house and put my head in at the door of the sitting room where Mummy was sitting in front of her typewriter looking thoughtful, and I said, 'You've jolly well got to go to America whatever happens, and I'll even go to Cecilia's. It can't be worse than the dungeons under the Tower of London and people lived for years in them.'

'You are a dear,' said Mummy smiling happily at me. 'I do want to go. But, Jill, there's something awful you haven't thought of and I hardly dare to say it – you won't be able to take Black Boy to Cecilia's. You'll have to leave him at the riding school. Mrs Darcy will be glad to have him and he'll be well looked after and exercised.'

'But – but – ' I stammered.

It was terrible. No Black Boy? No riding? I choked, and dashed up to my small bedroom. This was what you got for being noble. I was being noble about Mummy going to America, and I might just as well be going to a dungeon myself. On my chest of drawers were the cups I had won with Black Boy, and his rosettes made a bright pattern pinned over the mantelpiece, and I should miss the last two shows of the season and I had been nearly certain of winning the under fourteen jumping and next year I should be too old, and if you can think of anything more utterly dismal than that you don't know anything about riding.

I did my level best to look on the Bright Side, only I honestly couldn't find one to look on. There was a book of Mummy's called *Barbie Bright-Side* about a girl who had both her legs cut off in a car crash and got such a name for looking on the Bright Side that practically everybody in the town used to come to her and ask her to find a Bright Side for them too, and she always did.

'Gosh!' I said aloud. 'If Barbie could find a Bright Side in this she ought to get the VC.'

Because funnily enough it is always easier to see a Bright Side for other people than it is for yourself.

I am sorry this book is starting in such a melancholy way, but that is how things did start, though it will get a bit better later on if you can hang out so long.

To think was to act with my mother, and to make a long story short, a week later school had broken up for the holidays, and Mummy had had a letter from Aunt Primrose, Cecilia's mother to say 'we shall be only too glad to have dear little Jill for seven weeks or as long as you like,' and I was all packed for the dreadful fray.

The worst moment – here I go all dismal again – was when Mrs Darcy's girl groom, Angela, came to take Black Boy away because one thing I had drawn the line at doing was taking him myself. I sat on the end of my bed and didn't even look out of the window to see him go and an air of heart-rending despair filled the cottage.

However I bucked up after a bit and went down and gave Mummy the farewell present I had bought for her, which was a Horselover's Calendar with a super photograph of a horse on every page and the date underneath, and I told her to keep it and bring it back for me when she had done with it.

She said, 'You've been awfully good about all this, Jill, and I want to give you a reward. We've talked about you having another pony – '

I knew what was coming then and I was thrilled. Black Boy had done awfully well for me, but he wasn't up to the higher jumps which I hoped soon to be taking when I got into the under-sixteens; and besides when you only have one pony you sometimes get let down, for instance when Black Boy went off colour the day before the Lynbourne show and I had to scratch though I had entered for everything and Susan Pyke got three Firsts and told everybody at school that I had funked it when I saw what I was up against, which was absolute rot because I had beaten her heaps of times.

So I brightened up when Mummy said that and wondered what was coming next.

She brought her hand from behind her back and in it there was a small black leather wallet.

'I have been talking to Mrs Darcy,' she said, 'and to Martin, and they both have a good deal of confidence in your judgment. You have been very sensible and reliable, Jill, and I feel I can trust you with money. So in this wallet I have put eight hundred pounds – '

I gasped.

'Yes, it is a lot of money,' went on Mummy, 'and I want you to give it to Auntie or Uncle to take care of for you. But I thought that if by chance you should hear or see a suitable pony while I'm away you would have the means to buy it. You ought to get a decent pony for eight hundred pounds. Anyway, it will be something to brighten up your exile, and here is another fifty pounds for your pocket money. Now do take care of it until you get to White Ferry.'

'Oh, how wonderful!' I cried and gave Mummy a huge hug.

So when the taxi came for me the next day I felt a bit better about going, and was already making up a story in which I went to an auction and a magnificent chestnut show-jumper was put up and it just happened that there weren't many bidders that day and I got him for eight hundred pounds.

2 Home life at Cecilia's

When the train got to Wayfield station there were
Aunt Primrose and Cecilia standing on the platform
waiting for me. In the train I had taken off my hair
band and combed my hair out so that it hung round
my face, and in my new grey coat I walked down the
platform thinking I looked at least fifteen. However,
Auntie P. completely ruined the effect by shouting
from about twelve yards away, 'Oh there you are,
Jill dear! You weren't frightened all alone on the train,
were you, dear?' And several people looked round
expecting to see someone about six.

Cecilia rushed up and greeted me very gush-
ingly, and said, 'I'm so glad you've come, Jill, and
tonight we're going to press flowers for my Botany
album.'

Cecilia is the sort of girl who never talks about
anything but school. Actually I couldn't think of any
more squalid occupation than pressing flowers when
the poor things look like dried-up corpses wilting all
over the place.

'At first,' said Auntie P. with a sarky sort of smile,
'we were afraid we'd see a horse's head sticking out

of the carriage along with you. But you seem quite a normal little girl after all.'

'I shall never forget,' said Cecilia, 'when I was staying with you and you were learning to ride. You did look funny.'

I didn't say anything, but I made a resolution that nobody was going to look after my eight hundred pounds but me.

We got into the car outside the station and Aunt Primrose drove. She went round the corners very suddenly without using her indicators at all, and brakes kept squealing behind us and a lorry driver shouted something and Cecilia said, 'We never take any notice of rude men.'

When we got to the house Cecilia took me up to my room, which was awfully pretty and tidy and had a fitted wash-basin which I thought was super-luxurious, as I had never been used to anything but a bathroom which everybody wanted at the same time.

As soon as she left me I opened my case and there on the top were my riding things which I had put in at the last moment, not because I had a hope of wearing them but I thought it would do me good just to look at them sometimes. I threw my jodhpurs over the back of a chair and at once the room looked homelier. Next I got out the wallet with my money and tied it in the thick cardigan that Mummy had made me put in for if it was cold, and put it at the bottom of a drawer with all my other things on top of it. I know that in books most people take care of money by putting it up the chimney or in the mattress where it is found about a hundred years later by somebody who buys the house or the mattress, but I wanted to have this myself, not my descendants.

Then I went downstairs, and I must say we had a very good tea with sandwiches and two kinds of jam and three kinds of cake. The minute tea was cleared away, Cecilia got out a big fat heavy-looking book and a box full of depressed-looking asters and things, and said, 'Come along, I can't wait a minute. Our Botany teacher is giving a prize for the best album of pressed flowers done during the holidays and I've simply got to win it. Can you print fairly decently?'

'Not too badly,' I said.

'Well, I'll stick them in and you can do the lettering underneath. I think this is going to be absolutely smashing!'

As I said before, I cannot think of any more dreary occupation for the holidays than pressing flowers, and all I could be thankful for was that I didn't go to the kind of school where they had the kind of teachers who were so far gone as to suggest it.

So I spent a grim and deadly evening printing things like 'Little yellow flower name unknown found on our tennis court' under the squashed corpses in Cecilia's album, and thinking of Mummy who was by now on her way to Liverpool, and trying hard not to think of Black Boy at Mrs Darcy's stables and perhaps missing me and wondering if I had left him for ever.

At eight o'clock Auntie P. sent us to bed, because she is the sort of person who always treats you as if you were six until you are about twenty-two.

I got into bed with the light on and thought I would read a bit. Somebody had kindly put three books on the table by the bed, and I picked them up hopefully on the mere chance that one of them might be about horses. Then I put them back with a groan. They were all school stories, called respectively, *The Third Form at St Faith's, The Fourth Form at St Winifred's* and *The New Girl at St Ann's*.

The next morning after breakfast my aunt said to me, 'Cecilia always tidies her room *before* breakfast, but I've done yours for you, just this once.'

I could feel myself going red, as I hadn't wakened until five to nine and had leapt out of bed and hurled some clothes on and dashed down as the last echoes of the gong were dying away, and of course I had left my room in the most frightful mess like a battlefield.

'I can't imagine why you've brought your riding things,' went on my soulless aunt. 'You won't need them here.'

'Oh, you never know,' I muttered hopefully.

'Well, I've put them in the cupboard on the landing with some mothballs. And now what are you two girls going to do? What do you usually do in the mornings in the holidays, Jill dear?'

'Ride,' I said.

'I simply cannot see any fun in that,' said Cecilia. 'I mean, just sitting on a horse while it ambles along,

I mean, it's all right for anybody that's ancient and decrepit, about forty.'

'Cecilia has either a dancing lesson or a music lesson every morning in the holidays,' said my aunt, 'so do you think you can amuse yourself alone from about ten thirty to twelve?'

'Oh, rather!' I said, feeling absolutely full of joy at the prospect. 'I'll go for a walk.'

'Well, don't get lost,' said my aunt.

'Oh, no,' I said. 'I've got a frightfully good sense of direction. Besides, I'm used to riding for miles.'

I could hardly wait for ten thirty for Cecilia to be gone, and directly she had left I rushed out of the house and down the road before my aunt could change her mind and take me shopping. Wayfield wasn't a bad place, and though much larger than Chatton where I lived it was surrounded by country, and country always had possibilities.

I walked to the end of my aunt's road and up another road, and then to my delight I saw a lane going off at right angles, so I ran down there and into another lane which had grassy verges and high hawthorn hedges, and I began to feel quite bucked up and whistled a bit, though I couldn't help thinking, 'Oh, Black Boy, angel, if you were here now, what a marvellous canter we could have along that grass. It's simply made for horses and here am I without a horse.'

Just at that moment I saw a horse. It was in a field, and was only a working mare with harness galls and a plaintive expression, but when I made enticing noises she came to me and nuzzled my shoulder across the gate, and I stroked her cheeks and her neck and talked to her for a bit, though I felt very mean at having nothing to give her, and I decided to make friends with my aunt's help and get her to dig me some carrots and stuff, because actually if you care anything about horses you should never go for a walk in the country without something for them in your pockets. And that is why you ought always to wear a sensible coat or mac with pockets and not a whimsy blue thing with frills like Cecilia wore to go to her music lesson or dancing lesson or whatever it was she had gone to.

Anyway, now I had actually talked to a horse I felt better and not so exiled among the soulless heathen, and the fact that I had rescued my coat and jodhpurs from the squalid cupboard where my aunt had put them also helped. I like my horsy clothes so much, and I am sure they can feel happy or miserable just like I do, and I thought that if I wore them, I wouldn't feel so bad about not being able to ride. Of course, I don't think silk dresses and things like that have any feelings.

When I had done talking to the mare I walked on, and suddenly I saw three people sitting on a gate.

They were two boys and a girl, about fourteen and twelve and ten, and they were the most miserable people I ever saw in my life.

3 Horsy people at last

I said 'Hello', because when you live in the country you get into the way of saying hello to everybody you meet, and they all looked at me, and the two boys didn't say anything, and the girl said, 'Hello', very dolefully.

And then she said, 'Who are you?'

'As a matter of fact,' I said, 'I'm Jill Crewe. Who are you?'

'Oh, shut up talking like Alice in Wonderland,' said one of the boys. And then he said to the girl, 'She looks quite decent, Bar. I saw her talking to the mare in Hobson's field.'

'Oh golly,' I said, 'you don't mean to say you're horsy people? That would be too marvellous.'

'Yes we are,' said the girl.

'But you look so frightfully miserable,' I said. 'What's the matter?'

'You'd be miserable – ' began the elder boy, and the girl interrupted. 'Oh, shut up, Pat. She won't understand.'

'If it's anything to do with horses – ' I said.

'It is,' said the small boy. 'Dad's going to sell our

pony, because he says we can't afford her.'

'You oughtn't to have said that, Mike,' said the boy called Pat. 'It's nothing to do with strangers.'

'Gosh!' I said. 'I once had a pony I couldn't afford to keep, but I did keep him, and I've got him now and he's called Black Boy, and he's won heaps of Firsts at shows.'

'What do you mean by shows?' asked Pat suspiciously. 'Do you ride at the Royal International Horse Show and terrific things like that?'

'Good gracious, no,' I said. 'Only in country events, but most of the children about where I live are pretty good on ponies.'

'We had a pony show here for the hospital last month,' said Bar, 'and Pat won a first and two seconds on Ballerina.'

'Nice work,' I said.

'Well, what's the use?' said Pat. 'Daddy's definitely going to sell her when he and Mother come back from Gran's next month. He says we ought never to have had her.'

I pictured their father as a harsh, cruel parent with a large black moustache and cold, pale eyes.

'Our Australian uncle gave her to us before he went back to Australia,' said Mike, 'and Dad said that cricket and football stuff for school would have been more to the point because it doesn't cost anything to keep up. And now Ballerina's out at grass, and she has to be sold before the winter. And we taught ourselves to ride too out of a book called *Hints for*

Young Horsemen. I suppose you went to a poshed-up riding school.'

'I did not!' I cried. 'I never went to a riding school at all, except to work there. And the man who taught me to ride had to sit in a wheelchair the whole of the time he was telling me what to do, because he was in the RAF and his plane crashed. And I didn't even have a stable for Black Boy.' And then I told them all about my pony and about Mummy and me, and all the weird things I had done to make enough money to feed my pony in the winter, in fact all the things I told about in my other book, *Jill's Gymkhana.*

They looked quite impressed and not nearly so miserable.

And then I told them about having to stay here at Wayfield with my unsympathetic aunt and cousin, and they were very interested and realised how marvellous I must feel to have met some horsy people like themselves when I hadn't any hope of anything but pressing flowers and listening to Cecilia yap on about school.

'Where do you live?' I asked.

'There,' said Mike, pointing to where a church tower showed over the tops of some trees.

'That's a church,' I said.

'Of course it is, you dope,' said Pat. 'We live at the vicarage.'

I didn't really mind him calling me a dope, because I know that when you are miserable it makes you feel both savage and rude, and I thought that if their father was the vicar he probably didn't have much money after all, and perhaps he wasn't really as bad as I had imagined.

'I say,' said Bar, 'why don't you come to our house now and see Ballerina? It's only across the field.'

'OK,' I said, and they got off the gate and opened it for me and we all started to run. It had just come to me like a flash that perhaps I would buy Ballerina and she would be the second pony I was looking for.

When we got to the vicarage I saw that it was a huge old-fashioned house, and it had a cobbled yard at the side with stabling for several horses, but all that was in a very bad state of repair because it probably hadn't been used for about fifty years.

In a small paddock adjoining the stable yard was Ballerina, with her head over the gate looking eagerly at us as we approached. She was a very pretty bay of fourteen hands, with lovely lines and a good head, but rather delicately made compared to the animals I was accustomed to.

'Is she a good jumper?' I asked.

'Well, I think she's got a Thing about jumping,' said Pat. 'I've seen her do a clear round at one metre, and yet another time when she wasn't in the mood she simply kicked her way through everything in the under-twelves at seventy-five centimetres. Mike was riding her at the time, and was his face red!'

'More often than not, she isn't in the mood,' said Mike.

So I at once decided that Ballerina wasn't the pony for me.

'Let's saddle up,' said Bar, 'and each have a canter round the paddock.'

'I'd love it,' I said, 'but not in this awful skirt.'

'Oh, you can wear my other shorts,' said Bar. 'Come in the house and put them on while the boys get the tack out.'

Well, I thought, this is a super way of spending the morning. If anybody had told me at breakfast that I should be up on a pony my very first morning at Wayfield I wouldn't have believed it. It just shows there are horsy people everywhere, even in the deepest desert.

In Bar's bedroom, which was frightfully plain with bare boards and just a rag rug beside the black iron bed, and a wooden chair and a shelf of books with lovely titles like *My Friend the Horse, Common Diseases of Ponies and How to Cure Them*, and *Riding in Britain*, we changed, and Bar put on some rather mothy jodhpurs and I put on her grey shorts, and then we went down and found the boys had saddled Ballerina and Pat was up.

Pat rode like a jockey on the pony's neck, with his knees too high, but he was very showy and it was nice to see how completely he and Ballerina were in sympathy. I could understand he would get the best out of her in a competition.

Then Mike got up and had to shorten the stirrups, and he was very fussy, but he had a good seat and a straight back and when he got going he did a lovely collected trot, and I clapped.

'Now you,' said Bar.

So I mounted Ballerina, and though I wasn't accustomed to her pace or anything I found her easy, and I was very happy on her as I cantered round the paddock.

Then Bar had a turn, and I thought she was a bit bumpy, but she was clever and did a circus trick she had practised, riding first in front of and then behind the saddle without interrupting Ballerina's pace.

When I looked at my watch, to my horror it was half-past twelve and I knew I would only just have time to get back for lunch if I ran all the way.

'Can I come again tomorrow?' I yelled, and they said, 'Yes, do!'

4 Exile or worse

I dashed up the steps of White Ferry which is the misleading name of Cecilia's house, just as the gong was going for lunch. I hadn't even time to wash my hands, as the dining-room door was open and Auntie P. and Cecilia were already sitting at the table. So I went straight in, and my aunt gave me one horrified look and said, 'Really, Jill, I can't have you coming to the table dressed like that, whatever your mother allows. Please go and change and we'll wait for you.'

Then I realised with dismay that I was still wearing Bar's shorts, and they had a lot of horse hairs on them and some whitewash which I couldn't account for.

'Sorry!' I gasped, and flew upstairs. My skirt was in Bar's bedroom and I hadn't another, so I had to put on my blue dress, and I washed my hands and did something about the parting in my hair which had disappeared in the general mop effect.

When I got down, Auntie P. and Cecilia were sitting patiently before their cold plates of soup, looking like martyrs.

'Oh, you shouldn't have waited,' I said.

'We *never* begin until everybody is served,' said Cecilia, and I felt awful and said I didn't want any soup anyway, so they drank theirs and Cecilia changed the plates and the mutton came in.

'And what has Jill been doing all the morning?' said Aunt Primrose.

'I talked to some people I met,' I said. 'Their father's the vicar.'

'Oh, I don't think so,' said my aunt. 'Mr Mulberry is a bachelor.'

'They are awfully nice,' I said, 'and they're called Bar and Pat and Mike, and I think their other name's Walters.'

'Oh, she means the vicar of St Mary's at Matley,' said Cecilia. 'But absolutely nobody goes to St Mary's. We go to St Jude's.'

'They were jolly nice,' I said, 'and they ride too.'

Cecilia and her mother exchanged pained glances, and Cecilia said, 'A girl at the dancing class told me there are some unusual purple flowers growing by the mill dam over the fields. I think we'll go there this afternoon and get some, Jill, for my collection.'

I had had such a good morning that I thought I could cheerfully face an afternoon with Cecilia, and after lunch we set out to walk while she happily gabbled on about school and the teachers and the games and how many marks she had got in all the exams.

'I thought tonight we'd just read,' said Cecilia, who had the most potty habit of planning in advance what she'd do instead of letting things happen. 'Did you bring a book? If not I'll lend you one I've just finished called *The Spirit of the School*. It's frightfully good.'

'Actually,' I said – which was a word you weren't supposed to use at my school under the fifth form – 'I have got a book. It's called *Recollections of a Woman Show-jumper*.'

'Oh, you are crazy about riding!' said Cecilia. 'Some time I'll introduce you to some friends of ours who know absolutely all there is to know about riding. Of course I could ride myself if I wanted to. Someone – I forget who it was – once told me I look splendid on a horse. I suppose you either do or you don't.'

'Do or don't what?' I said.

'Look well on a horse. I'd have a horse with spirit, anyway. I can never understand those people who go along like a funeral.'

'By going along like a funeral,' I said, 'I suppose you mean riding at a collected walk. If ever you see anybody doing that it means the rider has perfect control of the horse, and until you can do a collected walk you're not fit to be in charge of a horse in any public place.'

'Oh, well, different people have different ideas,' said Cecilia. 'I have ridden once or twice and I found it frightfully easy.'

'Like when you were staying with us,' I could not resist saying, 'and you got up on Black Boy and bounced about all over the place and then fell off backwards.'

Cecilia went scarlet and said, 'I naturally wasn't prepared to be put on a rough, untrained pony, and then he reared and threw me. Everybody knows that no well-bred pony ever rears.'

'He never reared before or since,' I said hotly. 'The way you went on he must have thought he'd got a mad gorilla on his back, or something. Poor old Black Boy.'

'You and your silly pony,' said Cecilia scornfully.

'Oh, shut up,' I said. 'I'm not going to have a row. Let's go and get these potty flowers.'

So we picked flowers, and I was quite sorry for the ones I picked because they were going to be pressed by Cecilia, and all the evening I read *Recollections of a Woman Show-jumper*, and Aunt Primrose said, 'Can't Cecilia find you a really nice book?'

Next morning to my delight I had a letter from Mummy to say she was just going on the boat and had posted me some more handkerchiefs from Liverpool because I lost such a lot; and another from Angela who worked at Mrs Darcy's Riding School and was looking after Black Boy.

Angela wrote:

'Dear Jill,

'I thought you would like to hear that Black Boy has settled down all right and is eating like a horse (joke!) I sent him out today with the eldest Holmes girl who as you know rides jolly well, and she was very keen on him and said, was he for sale? I said, "You'd better not say that to Jill Crewe or she'll go up in flames." So she said, "Oh is this Crewe's pony that did so well at Chatton Show? Well don't you let anybody ride him but me till Jill comes back." So you see he'll be well taken care of.

'I have just finished the grooming and feeds, and it reminded me of what fun it was that time you worked here. I am actually sitting on an upturned bucket waiting for Mrs Darcy to come back so I can go off duty. She has gone in the shooting brake to see a pony at Forder.

'Are you getting any riding? I can't imagine you not doing, it would be worse than death. Yesterday I took Cocktail over to North Spinney, we went by the fields and she simply sailed over everything, it was grand. I thought of you.

'So no more now,
    'Love from Angela.'

As I read this nice letter and pictured the fields at home and the sun sparkling on the hedges and horses flying over timber with inches to spare, I gave a gulp, and unfortunately a piece of toast I was eating popped right across the table and went ping against the silver marmalade jar. I wanted to giggle, but Auntie P.'s eyes went enormous and Cecilia just looked pained and began to cut her toast into tiny little bits and put them into her mouth with frightfully exaggerated daintiness. I thought how differently people take things like that, and how Mummy would have giggled too, though we hadn't a silver marmalade jar for anything to go ping against and it would have hit our ordinary grocer's glass one and given out a feeble pong.

This made me feel exactly like the Irish exile in the song, and I thought what fun it was at home at the cottage, getting up early to muck out the stable and feed my pony, and then dashing in to find the kettle boiling all over the place and taking Mummy up a cup of tea, and then eating my porridge with all the enthusiasm of a starving sailor, and Mummy coming from the hens and saying, 'Gosh, isn't it marvellous, Martha's laid again!'

Compared with Cecilia's luxurious home some people might think mine squalid, but I thought it was just great. You jolly well don't appreciate things till Fate ruthlessly snatches them away from you, so if any of you who read this book think it is pretty grim at your home doing all the usual things every day, wait till you go and stay with some relations who do everything properly, and you'll see what I mean.

I made a silent vow that as long as I lived neither I nor any of my descendants would have anything on the table so soppy as a silver marmalade jar.

When breakfast was over, having nothing else to do I looked out of the window until half-past ten when the hour of my release approached and Cecilia came out of the drawing room with her music case, all ready to go to her lesson.

5 Ideas about Ballerina

'I've been thinking about you people all night,' I said to Bar as she greeted me at the vicarage gate.

'I'm jolly glad you've come,' she said. 'I thought you might be a bit fed up with us and not bother. And Agatha said, where did that skirt come from and where were my shorts.'

'Who's Agatha?' I said.

'She's our housekeeper that looks after us when Father and Mother are away. At least she calls it looking after, but we call it the iron hand in the iron glove.'

'You mean the velvet glove,' I said.

'Velvet my foot!' said Bar. 'Is that newspaper parcel my shorts?'

I handed them over, and said, 'You should have seen my aunt's face when I dashed in to lunch with them on, all horse hairs and whitewash. I don't know where the whitewash came from.'

'Oh, all my clothes have whitewash on,' said Bar. 'Your skirt's in the kitchen.'

'Good,' I said. 'I'll change out of this awful frock,

and actually I've brought my jodhpurs and a sweater, they're in the parcel with your shorts.'

Then Pat and Mike came running out, and we all went and leaned over the paddock gate like horsy people do and chewed straws and looked at Ballerina.

'As I said,' I began, 'I've been thinking about you people a frightful lot in the silent watches of the night and all that sort of thing. You do want to keep Ballerina, don't you?'

'Want to?' said Mike. 'What do you think!'

'Well,' I said, 'there's only one way. You've got to show your father that she isn't going to cost him anything to keep. She's got to be self-supporting. You've got to turn her from a frozen liability into a profit-producing asset.'

'Gosh!' said Pat, staring at me in admiration; and Bar and Mike said together, 'How?'

'Well, what can you do with a horse to make money?' I said.

'We did once think of a circus,' said Bar, 'and getting people to pay to come in, but we couldn't get enough turns. I can do three different tricks on Ballerina, and Pat and Mike thought they might practise jumping on and off bareback, only we didn't have any clown's clothes and I asked Mummy if I could cut up the spare room curtains – I mean, nobody ever uses the spare room, and they are sort of yellow and black check – but she said no. So that idea died on us, and we haven't thought of anything else.'

'You might use her to give a few lessons,' I suggested, 'if there are any kids about here who want to learn to ride.'

'Oh help!' said Pat. 'We can't ride well enough ourselves to teach anybody else. We'd get put in prison.'

'Actually there are kids,' said Bar, 'but I don't think we'd be very hot as teachers. I wouldn't even know how to tell a kid to mount a pony.'

I looked at her doubtfully, as I had read somewhere that teachers are born and not made and I suppose that applies to riding as well as maths and things.

'Well,' I said, 'if you don't know how to tell anybody how to mount a pony you jolly well ought to get a book and learn. Stand on his left side, by the shoulder, with your back to his head. Place the reins in your left hand and put it on the withers in front of the saddle. Next take hold of the stirrup with your right hand and place your left foot in up to the instep, and then take hold of the waist of the saddle with your right hand. Then spring from the right foot – '

'You can write it out for me some day,' said Bar, and I blushed and said, 'I wasn't showing off.'

'Oh, cut it out, you two!' said Mike. 'The circus is off and the riding lessons are off, so what do we do now?'

'Let's go and have our elevenses,' said Bar. 'It may give us an inspiration.'

So we went in the house, and the elevenses proved to be very good indeed, consisting of coffee and hot toast with jam on, because the Walters' Agatha, though lacking in what you might call endearing qualities, Believed In Food.

'There's one thing about us,' said Bar, 'we're always willing to learn. If there's anything wrong with my riding I hope one of you will always tell me. I have a dread of getting ham-handed, because someone once told me that people who are naturally light-handed are so sure of themselves that they grow hammier and hammier as they get older. You can go on for ever learning something new about riding, can't you? Even when you're the Pride of the Quorn, and all that.'

'My cousin Cecilia,' I said, 'says she knows some people who know everything there is to know about riding. They must be blots, mustn't they?'

'Of the first water,' agreed Bar. 'I suppose your cousin wouldn't have any ideas about making a horse self-supporting?'

I gave her a withering look, and Pat said, 'We are a dumb crowd. There *must* be something you can do with a perfectly good pony. In the old days, if a man had a horse that seemed to be all he needed.'

'Are you suggesting we should be highwaymen?' said Mike.

'I wouldn't mind having a stab at that,' said Pat, 'only we'd have to do a bit of explaining to Father if we came staggering in every night dripping with gold watches and diamond rings.'

We stuck our elbows on the table and thought.

Looking idly out of the window, I said, 'Gosh, you've got some marvellous premises here. When I was a kid about two years ago I used to say the dream of my life was to keep a stable. You could keep a smashing stable here. There's room for six horses.'

'Well, what do you do with your stable when you've got it?' said Pat. 'Sit and look at the horses? Or just tie ribbons in their foaming manes?'

'You're so frightfully funny,' I said, 'I wonder you don't die laughing at yourself! Near us at home there's a woman called Mrs Darcy who has a stable. Actually she's looking after my pony while I'm here. She runs a riding school, and she hires hacks, and she's got a most lovely foal that was born in the stable and she's going to sell him when he's older. I'd be content just to have a hacking stable, because I love grooming horses and cleaning stables and I once did it professionally at Mrs Darcy's when I needed some money for my own pony.'

They all looked at me with awe and respect, and Bar said, 'Well, that sounds all right, but we can't do much with only one horse, even if we have got stables. And you should see the inside of them! Talk about the dirt of ages! Ballerina's stall is the only decent one.'

'I know what I'd like,' I said dreamily. 'I'd like to see a notice on your gate saying, "Hacks for Hire".'

'Well, stick one up,' said Mike cheerfully. 'If anyone comes to hire one we can trot Ballerina out and say, "unfortunately this is the only hack I have in the stable at the moment, sir", which would be quite true.'

'Too blooming true,' said Bar.

'I don't want to hurry you,' said Pat, 'but it's nearly twelve o'clock.'

'Oh, how sickening!' I groaned. 'I'll have to go.'

'Come on!' said Bar. 'Let's have a canter first. You can have first go, Jill. And you could show me how you do that figure of eight?'

So we dashed into the paddock and did figures of eight on Ballerina, more or less correctly, and then I really had to go.

'Do see if you can come this afternoon,' said Bar. 'I'm sure we shall think of something if we have more time.'

I didn't think there was a hope of this, but as you know, grown-ups are quite unpredictable, and my aunt said, 'Well, I want you to stay in this afternoon, Jill, as some people are coming to tea who know your mother; but as you are going to be here for several weeks it won't be a bad idea if you can find some means of amusing yourself. I've been making inquiries, and the Walters children seem to be All Right.'

'Oh, thanks very much,' I gasped, and flew upstairs to write to my friend at home, Ann Derry.

'Dear Ann,' I wrote, 'You will be glad to hear that things are not so grim as I thought they were going to be. I have been lucky enough to make friends with some horsy people and once more we are up against the old problem of Ways and Means, like I was with Black Boy. Can you think of any ways of making One Horse self-supporting? If so, just send me the details.

'How is Seraphine? I hope that swelling on her hock went down, in time for the Bank Holiday show. I am dying to know what happened, but if Susan Pyke won the jumping you needn't tell me or I shall die of rage. Did your kid sisters enter for the under-tens Showing class on their Shetlands? I bet they looked sweet.

'You might pop up to Mrs Darcy's some time when you've nothing to do and take an apple for Black Boy. I'd give everything I've got for just one good ride.

'Love from Jill.'

In the evening my uncle came home from London where he had been on business and said that for a treat he would take us to the pictures, as Auntie P. said there was a picture that was suitable for young girls. What she meant was, suitable for kids, as it was a very weepy picture about a kid of ten who lived in dire poverty in a slum in the Big City. This kid was a marvellous singer, and the funny thing was that whenever she burst into song either in the street or in her dirty kitchen, a fifty-piece orchestra would pop up from nowhere and accompany her. This kid had a dog she adored, a St Bernard weighing about half a ton, and I couldn't help wondering how her parents who were so poor could afford to feed it. Well, one day this dog got run over and killed in the street, and it was rather unfortunate that this was the day when the kid was having an audition at the Opera House, with Cartoni, the great impresario. She was so upset about the dog that she made an awful mess of the audition, and Cartoni was furious, thinking he had been brought all that way to hear a kid that couldn't sing for toffee. So out she went into the snow, but somebody told Cartoni about the dog and he was filled with remorse and went after the kid. He arrived at her meagre home to find her scrubbing the floor, at ten o'clock at night, and crying great big blobby tears that stuck on her face, and singing bits out of *La Bohème* so beautifully that he just rushed at her and cried, 'A New Star is born'. The next thing, she was singing *La Bohème* at the Opera House and a vast audience was clapping, and when it was over she put on a long white ermine coat and the impresario presented up a new St Bernard dog (which I think was the same one as I particularly noticed its markings) and she put her arms around its neck and sang 'Stille Nacht'. And that was the end.

I found I was very unpopular when we got outside, as I had giggled in all the bits where I saw the funny side of it, as Mummy and I always did when we went to the pictures together, and my aunt and Cecilia had both cried.

6 Three more horses

The next morning I went haring off to the vicarage,
feeling particularly thrilled because I had the whole
day in front of me and my lunch that I had begged
from my aunt's maid, in a parcel. I had on my
jodhpurs and a fawn sweater with a turtle neck that
Mummy had knitted, and I didn't even care when
Cecilia said, 'I shouldn't think it would do your
marvellous riding any good to ride on any poor old
broken-down horse that the Walters might have. But
you should know.'

It was a cold day for August and the sky was
grey, but I was happy and I whistled as I ran, and
thought of my unfortunate mother battling with the
raging main and hoped she was finding consolation in
looking at the magnificent pictures in the Horselover's
Calendar.

When I came in sight of the vicarage I knew
something had happened because Mike was standing
up on the wall looking out for me, and as soon
as he saw me he jumped down and ran off to tell
the others, and when I got to the gate they were
all there.

'Bags I tell her!' shouted Mike. 'I say, Jill, we've got three more horses!'

'What!' I gasped.

'Three more horses!' shouted Mike. 'We'll be able to start the stable now.'

'It's this way,' said Bar. 'We have an uncle we call Uncle Toots, who's a vet and lives about two miles from here. He's been ill and has gone away for two months and left a locum at his house, but he's also left three horses out at grass in his field, and before he went he said sort of jokingly to us, "You can give those horses a bit of exercise if you feel like it," but of course we didn't bother about it at the time and it had slipped our memory. But the point is, we can *have* those horses if we want them. Nobody wants them while Uncle Toots is away.'

'How absolutely gorgeous!' I said. 'Why, we can start a stable straight away.'

'The snag is,' put in Pat, 'that there are horses and horses.'

'What do you mean?' I said, with visions of gorgons and other monsters floating before my eyes.

'Pat means,' said Bar, 'that as riding horses these of Uncle Toots' aren't so hot, so don't get any idea of shining hunters or even decent ponies like Ballerina. In the first place, there's Bungie who's twenty-seven. In the dim, dark ages he was Uncle Toots' riding horse; now he's pensioned off. He sags in the middle just like a hammock, and half the time he's fast asleep. But on his best days, which are few and far between, he's just rideable. Then there's Mipsy, the cob that pulls the trap, because Uncle Toots is old-fashioned and won't use a car. He always glares at me and shows his teeth, and actually nobody can do much with him but Uncle Toots. And then there's Dot, the Shetland, that Uncle Toots' daughter grew out of. And that's the lot.'

She sounded more than doubtful, but to me horses were horses, the most wonderful creatures in the world and full of exciting possibilities, so I said at once, 'Can we go and see them? *Now?*'

'Yes, let's,' said Pat who was always practical. 'Let's go on the bikes. I'll ride Mike's with Mike on the crossbar, and Bar can ride mine and Jill can have Bar's.'

So we whizzed off to this place of their uncle's, and as we got there we saw a car standing at the gate and the young locum was just coming out in a white lab coat, with a spaniel under his arm.

'Hello!' said Bar. 'We've come to have a look at the horses out at grass, if that's OK by you. Uncle Toots said we could exercise them if we liked.'

'It's OK by me,' said the young vet. 'Help yourselves.'

'And if we thought of taking them away to our place?' said Bar.

'Nobody's using them but you,' said the young vet, placing the spaniel very carefully on the back seat of the car, as it had a splint on its off-hind leg.

So we went round the side of the house and across

the yard, where there was a long row of outbuildings from which issued interesting noises like the yowling of bored cats and the yapping of dogs and the bleating of sheep. I thought it was all fascinating and would have liked to have a look at the patients; in fact I decided at that moment it would be rather fun to be a vet as a sort of sideline to the stable I meant to run some day. But there wasn't time to stop, so we went straight to the gate which led into the field, and there were the three horses.

The old horse was quite nearby, standing under an oak tree with his eyes shut and slightly swishing his tail in a vain effort to discourage the flies. He was a nice chestnut with black mane and tail, but his head was very bony and heavy and he certainly sagged in the middle, very hammockishly.

The cob, also a chestnut but with a curious effect as though a bottle of ink had been sprinkled over his withers, stood a little way from us and looked at us with a suspicious eye, then lifted his front lip and whinnied at us.

The Shetland, who was grazing on the far side of the field, didn't even bother to look up. She was a nice little animal with good lines, but too fat.

'Well, there they are,' said Pat. 'What do you think of them?'

'Of course they're not exactly bloodstock,' I said, 'but I do think they've got possibilities. For instance, the Shetland is an asset in any stable. Kids love riding on a Shetland, and the mothers think they're so sweet and innocent, though they sometimes have quite awful dispositions – the Shetlands, I mean, not the mothers. Then the old horse might be useful if we get a very nervous client who wants something quiet and steady. By the way, I never asked, but are the cob and the old horse broken to the saddle?'

'Oh, yes,' said Bar. 'The old horse used to be Uncle's riding horse about a hundred years ago, and he bought the cob from a farmer who used to ride him.'

'What about tack?' said Mike.

'Well, Dot has her own, and Bungie's old saddle must be somewhere around, and I know there's loads of stuff lying about in the harness room. Come on, let's see.'

So we went to the harness room, which was full of all sorts of things like old kitchen chairs and medicine bottles and a pram and a pile of fire logs, and we discovered the Shetland's saddle and a snaffle bridle and a double bridle much the worse for wear, and also Bungie's tack which was filthy, and an odd saddle that would do for the cob, and two more bridles, and some stirrups that looked as if they had been at the Battle of Waterloo, and some mothy-looking rugs, and a box of dirty dandy-brushes and other cleaning things, and a tube for blowing pills down horses' throats, and a lot of other things all mixed up with the dust of ages.

'Crumbs!' said Pat. 'How are we going to get all this junk to our place?'

'It's going to be even crumbier getting it clean,'

said Bar. 'But actually that carrier – what's-his-name Evans – would fetch it for us cheaply. Let's drag all we want out into the yard!'

So we did, and by this time we were filthy and jolly hot. Then we went into the harness room again and poked about looking for halters, and we found three very dirty and knotted ones in a box labelled 'Glass With Care'.

'Come on, let's get the horses,' said Mike. 'They'll take some catching after being out at grass for two weeks.'

'Listen,' I said. 'This has got to be properly done in a professional way as befits people who are going to keep a well-run stable. Before we take the horses we've got to tackle those stables at your house. They're not fit to put a gorgon into.'

'Well let's take the horses now and put them in our paddock with Ballerina,' said Pat.

'Look at them!' I said. 'They've got to be clipped before we can begin to groom them, and probably re-shod. Is there a place near where that can be done?'

'Oh, yes,' said Bar. 'There's a farrier's nearly opposite. We could tell him to carry on with the horses while we're getting the stables ready. But the point is, who's got any money?'

'I can raise about ten pounds,' said Pat, and Mike said he had six and Bar said it was a pity but she'd have to take something out of the Post Office.

I said, 'We'll wait till the farrier's bill comes in and then divide it between us. We'll have to keep some books and put down all our expenses and takings.'

'Takings!' said Pat. 'Ha. Ha. Ha.'

So we went across to the farrier's, and he said he would collect the three horses and clip them and replace any worn shoes, and give us a ring at the vicarage when they were ready, and then it was half-past twelve and we thought we'd done a jolly good morning's work, so we biked back to lunch.

After lunch – at which I added my sandwiches to the general mêlée – we thought we would go out and have a look at the grim and ghastly sight which lurked in the stables.

This was even worse than the direst dreams of a fevered imagination could depict. (I got that out of a library book, and copied it in my notebook to use sometime. Whenever I use really highbrow phrases like that, they are out of my notebook and the fruit of some distinguished author's gigantic brain, not mine.)

In the first place, the vicarage stables didn't even smell of stables, which is – I think – a beautiful and inspiring smell. They smelt of dirt and spiders and cats and old sacks. That is, all except the small one where Ballerina had her stall, and even that wasn't up to my standards. And when we got inside you could understand why they smelt of dirt and spiders and cats and old sacks, because that is what they were mostly full of. I shouldn't think they had had any horses in them or been cleaned since about the year Queen Victoria came to the throne.

'Gosh!' said Mike. 'It's past hope.'

'No, it isn't,' said Bar. 'It's just a terrific job, isn't it, Jill?'

'OK,' I said. 'Now we've got to get cracking on this. This afternoon we'll pull all the old sacks and things out and make a bonfire of them. Then we'll pool some money and buy cleaning things and whitewash. And then we'll jolly well all four go at it till the stables are fit to put our horses in. And after that we'll have all the tack fetched from your uncle's and clean that. It's about a week's solid work, I should say.'

'Let's go in the house and make a list of the cleaning stuff,' said Bar.

So we went in and made a terrific list, beginning with scrubbing brushes and ending with saddle soap and metal polish, and as ready money was needed for these we pooled what we had and the boys offered to go to the hardware shop and do the buying.

I promised to be round early to start the good work, and with that I took my leave and departed from my nice, horsy world to the dreary pink-cushioned one in which I was doomed for a time to wilt.

I washed and changed for dinner, and in the evening mended my string gloves and hoped I should soon be needing them.

7 Walters and Crewe Ltd

Next morning we got right down to work on those awful stables. We were wearing the weirdest assortment of garments, in fact any rags that we could unearth, and we had ransacked a box in the attic of the vicarage which was really intended for bombed-out civilians, but that seemed a bit out-of-date anyway and the things could all go back when we'd done with them, if nobody minded a few spiders, sploshes of whitewash, and large damp patches of a peculiar-smelling chemical stuff called Stablo which is meant for cleaning out stables and proved to be jolly good.

First we lighted a bonfire and burned all the rubbish. It was a bit unfortunate that Agatha had just washed some pillowcases and hung them out to dry, and the result was heated words on both sides, but as we obviously couldn't move the bonfire she kindly agreed to move the pillowcases, and they weren't really very smoky and would probably look quite clean when dry.

Then we got up on ladders and washed the walls down – this was an awful job as all the water which had been on the walls descended on us and we couldn't wash for spluttering – and when this was done we swilled all the floors with hot water and Stablo and brushed them with yard brushes.

Then we left everything to dry, and that was a whole day's work.

The next day we whitewashed, and that was another whole day's work; in fact I had to go before it was finished and the others nobly carried on all the evening while I languished in the hated bonds of social life, handing round cups of coffee to some friends of Cecilia's who had come to talk about starting a school Madrigal Club. When they had sung a few madrigals, a girl called Phyllis Barnes said to me, 'Which do you like best?' and without thinking I answered, 'Whitewash,' and Cecilia said, 'Don't take any notice of her, Phyllis, she isn't quite all there.'

But on the whole Cecilia was glad to get rid of me in the daytime, so that she could go out to coffee with her friends and practise the piano for some school prize that she wanted to win, and write letters to one of the teachers that she had a crush on.

Meanwhile the stables were finished and a credit to us, and we got a plumber in to make the taps work and a man to clean out the drain which proved to have a family of mice in it, and we set to work like mad, cleaning tack. We banged clouds of dust out of the saddles, and then we brushed them and soaped them and rubbed them up, and we did the same for the leathers and the girths and bridles, and then we polished all the bits and the stirrups – and it took hours to get the dirt off, never mind putting a shine on them – and then we washed all the dandy-brushes and stable rubbers and other things and arranged them neatly on the shelves, and we arranged the tack in the cleaned-out harness room after we had shunted the vicar's old books out if it, and we had now been at it for five days and were ready for the horses.

It was a great moment when we walked over to Uncle Toots' to fetch them. The farrier had made them look quite decent and put them back into the field, so we paid his bill, and by then everybody but me was insolvent. In fact I had such terrific faith in the stable idea that I thought I might as well go the whole hog, and I had ordered a lot of fodder from the local corn merchant, hoping that we should have made some money before the bill came in.

Bar, Pat, and I each took a halter and Mike acted as rounder-up. We got the Shetland easily because she was too fat to move away from us, but the cob led us an awful chase as he was very nappy after a few weeks off work; and Bungie the old horse was also a problem, because though we got the halter on him he just didn't get the idea of moving and it was like trying to shift the Pennine Chain. Though as a general rule I never hit a horse and think nothing of riders who use crops in the show ring, on this occasion there was nothing else for it, so I cut a hazel switch and gave Bungie just one flick on the flank, and he jumped as though I had put a squib under him and gave me the look of a Victim to its Murderer. However, he ambled off, and then Mike running beside him did his circus trick and leapt on to Bungie's back. There he sat, grinning and waving, and looking so like a monkey in a sailor's hammock that Bar and I could only giggle.

So we got the horses home, and though Pat and Mike were all for saddling up and trying them, Bar and I said no, they must have a chance to get used to their new home first, so we opened the gate of the paddock and shoved them in. Ballerina looked most haughty and resentful, just as you probably would if someone unceremoniously opened the door of your house and shoved in three rather weird-looking strangers, but after a bit her curiosity became too much for her and she sidled up to Mipsy and they began to graze together. Dot didn't bother at all, but found a nice spot and planted herself in it as though she belonged, and Bungie just stood inside the gate and went to sleep.

By now it was lunch-time, but we were too excited to bother much with food and golloped it down, and unfortunately Mike choked and was sick and Agatha made him lie down on the kitchen sofa.

The next thing was to try the horses. We collected them and got them saddled, which wasn't as easy as it sounds as they weren't a bit keen on the idea after their lazy life at Uncle Toots', and then I being the lightest went on Dot while Bar mounted Mipsy and Pat took old Bungie.

I found that Dot wasn't too bad at all. She had

at one time been properly schooled and the vet's daughter who rode her must have known something about the principles of horsemanship, and Dot even obeyed my diagonal aids quite nicely; but Bar wasn't having such a good time on Mipsy. Mipsy was just silly, bucking and shying, showing his teeth and pretending to be a poor little nervous horse, which he certainly wasn't, but after a bit he realized that Bar knew what she was doing and he settled down. He had never been properly schooled, but he knew enough to be a decent hack for anybody who could ride. As for Bungie, he turned out better than we had expected. There were only three things about Bungie, Start, Walk, and Stop, but when Pat got him started he went on walking until made to stop, and he wasn't stubborn or awkward about it, so we thought he would do quite all right for any client who wanted a really quiet horse.

Then Mike came out feeling all right again, and Bar mounted Ballerina, Mike took Dot, I took Mipsy, Pat stayed on Bungie who seemed to like him, and with Ballerina leading we went round and round the paddock as though it were a riding school, making our horses do more or less what Bar did on Ballerina.

Thus the afternoon slipped away, and finally we took the horses to their nice clean stalls, rubbed them down, and fed them.

'That's all for today,' I said. 'Now what about tomorrow?'

'Grand opening,' said Pat, and we all dithered with excitement. 'Look here, we boys will muck out, and then you and Bar can take over.'

'That's jolly sporting of you,' I said. 'And I'll come early in time for the feeding, and then there's all the grooming to do. I vote we open in the afternoon.'

So I dashed off, and by the time I got home I was nearly too tired to crawl, but fortunately for me Cecilia wanted to spend the whole evening practising her prize piece so I was able to go to bed early.

I arranged with Doris, my aunt's help to call me at seven and I was quite prepared in my enthusiaism to cut out breakfast, but Doris proved to be a really super person and called me with two cold sausages and a pile of bread and butter which I ate while I was putting on my new yellow shirt and jodhs and tying my fawn tie.

I then scribbled a note to my aunt which read,

'Dear Aunt Primrose, please excuse me from break-fast as I have to go out on business. I will be sure to be back about five. Love from Jill.'

I dashed downstairs and put this on the dining-room table, then I collected the sandwiches which the worthy Doris had been making while I dressed and I simply flew, before anybody could stop me.

When I got to the stable I beheld a scene of terrific activity. All the mucking out had been done, and Pat and Bar had already started the feeding. So we finished that, and then we were ready to groom our four horses.

First we washed all their sixteen feet and then we got to work with the dandy-brushes and by the time we had finished that we were all scarlet in the face with exertion and excitement and working at top speed, quite apart from the fact that Mipsy and Dot didn't want to be groomed and you know what that means! Ballerina was an angel and a great help, holding up her feet for Bar to wash them while Pat and I struggled to make Mipsy bend his joints.

'Could you by any chance lay your hands on a few soap flakes for their tails?' I said. 'I always have to get mine at home when Mummy isn't looking, as she thinks that soap flakes are destined for higher things than washing horses' tails.'

'I can do better than that,' said Bar. 'If we can get Agatha out of the kitchen I'll pinch her liquid shampoo. It's wizard for tails.'

'I'll go into my bedroom,' said Mike, 'and yell out to Agatha to come and find my other shirt, and then you can nip into the kitchen.'

This worked like a charm, and once Agatha was out of the kitchen Bar got in and found the liquid shampoo in the corner cupboard. It was called Gleemit and there was a picture on the bottle of a most beautiful girl with millions of shining curls, and it said underneath, 'You too can have hair like this if you use Gleemit regularly.'

I doubted this, and certainly Agatha's hair wasn't

in the least like the beautiful girl's, but the shampoo turned out to be marvellous for horses' tails and we thought when we had time we would write and tell the makers who would probably be glad to know and could use it in their advertisements.

Finally Mike, who was good at making wisps – which isn't a bit easy and actually quite a gift – made some wisps, and we finished the horses off, and we left them standing with their tails drying and they really looked very nice indeed. The whole place looked frightfully clean and efficient, and I wouldn't have cared if Mrs Darcy herself had inspected it, in fact I wished she could.

Then we took off our rags and put on our riding things, and Bar and Pat and Mike had awfully nice breeches and boots that they had spent the money on that their Australian uncle had given them for tips when he left, though their mother wanted them to spend it on dreary tennis and football kit that you have to have for school in any case. Bar and Pat had white shirts and Mike had a blue one, and we tied our ties with great care and brushed our hair.

Finally I produced my surprise. A few days before I had bought some cartridge paper and some Indian ink at an art shop, and in my room in the silent watches of the night I had made a big placard which read:

WALTERS AND CREWE LTD
HACKS FOR HIRE

The others said they thought this was simply smashing, so we got a hammer and some tacks and went out and nailed it up on the oak tree by the gate of the stable yard.

Mike didn't know what LTD meant, so I explained that it meant this was a proper business to make assets, not just a game.

As I had a bit of cartridge paper left over I had done another little thing, with a drawing of a horse and rider flying over a five-barred gate and underneath the pleasant words:

> Hands down and head up,
> Heels down and heart up,
> Knees close to your horse's sides,
> Elbows close to your own.

This we tacked over the stable door where our clients would be able to see it.

Then we went in and had lunch, and Agatha said, 'I don't know what your mum and dad would say, but I suppose it isn't my business,' and Pat said, 'We couldn't agree more.'

8 People want to ride

And then when everything was ready and we were actually waiting for the clients, you will hardly believe it but we all had an acute attack of the needle and started quarrelling like mad.

Bar began it by telling Mike for goodness' sake to keep out of the way when any clients arrived, as they might not think much of an establishment that had people in it who were only ten; and I stuck up for Mike and said that he had done his share of the work and Bar was just being beastly on purpose; and then Pat stuck up for Bar and told me that considering it was *their* stable and *their* horses, wasn't I throwing my weight about far too much? And I said, whose was the idea of the hacking stable anyway, and who had made all the suggestions? And if it wasn't for me they'd still have been feebly sitting on a gate moaning about having to part with Ballerina, but if that was how they felt I knew what to do, and I began to stride towards the gate, but Pat yelled after me, 'Come back! I apologise!' and Bar said, 'Oh, do shut up, everybody. You know it's only because we all feel like just before you go into the ring at a show.'

Then Pat remembered that he had left the tap running, and Mike said there was a pitchfork just where anybody would fall over it when they went into the harness room, so they both went off, and Bar said, was her hair all right and would she look older with a hat on? And just at that moment a very tall, oldish, military-looking man in tweeds came into the yard.

We both gasped, and the man came up to me and said, 'Anybody in charge here? Jolly glad to see I can hire a horse here occasionally. Left all mine in India.'

'We're in charge,' said Bar quite coolly. 'Anything we can do for you?'

He looked a bit taken back, and said, 'Well, I want something up to my weight. Well-mannered, and not a slug. Do you charge by the hour?'

Will you believe it, in all the excitement of getting the stable and the horses ready that was one thing we had never discussed, what we should charge! So I had to think awfully fast and make these world-shaking decisions alone.

I looked at Bar but she just gaped helplessly back at me, so I thought a minute and then said, 'We charge five pounds an hour, or thirteen pounds for a whole morning or afternoon, or twenty pounds a day if you want to go for a riding picnic.'

'Well, let's start with one hour,' said our client, looking a bit grim. 'What have you got?'

'Excuse me while I speak to my partner,' I said, and Bar and I walked a few yards away.

'We daren't show anybody like him anything but Ballerina, she said.

'Why not Mipsy?' I said. 'He's stronger than Ballerina.'

'Yes, but it's one of Mipsy's bad days. He nipped Pat while he was mucking out.'

'Well, let's show them both,' I said, 'and trust to luck.'

So Bar and I led out Ballerina and Mipsy, and Ballerina looked all smug and ladylike, but Mipsy made faces and pecked, and I was ashamed of him.

'I'm afraid this is all we have in that would suit you,' I said to the client. 'You see, we didn't actually expect – '

'This establishment actually only caters for children,' said Bar in a very dignified way.

'Good heavens!' said our client, looking at the animals, and added, crossly. 'Of course those won't do. The mare is a lady's pony and I couldn't possibly see myself on a cob. Your notice says Hacks for Hire. If what you mean is children's ponies you ought to say so.'

And away he went without a backward glance.

'Well, that's that!' said Bar. 'What a beast! Do you think all our clients are going to be as beastly as that?'

Then Pat and Mike who had been in the harness room and had heard every word came out, and Pat said, 'We ought to get some money from somewhere and buy one decent horse, a hunter or something.

This is just *playing* at keeping a stable,' and I was furious and said, 'All right, you get out and we'll play at keeping a stable by ourselves,' and Bar said, 'Oh, shut up!'

'While we're on the subject,' I said, 'I do think we ought to change the horses' names. I mean, I can't think of any more utterly revolting names for horses than Mipsy and Bungie and Dot. I mean, it's so mean-minded to give horses names like that. They ought to be called Starlight and Cameron and Golden Girl, or something like that.'

'Well, you can call these horses Starlight and Cameron and Golden Girl till you're blue in the face,' said Pat, 'but they'll never answer to anything but Bungie and Mipsy and Dot. They're too old.'

'Well, I shall call them Starlight and Cameron and Golden Girl to the clients,' I said.

Bar giggled.

'Can't you just see one of our clients saying, "Come up, Cameron" to Mipsy?'

'Oh, look!' shrieked Mike. 'There's somebody coming! A mother and a little boy.'

Sure enough, a very fashionable-looking mother all in grey with a red hat with birds on, was coming into the yard holding the hand of a kid of about six in a beige coat and gloves.

We all brightened up, especially when the mother who said her name was Mrs Charles asked if we had a nice, gentle little Shetland that would do for her little boy, who was a lovely little rider and missed his own pony very much while they were staying at Wayfield.

So of course we led out Dot, and Mrs Charles said, 'Get up, dear,' and the little boy struggled into the saddle in a rather sack-like manner, and Mrs Charles said, 'Doesn't he look adorable? I'd like to engage the pony for the whole week that we're here.'

Bar said, 'You'll water her and rest her well, won't you? And please bring her back each day before five.'

And Mrs Charles said, 'Oh, of course. Cecil goes to bed in the afternoons in any case, so he'll only actually be riding for a bit in the morning and after he's rested, but he'll like to feel the pony's there, just like his own at home.'

So I said, 'Well, we charge twenty pounds a day, but we might make a bit of a reduction for a week,' and Mrs Charles smiled and said, 'That's quite all right.' And off they went.

'Nice work!' yelled Pat and Mike together.

'Isn't that smashing?' I said, multiplying twenty pounds by five, six, and seven, according to how many days Mrs Charles called a week. 'It'll be one hundred pounds at least!'

'One hundred pounds!' said Bar in an awed voice. 'Why, the stable's practically supporting itself already.'

However, nobody else turned up, and about half an hour later Pat said, 'We really ought to have taken Mrs Charles's address. Suppose she makes off with Dot and never brings her back!'

At this grim thought we went cold all over, and were frightfully uneasy for the rest of the afternoon, but to our relief at five minutes to five Mrs Charles and Cecil arrived back with Dot, and Mrs Charles said, 'Well, we've just had the afternoon and we'll be back for Dot tomorrow morning early, so shall we wait till the end of the week and I'll give you a cheque?'

We were so thrilled that when she was gone we went quite mad and did a sort of circus all round the yard, and then we brought in the horses and fed them and I went home.

To make a long story short, Mrs Charles and Cecil had Dot out for five days running, and on the fifth evening she said, 'Well, tomorrow will be our last day as we are leaving for home,' and I said, 'We'll get the account ready for you when you come tomorrow.'

But she didn't come tomorrow; in fact she didn't come any more, and we never saw or heard of Mrs Charles and Cecil again. What was more, when we tried to ring up the hotel where she said she was staying the exchange told us there was no such hotel.

This was a revelation to us, as we didn't know there were such beastly people in the world, and Mrs Charles probably thought she had been very clever in getting a free pony for her little boy for five days and an afternoon and then disappearing, just because we didn't look very old or experienced. But actually though we were awfully sick when we thought of the one hundred pounds we ought to have had, we were very sorry for poor little Cecil too for having such a beastly mother.

But meanwhile we hadn't been doing too badly. There were two very nice sisters called Diana and Brenda Prince who had been out three times on Ballerina and Mipsy, and a rather shy boy called Bill had been out on Bungie because he was just a beginner and his father who went with him wanted something awfully quiet for him, and an older girl of about eighteen who was dancing at the local theatre had taken Ballerina out four separate hours and rode beautifully, and a school friend of Pat's had taken Mipsy out once, and if only we had had Dot free we could have used her several times for small children. So at the end of the week we did have some money, and we were solvent as it says in books.

9 Stable Trouble

'What on earth do you do all the time at that place?' Cecilia said one day.

'Oh, just mess about with horses,' I said with a frightfully cool shrug of my shoulders.

But I could see that she was simply eaten up with curiosity, so I wasn't surprised when she said, 'I want to come and see what you do,' and as I was actually staying with her and had to obey the binding laws of hospitality I couldn't say, 'No, you jolly well won't!' so I just said, 'OK,' and hoped she'd forget.

When I got down to the stable I found everybody in a state of fuss over Mipsy. It had been wet the day before and he had been out with a boy friend of Pat's and had got thoroughly messed up, so Pat had spent ages that morning grooming him and had then told Mike to lead him up and down the yard to air off. But Mike had suddenly thought of something he wanted to do, and had popped Mipsy in the paddock by himself, whereupon Mipsy made for that muddy spot under the trees and lain himself down and *rolled*.

Gosh, you should have seen him!

Pat was engaged in flattening Mike, and Bar was saying, 'What shall we do? He's got to be ready for an hour with the Parker boy, and look at him!'

'I'll do him,' I said. 'I'm fresh. You get the others ready.'

So I set to work with the water-brush, meanwhile telling Mipsy just what I thought of him, and I did his eyes and nose and ears which were all muddy, and I finished him with a wisp and a rubber, thanking goodness that he was docked, though as a rule I don't approve of docking as I think it is cruel to deprive a horse of his natural fly-whisk, and I gave him a final slap just as the Parker boy came into the yard.

'Phew!' I said, for I was boiling hot and jolly well aching too. But I couldn't help thinking how beautiful the stable yard looked in the morning sunshine, with the doors open to show clean stalls and the shining horses waiting for their riders.

Just then Mike came up to me and said, 'There's a girl outside asking for you. I think it's that Cecilia.'

It was Cecilia all right.

'Good gracious!' she said, gazing round with a look of astonishment on her face and walking backwards into Ballerina, who was standing ready for work and obviously hated being walked into.

'Oh, hello, Cecilia,' I said without enthusiasm.

'Good gracious!' she said. 'You are dirty.'

'So would you be,' I said, 'if you had just been grooming a muddy pony.'

'Oh, do you do that?' she said. 'I do think Mummy

would be furious. I can't imagine anybody liking to do such dirty things.'

'Well, some people do,' I said.

'What is this horse waiting for?' she went on, and Bar who had just come out of the harness room said, 'It isn't a horse, it's a mare.'

'Well, it's all the same,' said Cecilia. 'Can I have a ride?'

'What time is Ballerina booked for?' I asked Bar, who replied that Diana Prince would be coming round in a quarter of an hour.

'You can try her in the paddock for about ten minutes,' I said to Cecilia, 'and for goodness' sake don't make her hot.'

So Cecilia, who had terrific ideas about her riding, scrambled up on Ballerina – I cannot call it mounting – and suddenly slapping her heels upon the poor animal's unsuspecting sides, dashed off into the paddock at a pace that nearly unseated her.

'Does she usually ride like that?' asked Bar.

'Oh, always,' I said. 'She calls it proper riding. She hates people who walk along as if they were at a funeral. She thinks, what's the use of a horse unless he's galloping?'

So we both laughed, and then were busy getting a girl called Hilda Southwood – a beginner – off on Bungie and a small child called Noel Something-or-other on to Dot, while his nanny stood by saying, 'Upsy-daisy, Nanny's little man,' which we thought was too revolting for words, though you have to be very tactful when you are running a stable and not laugh at the clients.

Then we started cleaning tack, of which there was always some waiting to be done, until Diana Prince looking awfully nice in fawn jodhpurs and a hacking coat of brown tweed came in at the gate, all ready for Ballerina.

'Hey! Where's that cousin of yours?' said Bar.

I had forgotten Cecilia, and I had just said, 'I'll go and find her,' when a horrible sight appeared at the gate of the paddock and my veins turned to ice, as it says in one of Grimm's fairy tales or elsewhere.

I honestly couldn't tell which was Cecilia and which was Ballerina, they were both so plastered with mud. Cecilia's legs and skirt and blouse and face and hair were just one solid lump of mud, and as for Ballerina! The only place on Ballerina that hadn't got mud on it was the part round her mouth and she was actually smirking, I suppose because she had successfully played up Cecilia.

'This b-b-b-beastly h-h-h-horse!' sobbed Cecilia, who was weeping real tears which trickled stickily off her muddy nose. 'He - she - it took me to where there was some mud and threw me into it and then rolled on me! It's a hateful horse. It ought to be shot!'

'Don't be silly,' said Bar in a fury. 'Ballerina couldn't possibly have rolled on you or your ribs would be broken. If she threw you, why didn't you get up and stop her from rolling? Look at her!

Who's going to jolly well clean her, I should like to know?'

'You are the limit, Cecilia!' I said. 'Right-ho, Bar, I'll do Ballerina. Cecilia's *my* cousin, and I might have known.'

'It looks as though my ride's off today,' said Diana Prince. 'I can't come this afternoon instead, so I'd better leave it till tomorrow.'

'There!' said Bar, as Diana walked away. 'That's ten pounds gone.'

'Can Cecilia go in your bath?' I said. 'I know she's a blight, but she can't go home like that.'

'OK,' said Bar, 'I'll take her,' and off she walked followed by the blubbing Cecilia, dripping mud as she walked.

You can guess how I felt at being confronted with yet another mud-plastered pony. However, I carried on manfully, feeling that one's relations are one's own responsibility and *noblesse oblige* and all that. After about three-quarters of an hour Cecilia came out, clean and wearing a skirt and jumper of Bar's, and with a long scratch on her nose, and said, 'Fancy taking money for giving people rides on ponies! I wonder you don't go on the sands.'

As a consequence of this, I was not surprised when later that afternoon Auntie P. said to me, 'I was rather surprised to hear that you and those children at St Mary's vicarage are actually giving children rides and taking money for it. I'm sure your mother wouldn't like that. I mean, it simply isn't the sort of thing that I should let Cecilia do.'

'As a matter of fact, Aunt Primrose,' I said, 'we are not giving children rides. We are running a proper hacking stable, and Mummy says there is nothing to be ashamed of in running a proper business concern.'

'Well, I think you're a very odd girl, Jill,' said my aunt, 'and I don't know if I ought not to forbid you to go to that place any more.'

I was so horrified at this prospect that I flew upstairs and sat on my bed for ages, thinking. Then I scrabbled about in my drawer and found a bit of paper and composed a cable to Mummy, and after altering it about ten times to make it less words, it finally read, 'HAVE GOT HONEST WORK RUNNING HACKING STABLE KNOW YOU WOULD APPROVE ALL FOR A GOOD CAUSE. PLEASE PLEASE TELL AUNT I MAY. JILL.

I then rushed downstairs and ran all the way to the Post Office where I handed in my message, and then ran all the way back, only to find that the tea gong had gone in my absence and I wasn't even changed, which made me rather unpopular.

I will say for Cecilia that she hadn't said anything about getting thrown by Ballerina into the mud, as I had feared she would make a terrific story about it – savage, unschooled ponies and all the rest of it – but I think she was really a bit ashamed of herself. I don't know what it was about Cecilia, but there really are some people who bring out the worst in horses and she was one. I mean, Ballerina was a well-mannered pony and had never before in her career even *wanted* to do such a thing as roll in mud till Cecilia got her; and it was just the same with my pony at home who actually reared for the first and last time in his life when Cecilia was up.

All the next day and the next I was in such a frantic state of suspense that my teeth simply knocked together, and when the cable from Mummy actually arrived my numbed fingers would hardly open it, as it says in novels.

But I might have known Mummy would be all right!

The cable just said, 'HAVE FAITH IN YOU TO DO RIGHT THING CARRY ON WITH HACKING STABLE BUT CONSIDER AUNTS FEELINGS IF POSSIBLE. MUMMY.'

I was so thrilled that, left to myself, I should have rushed all over the house making hunting cries, but I thought I had better consider my aunt's feelings, so I showed her the cable and said, 'I honestly don't want to be a nuisance, and please tell me if I do anything wrong, Aunt Primrose,' and she said, 'Well, if your mother says so I suppose it's all right,' and I felt so awfully pleased and forgiving that on my way home from the stable that afternoon I went into town and bought some wool to start knitting a pair of Fair Isle gloves for Cecilia in my room in the silent watches of the night.

The stable was now doing very well, and we had paid ourselves back what we originally put into it and could pay the corn merchant's bill and regular expenses like shoeing. We had started a new idea, for very small children who could have half an hour on Dot for two pounds fifty, being led round the paddock by Mike, and some children came every day for this with their mummies or nannies.

Of course the stable was by now not a game but jolly hard work. Every day we had four horses to feed and groom, to say nothing of mucking out and keeping the stables clean and cleaning all the tack. We started work at eight every morning, after the boys had mucked out, and we were busy until about five. Wet days were our despair, because really keen riders went out in all weathers and brought the horses back wet and splashed, and if you know of anything worse than being confronted by one or two really messed-up ponies when you want your tea, I'd like to know what it is!

But of course that is all part of keeping a stable, and to be absolutely frank and honest I was beginning to cool off a bit from the idea of having a stable of my own for ever and ever.

10 How not to buy horses

I hope you have not forgotten the pony money which my mother had given me on the occasion of our dismal and sad parting. What I really wanted to buy with this money was a show-jumper, but I hadn't had time to think about looking for one and anyway there didn't seem much chance of finding one in the neighbourhood of Wayfield. Besides I had another idea in my mind. As Pat had once said, the stables were theirs and all the four horses were theirs, and though I am sure he didn't intend to be mean and probably forgot the words as soon as he had said them, I sometimes remembered them in the silent watches of the night, which as you may have noticed elsewhere in this book I often refer to. After all, I called myself a partner in the stable but I hadn't actually given anything to it compared with the Walters. What I was thinking was that some of our clients had said their older brother or sister would have liked to come for a ride if we had had a horse big enough for grown-ups, and Pat had said it was a pity we hadn't anything in the hunter class.

Well, about two o'clock one morning I woke up

suddenly and decided I would buy a horse of about 15–16 hands, and use him in the stable, and then sell him again. I thought it would be a rather noble thing to do and would please Bar and Pat frightfully.

I then went to sleep again, and when I woke up properly in the daylight this still seemed a good plan, which was unusual, as things you plan in the middle of the night generally seem perfectly idiotic in the morning.

When I told Bar she thought it was a splendid idea, and Pat said, 'There's a sale of horses at Farbury next Thursday. I saw it advertised. Let's send for a catalogue.'

So the catalogue came and there were actually about sixty lots, though I think it is most squalid to call such wonderful creatures as horses 'lots' even when they are in a dreary saleroom.

We pored over the catalogue. I don't know what pored means, but people always do it in books. I think it means leaning right over the table and breathing on the paper, like we did.

'Gosh!' said Bar. 'Listen to this. "Grey hunter, Albatross, 17 hands, 3 years, from Earl of Sattingham's stable, by Hercules out of Ocean Bird – "'

'That'll be about six thousand pounds,' I said, 'unless there's something wrong with him.'

'There'll be something wrong with him or they wouldn't be selling him at Farbury,' said Pat. 'How about this one? "Bay mare, Strawberry, 15 hands, 5 years, has hunted – "'

'I don't like "has hunted",' said Bar. 'It sounds jolly sinister to me.'

'That sounds a good pony,' I said, pointing to "Grey pony, show-jumper, 14.2, four years, spirited, one owner", and wondering whether I had been a bit too rash in promising to buy a hack for the stable instead of a pony for myself.

'But we don't want a pony,' said Pat. 'Oh, look here! "Lot 36. Chestnut mare, Begorra, 16 hands, 15 years, ridden by lady, very sound, useful hack." I wonder how much she'll fetch?'

We talked a lot more, and then decided that Bar and I would catch the nine o'clock bus for Farbury on Thursday morning which would get us there about nine forty-five and give us time to look over the horses before the sale started at eleven.

I was there by ten past eight, and we began to get ourselves ready. We thought this was very important, as we wanted to look thoroughly hard, experienced horsy people who couldn't be taken in. It was a very hot day, and I had on my jodhpurs and boots, and a clean white shirt and my fawn tie with foxes' heads. Unfortunately, I couldn't do much with my hair as it looked worse out of plaits than in them, but I put on some lipstick that I had bought for the occasion at Woolworth's and then I asked Bar how I looked.

'Well, quite honestly,' she said, 'you only look about thirteen, which you are. You'd better try my best coat and skirt.'

So I got into the grey coat and skirt which was

a bit too big for me and rather long, and made me look much older, and I put on my string gloves, and Bar found a pair of sunglasses with tortoiseshell rims and pushed the dark glass part out, and I put them on and when I saw myself in the mirror I did look very impressive.

Bar had on her breeches and boots, in spite of the heat, and a tweed coat with leather patches on the elbows, and her bowler, and she had frizzed out her hair a bit at the sides and used my lipstick, and she looked marvellous and about sixteen.

The boys thought we looked jolly good and that one look at us would make the auctioneer realise what he was up against, and then Pat said, 'Have you got the money, Jill?'

'Of course,' I said. 'It's folded into a handkerchief and pinned inside my jodhpurs with about seven safety-pins.'

'But you haven't got your jodhpurs on!' said Mike.

'Oh, help!' I yelled, and tore back into the house and up to Bar's room and found my jodhpurs and unfastened the safety-pins, and my fingers were all thumbs. Then I had to do them all up again to fasten the money inside the lining of my coat, and that made us late for the bus and we had to run all the way and just caught it as it was moving, so for about five minutes we could only lie back on the seat panting with our mouths wide open; and it was a bit of a blow for us because when the conductor came and I gasped, 'Two returns to Farbury, please,' he said, 'Do you want halves?'

'What do you mean?' said Bar haughtily.

'Under fourteen half fare,' said the conductor, and before we could stop him he had clipped them. It was more humiliating for Bar than for me because she was actually fifteen the next month.

When we got to the salerooms and saw all the horses waiting to be sold to any hard-hearted and unscrupulous purchasers that might come along, I wished I was a millionaire so that I could buy them all and put them into lovely paddocks, but when I told Bar this she said, why should I think that other purchasers were any more hard-hearted and unscrupulous than we were? So it was a bit more comforting to look at it like that.

'It's no good wasting time looking at things like Albatrosses and children's ponies,' said Bar. 'Let's look for ones that would be useful to us.'

So we walked along the rows of horses and ponies which were all tied to rings in the dirty walls, and we stopped when we saw anything we liked. Actually, we were afraid that anything we wanted was going to be too dear for us, because I had decided that I wouldn't spend more than about six hundred pounds. We passed the farm horses and the tradesmen's cobs, and then Bar said, 'Here's Number 36 that Pat read out. She looks rather decent, doesn't she?'

She did look decent, and though she was fifteen years old she had nice, clean lines and a lovely clear eye, and when I went to examine her legs and feet she nuzzled me gently and I could tell that somebody had once been very fond of her. I began to make up a story about her mistress having died, and a soulless lawyer thrusting poor Begorra into the cold world to be sold until I nearly started weeping.

'Seems all right,' said Bar in a most reassuring horsy kind of way. 'Do you think there's something wrong with *all* horses at *all* sales?'

'Oh, there couldn't be,' I said, 'or really intelligent people wouldn't buy them would they? – and some of the people here look frightfully intelligent.'

'When does the auction start?' Bar asked a man who was standing near, and he said, 'It's started, miss. He's sold fifteen lots already.'

We had been so busy looking at the horses that we hadn't noticed a small crowd gathered round the auctioneer at the far end of the room, which wasn't really a room at all but a sort of long tram shed.

'Oh, come on, Jill,' shouted Bar. 'We may have missed something.'

However, we weren't interested in what was being sold for a long time, though we learnt a lot from watching other people bid.

Albatross went for two thousand pounds, which seemed to worry the auctioneer quite a lot as he kept telling the buyers that this hunter was worth at least eight thousand, which I don't think could have been true. He had a mean-looking head and no hocks to speak of.

I was interested in the grey pony, the show-jumper, because though I had purposely not examined him for fear Bar would think I was trying to get out of my bargain, I couldn't help thinking he might have done for me. It was almost a relief to me when he fetched twelve hundred pounds, more than I could have given in any case.

'Here's ours!' whispered Bar excitedly, as a groom led Begorra out and began to show her paces up and down before the crowd. 'I say! We never looked at her teeth. She may be fifty, not fifteen. Are we going to bid for her?'

'Yes,' I said. 'I like her. Sssh! He's started.'

'Now here's a nice animal,' said the auctioneer. 'Best bargain of the show, I call this. Fifteen years old but been well looked after. Absolutely sound, nice action – look at that, ladies and gentlemen. I've seen animals in the hunter class no better than that fetch fourteen hundred pounds.'

'Oh, help!' said Bar.

'It's all right. He doesn't mean it,' said a rather nice, oldish man who was standing next to us. He looked as if he knew a lot about horses, and I suddenly, whispered, 'Oh, do please tell me. Do you think that's a good mare?'

'What do you want her for?' he whispered back.

'Hacking stable,' I said excitedly.

'She'll do nicely,' he said.

'Now somebody start me for this fine mare,' said the auctioneer. 'Best hack I've seen in years for her age and description. Anybody start me at six hundred pounds?'

'Ooooh!' Bar groaned.

'Four hundred pounds?' said the auctioneer, and I shouted out, 'Yes!' at the top of my voice.

Everybody turned round to have a look, and a rather harsh voice at the front said four hundred and twenty. Then somebody else said four forty, and I got thoroughly worked up and said four fifty, and about two minutes later I was saying five fifty, and there was only me and the harsh voice left in the bidding. He said five seventy and I said six hundred, and thought, oh dear, this is the fatal end. Then there fell a grim hush, and just as I thought it was all over the man at the front said six twenty in a faint, hesitating sort of voice.

'Go on!' said Bar. 'You can tell he's shot.'

So I said, 'Six forty,' awfully firmly, and this time the pause lasted several seconds longer and then the auctioneer crashed down his hammer and looked at me and said, 'Name, please.'

I was too overcome to utter a sound, but Bar called out very coolly, 'Walters and Crewe, St Mary's Stables, Wayfield.'

The auctioneer looked very impressed with this splendid-sounding address.

'Congratulations!' said the nice man next to me. 'You've got a bargain.'

'I call that super,' said Bar. 'Let's go now.'

So we went to find the place where you paid, and

I felt an awful fool unpinning all those safety pins to get my money out when other people just brought out wallets bulging with notes or wrote cheques.

Anyway, Begorra was mine, and it does give you a wonderful feeling to have bought a horse all by yourself.

'How do we get her home?' said Bar to one of the grooms.

'If you've got the tack you could ride her, if it isn't too far,' he said, but we said we couldn't do that, and in the end it was arranged for Begorra to be delivered by van next day, and we paid in advance for this, because I like to know how much I am spending all at once.

I threw my arms round her neck, and we both made a fuss of her, and you could see that she liked us, and she said as plainly as anything while I stroked her neck, 'Thank you for buying me. I know I'm going to be awfully useful to you,' and I said to Bar, 'Wouldn't it be marvellous if her dead mistress could see what a good home she's going to?' and Bar said scornfully, 'What on earth are you talking about?'

We felt wonderful when we came out of the dark and smelly saleroom, and we decided to go and have some lunch at a café before going home.

'I hope that hasn't ruined you completely,' said Bar as we sat over the sausages and chips. 'I think it's jolly decent of you to have done it – we all do – and it will be a great asset to the stable, and after all you can sell Begorra again and probably make more than you gave. I think you'd better let the stable stand the twenty pounds for transport.'

'OK,' I said. 'With what I've already spent and the six hundred and forty pounds, that leaves me – one hundred and twenty pounds.'

So after lunch we went round the shops at Farbury which weren't very good and bought some hair grips and things, and then we went to the bus.

11   And as for Pedro –

I don't know what you feel about it, but I always think that on days when anything terrific happens, something else terrific happens almost immediately after. I mean, you go on the same old round of school and eating meals and having a ride before you start your homework for days and days and even weeks and weeks, and all of a sudden something happens to you almost as though you were in a book and before you get your breath something else – if you see what I mean. I mean, I think it was a pretty terrific thing for me to go and buy a horse for six hundred and forty pounds, but if anybody had told me that before the day was over – but I'd better get on with it.

When we got off the bus Bar said she'd better go to the cake shop and get some buns for tea, so I waited outside for her. And right opposite where I was standing at the kerbside was the poorest, dirtiest pony I ever saw in my life. I couldn't help staring at him because he was so wretched, and it made a little cold feeling start in my middle and work right up to my neck. You couldn't see what colour he was, he was so dirty; and yet in spite of it all, and in spite of his miserable, downcast head, he had nice lines and good legs and I think it was partly that which made me look at him and think what an awful pity it was he was so neglected.

He was harnessed with filthy, string-mended harness to a little cart with a few sticks of firewood on it, and on the side of the cart was painted in very dirty paint, J. Biggs Timber Merchant.

Just then J. Biggs himself came out of the pub, and he was just as dirty as the cart and the pony, but they couldn't help it and he could.

The first thing he did was to say a horrible word, and then he picked up the reins which were trailing in the gutter – which was his fault – and lashed the pony across the face with them. Then he gave it a bang on the flank with his fist, and it staggered and slipped and he gave it another bang.

Well, I don't know what you would have done, but you can do all sorts of things when you lose your temper that you wouldn't dare to do in cold blood, and I rushed at the man and said, 'Don't do that, you beast.'

He looked very surprised, and I said, 'I've a jolly good mind to fetch a policeman.'

I think he would have said a few things to me then, but a man who was passing stopped and said, 'Good for you, little girl,' and a lady also stopped and said, 'Poor little pony! It looks half-starved. He ought to be reported. Take his name and address.'

Just then Bar came out of the cake shop and said, 'What on earth's going on?'

'Oh, Bar!' I gasped. 'Did you ever see such a poor miserable pony? And he's sweet too. And this horrible man – '

Seeing that everybody was against him, the horrible man thought it was time to change his tune, so he said in a wheedling voice, 'I'm sorry, miss, I lost my temper a bit. You see, I'm a poor man and I've had a lot of trouble. I've got a sick wife and seven hungry kids at home, I have.'

'Well, you've no business to hit that pony – ' I began, and Bar interrupted, 'You don't deserve to have a pony. People like you make my blood boil.'

'Well, it's like this, miss,' said the man, 'I had to take this pony as part of a debt and he's been a bad bargain. No use to me in my business, he isn't. He's a dead loss, as you might say. Don't understand kindness, he don't. I have to nearly kill him to make him go at all, I do.' And he turned round as if he was going to hit the pony again, just to show us.

'Stop!' said Bar; and at the same time I heard myself saying, 'You shan't take him away and beat him. I'll buy him from you. How much do you want for him?'

Bar and the man both stared at me, and the man found his tongue first and said, 'Well, I'd want a good lot for him, you know. I'm a poor man, I am. A hundred quid I'd want for him.'

'All right,' I said. 'Here's one hundred pou – I mean,

quid.' And I took my one hundred and twenty pounds out of my pocket and peeled off a twenty and held out the rest to him. This is the sort of thing you do when you're in a blazing temper.

The man looked absolutely thunderstruck, I suppose thinking he had suddenly come across a millionaire child, and said, 'Did I say only a hundred? I meant a hundred and – '

'Oh, no, you didn't,' said Bar, and some people who were standing by said, 'You said a hundred! Take the money and give the little girl the pony!'

'Well I'm blowed!' said the man, only he didn't say blowed.

'Get him unharnessed,' I said, 'and we'll make a halter out of that bit of dirty rope on the cart and take him with us.'

'But what am I going to do with the cart?' said the man, and some people in the crowd which had by now assembled said, 'It wouldn't hurt you to push it home yourself.'

Actually I think he was awfully glad to get the hundred pounds, and just at that moment a policeman came along and began to say, 'Pass along, please,' and believe me, in about two minutes everybody had melted away, including the man and his cart, and there stood Bar and I with the dirty pony between us and the end of his dirty rope in my hand.

'We're both absolutely mad,' said Bar. 'Here, Butterfingers, let me make that into something like a halter.'

'I know it was mad,' I said as we walked towards home, rather slowly to accommodate the pony which seemed bewildered, poor little thing, 'but I simply had to do it. Something made me.'

'I'd probably have done the same, if I had one hundred pounds,' said Bar. 'Gosh! Let's get home quick before we buy any more horses!'

It was only about a mile, and when we came in sight of St Mary's vicarage we saw the boys in the garden on the look-out for us. As soon as they caught sight of us they came running, and if you had seen their faces when they beheld Bar and me, one on each side of that wretched pony! It dawned on us they must be thinking that was what we had bought at the sale!

'No, no!' shouted Bar, and I yelled, 'We didn't buy it, this isn't it; I mean, we did, but it isn't, I mean it's coming tomorrow, not this one, the proper one!'

We got into the yard at last, and the pony seemed thankful to stand still, shivering a little and looking miserable, his head hung down. The boys gathered round, and somehow between us Bar and I managed to tell the whole tale of the day's adventures.

'I think you did quite right, Jill,' said Mike, walking round and round the pony. 'And I think he's a nice pony – if he was clean and you could tell what colour he was. If I had a million pounds I'd do nothing but buy poor ponies like this one, and I think a hundred pounds was jolly cheap. I bet the man stole him and was glad to get anything for him before he was caught.'

'He isn't small, either,' said Pat, 'about 14 hands if he wasn't so sort of wilted.' And he put his arm round the pony's neck and began to stroke his nose. The pony flinched as though he expected to be hit, but he stood still and seemed to be slightly enjoying it. He even turned his head and had a look at Pat out of what would have been a lovely eye if it hadn't been so bloodshot and messed up with flies. Pat found a lump of sugar in his pocket and held it out for the pony, but the poor thing didn't seem to know what to do with it, which we thought was awfully touching.

'What are you going to do with him now?' said Bar.

'Well, is it all right if I put him in the box stall at the end?' I said. 'I mean, it's your stable.'

'Why, of course!' said Bar. 'He's going to live here, isn't he, boys – as long as Jill wants him to?'

'You bet!' said Pat and Mike.

'Thanks a million,' I said, because after all it *was* their stable and I had wished this poor pony on them. 'I'm going to put him in the stall with heaps of clean straw, and give him a bran mash and leave him to rest until tomorrow. He'll feel better by then.'

'Goody!' said Mike. 'I'll go and fetch the straw.'

So we made the stall very comfortable, and we put the pony in, and he looked more bewildered than ever but just a bit pleased, and I fed him. He only hesitated a minute, and then he began to eat. Eat! I got frightened, and tried to slow him down, but I hadn't the heart to stop him really though I was a bit afraid he would swell up and burst during the night.

'Well, that's that,' said Bar as we fastened the door and came back into the yard. 'And we've hardly talked about Begorra at all!'

'And how's business been today?' I asked.

'Quite good,' said Pat. 'Dot did children's rides for two hours this morning and went out for an hour this afternoon with the Burton kid and its nanny. And Bungie is out with that Irish girl who likes him because he's so quiet, and I've been schooling Mipsy all afternoon and he's booked for the day tomorrow. And Ballerina is still out with Brenda Prince. And there'll be an awful lot of competition for Begorra, because absolutely everybody's big brothers and sisters want to ride. Everything's just great.'

Of course, when I got to bed that night I couldn't sleep a wink for thinking of what I had done and all the money I had spent on buying horses that weren't a bit what I wanted or what my eight hundred pounds was intended for. I mean, fancy having eight hundred pounds given to you by your loving mother to be spent on a show-jumper and then going and spending seven hundred and forty of them on a fifteen-year-old hack and a dirty neglected pony with grazed knees and harness galls, which I regret to say my latest pony had. I sat up in bed in the silent watches of the night and I'm sure my hair was standing on end. And yet I'd have done it all again! And I wasn't worrying over only having twenty pounds left, as the stable was doing so well and we were just about to have a share out.

I got up at seven and ate a hurried breakfast at the kitchen table, which my aunt now allowed me to do, and simply rushed round to the stable. The pony hadn't burst in the night, in fact he looked heaps better already and was holding his head up! I called Bar and Pat and they agreed that he looked heaps better, and then Mike turned up and the first thing he said was, 'I say! He looks heaps better, doesn't he?'

'First of all,' I said, 'I'm going to get the vet round to see him because I want to be sure he isn't dying of some frantic disease, and then if he isn't, we'll groom him, Bar.'

So we rang up the vet – who was Uncle Toots' locum – and he happened to be coming past our way to see a cow at one of the farms, so he called in about half an hour and saw the pony and said there wasn't a thing actually the matter with him except neglect and starvation and he thought he had the makings of a nice pony and we might be surprised some day, which was quite cheering.

So Bar and I got to work. We laid on with dandy-brushes and water-brushes but they didn't seem to make the slightest impression on the dirt which was simply clotted on like an overcoat. So I'll tell you what we did, though it isn't usually done in stables. We waited until Agatha went out of the kitchen and upstairs, and we pinched the soap flakes out of the scullery. We got some hot water from the scullery tap and we read the instructions carefully, and we used the whole packet of soap flakes, and the pony looked exactly like a film star in one of those foam baths. And the dirt came off in *chunks*. And underneath he was a lovely dark bay. And then we worked with the dandy-brush, and we washed his feet and his nose and eyes and mane and tail, and we polished his hoofs and rubbed him up with a rubber and finished him off with a wisp, and then we just stood with our tongues hanging out, panting like dogs.

When Pat and Mike came along to look they didn't recognise him, which wasn't surprising, he looked so nice, though we couldn't disguise his thinness and the harness galls.

'And now I'm going to feed him up like anything,' I said. 'He knows me, don't you, darling?' And as I said it, to my amazement he turned his head and looked at me and then made a lovely little whiffling noise and nuzzled my shoulder. I loved him from that very minute.

'Look at that!' said Bar. 'I believe this pony's got a history. We'll never know, but I think at some time he's been cared for. And he's a *good* pony. Look how he stands – and he lifted his feet for me to wash them as if he'd once been used to it. What are you going to do with him now, Jill?'

'Well, I should think he's pretty exhausted after all that washing,' I said. 'Besides, he's weak. The vet said rest him, so he can go back in the stall and tomorrow we'll put him in the paddock while the other ponies are out. And' – I added – 'I've just thought of it, I'm going to call him Pedro after Pedro the Fisherman which I think is a jolly good song!'

Just then Pat began to run to the gate as a horse van drew up. Begorra had arrived!

12 Begorra is a success

We all turned out to form a welcoming party for Begorra, and Bar and I simply swelled with pride, she looked so nice as she came down the ramp of the van with her head up and just dancing a little on her toes, and her coat was shining too as somebody had taken the trouble to give her a rub up.

'Oh, I say!' cried Pat. 'What a smasher!'

'Doesn't she look enormous?' said Mike, and of course she did compared with all the other horses, for even Bungie in her prime was only 15 hands. 'I should think a king would like to ride her.'

We took Begorra straight to the paddock which was only occupied by Bungie as the other ponies were being got ready to go out, and we introduced her to Bungie and then left her to get used to things while we got on with our job of saddling Mipsy, Ballerina, and Dot, a procedure which seemed frightfully tame after all the excitement.

However, when our clients arrived we had their ponies ready, and I was just helping a very fat nanny to heave an absolutely square child up on Dot when Mike came up to me and hissed, 'I say! Trouble ahoy!'

'What do you mean?'

'It's that man again,' said Mike, and looking up I saw the oldish, military-looking man who had been our first – and disappointed – client. He was just coming into the yard, and he had by the hand a small kid in a velvet riding hat and too-big jodhpurs which small kids often have to wear because their mothers can't get their size or else want them to have something to grow to.

He came straight up to me, and said very politely, 'Am I addressing Miss Walters or Miss Crewe?'

'I'm – I'm Crewe,' I said, a bit taken aback.

'We met on a previous occasion,' he said, 'and I must ask your pardon for having made a bad impression which I'm sure I did. But I've been hearing a lot about your stable, and I understand it is a well-run place. It looks clean and orderly – ' he went on, looking round, ' – and if there's one thing I admire more than another it is people who do something with horses and do it successfully.'

'Oh. Thank you,' I stuttered.

'You boys and girls have done a splendid job,' he went on, while I wondered if I was dreaming or had got into Alice in Wonderland, 'and I want to congratulate you – and encourage you. I wonder if you'd let me have a look round? By the way, this is my grand-niece, Alison Foster, and I don't think I told you, my name is Major Foster.

'Oh, thank you – how do you do – I mean, of course – yes, if you like,' I mumbled, all in one breath, and then pulled myself together and wondered where on earth Bar and Pat had got to – they were probably hiding on purpose – and said, 'Some of the horses are out. The Shetland is giving a child a ride in the paddock, and there are two horses grazing in there. But you can have a look at the stables with pleasure.'

So I took him into the stalls, and thank goodness they were clean, and he seemed most impressed, and when we got to the box stall at the end, there was Pedro.

'Why, what's this?' said Major Foster, and I tried to explain a bit, and before I knew where I was it was all coming out, about the eight hundred pounds Mummy had given me to buy myself a jumper, and about how Bar and I had gone to the sale at Farbury and bought Begorra, and about how we had found Pedro with the firewood cart, and all the rest.

Major Foster couldn't have been more interested or nicer. He had a look at Pedro, and said, 'I think you've got something here much better than you think, but time will show' – which I thought was a lovely, grown-uppish thing to say, as from one horsy person to another, and then he took out his notebook and scribbled something on a page and tore it out and gave it to me, saying, 'Get that made up at the chemist. It'll cure those harness galls before you can say knife.'

We came out into the yard, and Major Foster said, 'About Alison here. Her mother wants her to learn to ride, and so do I for that matter. What I wondered was, do you give lessons?'

'Well, this isn't a riding school,' I said, 'but I think we could teach Alison to ride. Both my partner and I are very experienced and have won a lot of firsts at shows.'

'Could she have a lesson now?' he said. 'And how much do you charge?'

'Oh, I don't know,' I said. 'I should think about two pounds fifty, if that isn't too much. If you like to leave her she can go up on Dot when that other child comes off, and when she's learned to sit properly and gets the feel of the saddle I'll teach her on Ballerina, who is the only properly schooled pony. Or would you like to wait?'

Major Foster said he would like to wait, so we went along to the paddock, and the first thing he said was, 'I say! What a fine-looking mare. And just my weight. Is that the one you bought yesterday? And have you got any tack for her?'

'Well, actually no,' I said, 'but there's a lot of tack up at Uncle Toots' – I mean, he isn't my uncle but that doesn't matter – and when Pat has time he's going to fetch some down here for Begorra and perhaps for Pedro too. As a matter of fact, we've only just got Begorra here about a quarter of an hour ago and we haven't tried her at all. She may be awful. Bar was going to try her with Bungie's saddle this afternoon.'

'Then I shall certainly come back this afternoon,'

said Major Foster, 'and I don't think she's going to be awful at all, and I intend to be your first customer for Begorra, and I shall want her for an hour a day – if not more.'

I opened my mouth, and shut it again, because I really wanted to say that I couldn't let anybody arrange to monopolise Begorra like that without consulting my partners, but he must have read my thoughts because he said, 'You see, I'm making a nuisance of myself, but of course I shall pay you double fees in compensation. And now I see that the fat child has finished with Dot, so shall we see what you can do with Alison?'

But just at that moment Bungie who was feeling inquisitive ambled up to us and began to snuffle round the pocket of Alison's jodhpurs as though in search of apples or sugar. Alison was terrifically pleased and threw her arms round Bungie's foreleg and held on, yelling, 'I want this horse! I want to ride this horse!'

'Oh, gosh, no, you can't learn on that horse,' I said, 'he's too big and he sags in the middle,' and Major Foster said, 'There's a nice pony here for you, Alison, just the thing to learn on, give you a good seat.'

But Alison who was apparently a very spoiled kid, held on to Bungie all the tighter, and yelled, 'I want this horse. I won't ride a pony! I'll ride this horse.'

I looked helplessly at Major Foster who shrugged his shoulders and said, 'She'll have to have her own way. Make the best of it.'

So in the end I saddled Bungie and put Alison up,

and Major Foster leaned on the gate while I taught the kid to sit straight and keep her hands down, though I couldn't do much about her legs and feet, Bungie being the wrong shape for her. She seemed to have naturally light hands and soon learned to hold the reins correctly, and I walked her round the paddock and she squealed with joy, and after half an hour Major Foster said, 'Good! You'll make a rider of her yet. I'll bring her tomorrow at the same time, and you'd better see that that horse is out of the way and give her something she can get her knees into. And remember I shall want Begorra!'

He then solemnly handed me the two pounds fifty pence for Alison's lesson, and they went away both turning back to wave at the gate.

The minute they were gone, as I expected, Bar and Pat arrived from nowhere.

'What did he want?' they both asked excitedly.

'I've a jolly good mind not to tell you, walking out on me like that,' I said, but of course I couldn't resist, and soon I had told them the whole story.

'Oh, I do hope Begorra's all right,' said Bar. 'Pat, the minute after lunch, put Bungie's tack on to her and we'll all try her. I simply can't wait. Mike, if you've done with Dot, go and see if you can hurry Agatha up a bit with our lunch.'

So after lunch, Bar went up on Begorra and there wasn't the slightest doubt about her. She had a nice, smooth action and quite a bit of spirit too, and she seemed happy and at ease.

'You all right up there?' yelled Pat. 'Any snow on the top?'

'Oh, she does feel high!' said Bar. 'But it's lovely. And she's narrow too and very comfortable. Look out, I'm going to do trot, canter, and gallop.'

So Bar put Begorra through her paces without any trouble, and then I had a try, and then Pat – though Pat wasn't so successful as Begorra didn't seem to like his jockey style of riding.

'We'd better cut out the gallop,' I said. 'She's panting like old boots, but she's full of spirit and she'll make a beautiful, easy hack if she isn't over-ridden. I think Major Foster will take good care of her; he understands horses.'

So Pat went off to Uncle Toots' on Ballerina to fetch the other tack, and Bar and Mike and I looked after the stable.

13 Cecilia's birthday

I had before me next day the exciting prospect of showing Pedro the paddock for the first time, but luckily I remembered that it was also Cecilia's birthday. Actually I could hardly have forgotten, because when I got back Auntie P. was in the kitchen icing a birthday cake, and on the hall table was a parcel labelled 'To Cecilia, not to be opened till tomorrow.'

So, in the silent watches of the night, I worked furiously to finish the Fair Isle gloves which still wanted two fingers and a thumb on the left hand, but I got them finished and they really did look snappy, with a natural ground and a very complicated pattern in black, green, red and white. Cecilia was so thrilled with them that I nearly fell down flat with the shock. She and my aunt seemed to be completely overcome by the fact that I could do Fair Isle knitting as well as things with horses, and they kept saying things like, 'When you can do such beautiful Fair Isle knitting, how can you *bear* to mess your hands up in stables?' – which I couldn't see the point of. I mean, it's all right to do Fair Isle knitting in the long winter evenings,

but to my way of thinking the summer is given us
for much higher things.

However, Cecilia said that apart from the gold
charm bracelet which her father and mother had given
her, she liked my present better than anything else she
had had, which didn't seem to me to be saying much
as the rest of her presents were such squalid things
as pink satin coat-hangers, a handkerchief case, and
a book called *Friends of the Lower Fifth*.

However, both Cecilia and my aunt were in a
frightfully good temper, and so was I as I had had
a long letter from Mummy in answer to one of mine
about the stable.

Cecilia said I must be sure to promise to be back for
her birthday party at four o'clock, and I said I would.
I would have promised anything as I was in such a
hurry to get to Pedro and see how he was.

When I got to the vicarage, Bar was dashing about
with a bucket, and she shouted to me, 'What do you
think of that?' waving in the direction of Pedro's
box. He was actually standing there with his head
over the half-door, taking an interest in what was
going on. When he saw me he pricked up his ears
and a sort of welcoming look dawned on his plain
features.

'We've fed him,' said Bar. 'We couldn't resist.'

'That's OK,' I said. 'I can't wait to get him out
to grass.'

So I opened the door and got Pedro's halter rope
and led him out, with Bar, Pat, and Mike clustering

round and we opened the gate of the paddock and sort of urged him in.

He stood just inside with a look on his face like you might have if you suddenly found yourself transported to scenes of tropical splendour. He had a long, slow look round, and then down at his feet as much as to say, 'Gosh, grass!' Then a look of terrific bliss shivered all over him and he put his head down and got a mouthful and munched.

It was a thrilling moment for us and gave me for one a bucked-up feeling as I'd always wanted to do this for a horse that wasn't having a good time in life and now I'd done it.

'He'll be all right,' said Pat. 'Go on, Pedro, get farther in, it's all yours.'

This last remark was necessary as Pedro was more than a bit stunned and remained standing just inside the paddock gate, eating the part round his feet.

So we all gave him a friendly shove and he went farther in, but I bet if he could have rubbed his eyes he would have done so.

'Well, that's that,' said Bar. 'We've got work to do.'

So we started getting the other horses ready for the clients, and then as we weren't very busy that morning Bar and I had a ride ourselves, she on Ballerina and I on Begorra – who was lovely to ride, though so high that I had to have shoving behind to mount her. It was a crisp, fresh sort of morning and we went to the common and let the horses enjoy themselves, and I could almost believe that I was on Black Boy at home and that Bar was my friend Ann. It occurred to me that I was leading what is known as a double life, and though I liked this half very much I should be wild with joy to get back to my real one. I had had a letter from Ann the day before which made me feel quite homesick.

She wrote: 'I am awfully glad you have got horsy friends and I hope you have got riding too by now. I have been to Mrs Darcy's twice to see Black Boy and he looks awfully happy. I hope this won't make you feel depressed because I expect he is really longing for you and hiding a broken heart with a smiling face, as they say. No, Susan Pyke didn't win anything at all at the show – can you believe that! – I think her star is on the wane (that's out of history and means Julius Caesar really), and I got second in the showing class under fourteen and commended in the jumping, but it wasn't half such fun without you, and won't it be super when you come back? Yours ever, Ann.'

In the afternoon Major Foster arrived, true to his word, for his ride with Begorra and brought Alison for her lesson. Off he went, while Alison hung back and said, 'I want my big horse' – meaning Bungie.

'She'll have to have him,' I said to Bar.

'Rot,' said Bar. And she fixed Alison with an eagle eye and said, 'Look here, kid, you're going on the Shetland and you're jolly well going to like it.'

I had never heard Bar sound so sergeant-majorish

and Alison looked flattened out. I don't think anybody before in her life had ever told that spoiled kid
what she had to do. She stood meekly by while Bar
led out Dot and helped her to mount, and then Mike
came to take her into the paddock for her lesson.
There she sat with her mouth wide open, staring
back at Bar but doing just as she was told by Mike,
a pleasant sight to see.

'She's settled,' said Bar dusting off her hands. 'We'll
have no more nonsense from her. I think I'd make
a jolly good riding teacher, don't you?' Then she
suddenly stood as though thunderstruck and said,
'Will you look at that?'

It was Pedro. He had been quietly grazing on the far
side of the paddock, now he lifted his head and looked
in an interested way at Dot, then suddenly set off at
a beautiful canter towards her, brushing the grass so
lightly that he nearly seemed to fly.

'Look at that action!' cried Bar. 'He's going to be
a lovely pony.'

I felt so happy as I looked at Pedro that I went all
choky in the throat. He stopped a few yards away
from Dot and began to crop grass again, but he
had shown us what he could do and we were quite
cretain that he had once belonged to people who had
cared for him and schooled him properly, and how
he came into the horrible hands of J. Biggs we should
never know, unless he had been stolen or sold by
soulless persons who didn't trouble to inquire about
the kind of home he was going to. I thought it was

a pity that Pedro couldn't write his own story which would probably make a much better book than any I write.

Then Major Foster came back, simply beaming all over and crooning Begorra's praises, and when he saw Alison on Dot he said, 'How on earth did you manage that?'

'Oh, just knack,' said Bar. 'It's all part of running a stable.'

At which Major Foster ha-ha-ed and said, 'Same time tomorrow,' and paid for Alison's lesson and his own ride, and went off looking like a sworn friend of Walters and Crewe Ltd.

Our clients finished fairly early that day and Mike came running out of the house with his camera and said, 'I've got a brilliant idea. Let's put the horses in their boxes with their six heads over the half-doors and we'll all line up in front and Agatha can take a photo of us. Then we can send it to *Country Life* or *Horse and Hound* and they'll probably put it inside instead of Lady Somebody.'

We agreed to this, but believe me, it took blue ages to organise, and the human beings were worse than the horses, as we had to wash, and brush our hair, and straighten our ties, and get some whitewash off Bar's shoulder, to say nothing of getting round Agatha to come out and take the photograph. Then when we were finally arranged Pat would keep dashing out of line to take another imaginary sweat mark off Mipsy's neck.

'I can't get you all in,' said Agatha.

'Well, back a bit,' said Pat.

'I am backing,' said Agatha. 'If I back any more I'll be in the swill bucket.'

Eventually she got jammed against the house wall and couldn't back any more.

'Which thing do I press down?' she said next.

'I'll come and show you,' said Mike, so he did.

When he got back into line Agatha said, 'Do I bring it up again when I've pressed it down?'

'It comes back automatically, you dope,' said Pat.

'Don't you speak to me like that,' said Agatha, 'or I'll have nothing to do with your camera.'

'Shut up, Pat,' said Bar. 'We apologise, Agatha. Go on, be quick.'

'Oh,' said Mike, 'we ought to have Slap and the cats in.' And he rushed off to find these animals. Slap their fox terrier about whom I have previously said nothing was a dog of awful character about whom volumes could be written by anybody who writes dog books, and there was a very big spoiled cat belonging to Agatha, called Edward, and a little grey cat which had rashly adopted the Walters.

At last Mike appeared dragging all these animals along, and he arranged them with great care in front of our feet, but needless to say they weren't having any and after we had wasted about ten minutes on them they all mooched away.

So Agatha took the picture, and then another to make sure. Then Pat said, 'I don't believe you turned the film,' and she hadn't, so those two were wasted and she had to take another, which was the last on the film.

To complete this story, when we got the print from the chemist the following week it was rather disappointing. To begin with, Agatha hadn't got it all in and Pedro and Ballerina who occupied the stalls at each end were off altogether. Bungie and Begorra were very good, but Dot had put her head down at the crucial moment and only her ears showed, and Mipsy had shoved his nose forward and looked more like an elephant than a horse. As for us, Pat and I were quite good, but Mike had moved, and what struck you most about Bar was the patch of whitewash on her shoulder which she hadn't got out as successfully as she thought she had. There was a sort of wavy thing across one corner which we couldn't place at all until at last Agatha realised that it was Edward's tail just disappearing as he made his dash for liberty.

So *Country Life* and *Horse and Hound* were done out of the marvellous picture they were going to get, and Lady Somebody was in as usual.

However, to get back to the moment when the photograph had actually been taken, I looked at my watch and said, 'Help, it's a quarter past four!' And I remembered I had promised to be at Cecilia's birthday party which began at four. So I dashed off like mad and arrived at the house at a quarter to five. I could see the party inside sitting round the tea table, I flew upstairs, sloshed a bit of water on my hands, dragged a comb through my hair, tore off my shirt and pulled on my blue frock. All this only took about eighteen seconds and then I burst into the dining room feeling as if flames were coming out of my ears and said, 'I'm frightfully sorry I'm late.'

'You certainly are late,' said my aunt with a sort of iciness under the sweetness. 'There's your place,' and I slunk into a chair between two girls I didn't know who didn't offer to pass me anything but just stared, so I helped myself to the last sandwich on the plate, and then Cecilia cut her cake which had pink candles on it and everybody beamed at her and they sang 'Happy Birthday to You' which I thought was too soppy for words.

Then tea was over and we all got up and went to the drawing room to play guessing jumbled fruits, and just as I was wondering why if they had to jumble something they didn't jumble something decent like kinds of horses, there was a roar of laughter and to my horror I realised that everybody was laughing at me!

I couldn't think what was wrong, and then I happened to glance down and the awful truth was revealed. I had forgotten to take off my jodhpurs when I put on my blue frock, and there they were below the blue hem looking most peculiar. I could have gone through the floor, especially when Cecilia said, 'Oh, it's just like Jill, she's quite crazy,' and all the horrible girls from her horrible school tittered

and giggled. All except one who to everybody's surprise said, 'Never mind, Jill – you are called Jill, aren't you? – I know just how you feel because the same thing once happened to me, only much worse because it was at a garden party my mother was giving, all bristling with important people. So just stop laughing everybody.'

And this girl came over to me and said – while all the others listened with pricked-up ears – 'Aren't you the girl who's running a very successful hacking stable over at Matley? I'm awfully interested, do tell me about it. Never mind your jodhpurs, you can take them off after.'

It turned out that her name was Mary Dangerfield and she was the head of the school and terribly popular. What was more Cecilia had a crush on her and everything that Mary did was just right.

So while I was telling Mary about the stable and she was listening in a very interested way, you should have seen Cecilia's face! And after a bit she came up and said, 'Jill knows an awful lot about horses. You don't ride, do you, Mary?'

'Of course I do,' said Mary, 'but I don't suppose I'm a patch on Jill. I've never had the nerve to go in for showjumping!' And then she added, 'Do let me come round to Matley and see your stable some time,' and I said, 'Yes, do come, whenever you like.'

From that day Cecilia and Auntie P. were quite different to me and treated me as the sort of person

Mary Dangerfield thought worth knowing. Which is very silly really, but it just shows you!

And it was much nicer for me and I was jolly glad I'd forgotten to take off my jodhpurs.

14   A great day at the stable

I can't go into details about all the things we did in the next two or three weeks. That is the worst of writing a book, if you put every single thing in it would be as big as an encylopedia, and yet you hate to leave anything out, and quite a lot of funny as well as rather paralysing things happened at the stable that I haven't time to describe.

One thing I must admit is that while we went on doing all the work that had to be done each day we were all secretly deciding that we didn't want to run a stable for the rest of our lives. It is funny how you get cured of things, isn't it? Bar said that she thought she would have a stab at being a commercial artist and doing railway posters which had a fascination for her, and Mike said he still wanted to be a vet because they had somebody to muck out and groom for them, and he thought it would be fun to do things to dogs for a change.

Pat said, 'You'd probably have to set old ladies' parrots' broken legs all the time,' and Mike said he'd quite like even that.

We spent a lot of time improving the horses,

except for Bungie who was past improving. Mike did wonders with Mipsy and Dot, schooling them both for part of each day, while Begorra proved to be a very nice jumper. She was popular with our older clients, as well as with Major Foster who had her out most afternoons.

I spent all the time I could spare with Pedro, because it was such fun to see him gradually remembering things he had been taught in his happier days. He was a nice pony to ride and very appreciative of anything you did for him. We discovered that he understood bending and musical chairs, though he was out of practice of course, and we wondered more than ever about the secret of his past, alas, never to be disclosed. The look of misery had quite gone from his eyes and he was filling out and his coat improving, and he had all the makings of a good pony.

So the weeks sped by, and one day when we were cleaning up at the end of the afternoon Bar said, 'I do wish something would happen to pep things up a bit.'

'Listen to this,' said Pat who was reading the local paper, sitting on an upturned bucket, 'It says, "According to the annual custom, the Earl of Sattingham's stables were open to the public last Saturday in aid of local hospitals. The Police Band was in attendance and rendered selections. Patrons included Lord and Lady – Something, etc. etc. etc." There you are! That's the thing we ought to do, have the stable open for inspection and invite all our clients.'

We looked round at each other to see how the idea was sinking in, and Bar said, 'It would be rather fun. They could bring their parents and things, to make a few more.'

'We'd have to have tea,' said Pat, 'or at least buns and lemonade. I wonder if Agatha would cooperate?'

'What shall it be in aid of?' I asked.

'Oh, horses in general.'

'You can't just say horses in general.'

'Well, say our horses in particular.'

'I'll tell you what,' said Bar, 'that thing Mummy went to at the Institute said "to promote friendship throughout the world". Couldn't we just say, "to promote the welfare of horses throughout the world" and then we could send the money to the Blue Cross?'

'Oh, *bong*!' I said. 'We ought to have some invitation cards. We could buy ordinary postcards and print them ourselves.'

'We could save a bit of money on that,' said Pat practically, 'by using Daddy's sermon paper which is just the right size for invitations and quite thick. I know where there's a whole drawer of it.'

'Will he mind?' I said.

'Oh, I'll stand the racket, if any,' said Pat.

So while Agatha was busy upstairs we all oozed into the absent vicar's study and found a large wad of the sermon paper.

Then we drafted out an invitation which read:

WALTERS AND CREWE LTD
invite you to inspect their model stables
next Wednesday afternoon at 3
Afternoon Tea
Price £1 or anything you like to give
Proceeds in aid of promoting the welfare
of horses
throughout the world

I thought the last sentence might have been better expressed as it wasn't very neat, but we couldn't think of anything better so we let it stand. We all thought that Bar was a bit rash putting in Afternoon Tea without consulting Agatha, but Pat said if the worst came to the worst we could make some lemonade ourselves, and buy a few buns.

However, to our surprise when we approached Agatha she seemed to cotton on to the idea like anything. I suppose she thought it would brighten her dull existence to see the yard glittering with exciting social life, and she said she would make tea and provide the cups and saucers only we would have to buy the food ourselves as the housekeeping didn't stretch to feeding swarms of people.

So then we all sat down round the vicar's desk and started copying out the invitations. We decided to do three dozen and include a few people we knew who weren't exactly clients, like Mary Dangerfield and Uncle Toots' locum.

'We'll have to watch Mike,' said Bar, 'or he'll spell words wrong.'

'I will not!' shouted Mike indignantly.

I kept an eye on him without him noticing me, and he was most careful, looking at the copy card for every single word, but at the end when we had finished it was four of Bar's cards that we had to scrap as she had forgotten the Afternoon Tea line and had spelt 'throughout', throgut.

Next day we distributed the invitations to our clients and they were frightfully thrilled and said they would all come and bring their parents. We then realised what a frightful lot of work we had let ourselves in for, getting the stables ready for inspection. We scrubbed and scoured and polished, and swilled the yard.

We asked Agatha if we could have the tea in the drawing room, but she took a dim view of this, and said that if it was a wet day on Saturday she'd have a week's work taking up the footmarks to say nothing of millions of crumbs trodden into the carpet. Then to soften the blow she said she would find time to make some shortbread biscuits.

'Tell you what,' said Pat, 'we'll put the tea in the harness room. We can take all the stuff out and put the kitchen table in the middle with all the plates of food laid out on it, and everybody can rally round and help themselves like they did at that potty wedding of Cousin Sheila's that Mother made us go to.'

'Oh, yes, a buffet,' I said.

So we made the harness room look as nice as we could, and Agatha said we needn't take the kitchen table, we could have the gate-leg one out of the morning room, so we put it up and laid a clean cloth on it, and Bar and I picked some dahlias and put them in a jug to go in the middle. It looked very nice. However, that same evening, which was the night before the party, a most ghastly thing happened. Over the harness room was the loft where we kept the straw and Mike had gone up to get some, forgetting that the flooring was a bit dicky, and his foot went right through the heaps of plaster and spiders and straw and chaff fell down on the beautiful table underneath.

You never saw such a mess. We groaned and groaned, and then we had to set to work and clean it all up again – which took hours – and Mike had to get round Agatha for another clean cloth, and I didn't get home till half past nine and Auntie P. was far from pleased, and we nearly wished the inspection at blazes.

But the great day dawned at last and it was fine. We had told our clients there would be no riding that morning, and we set to work and groomed the horses till they fairly glittered and washed their tails with Gleemit, of which we had bought ourselves a bottle, seeing how successful it was, and we tethered them all in the paddock in the shade of the trees so that nothing awful could happen to them.

Then Bar and I rushed down to the confectioner's shop in Matley village to buy the food. We bought two dozen teacakes and six dozen mixed buns, which we thought should be enough, but when we got home with them and Agatha saw the teacakes she said, 'What am I supposed to spread on these? Not your father's butter, I hope?'

So we decided to spread jam on them and Mike said he would do it, though he rather overdid it and the jam oozed out and a lot of wasps gathered round, but it might have been worse.

At last everything was ready and it did look good.

I don't know whether you have ever arranged an affair of this kind, but I remember Mummy saying that one of two things always happens, either too few people turn up or too many.

Ours was one of the 'too many' occasions.

I suppose our clients' parents were all interested and wanted to see for themselves what the stable was like, and then people like Mary Dangerfield came because they thought it would be fun, and a lot of public-minded people that we hadn't actually invited came along because they wanted to do something for the welfare of horses throughout the world.

It was all right when they started arriving in twos – because for a minute during our scrappy lunch we had had an awful feeling that perhaps nobody would come at all – but when they started coming in sixes our blood ran cold, as the saying goes.

We thought perhaps they would walk round the stables, cast an eye over the horses in the paddock, eat a bun and go, but they didn't. They stayed, and more and more came.

'What on earth are we going to do with them?' said Bar.

'Oh, let them rip,' I said. 'They're enjoying themselves, strange as it seems.'

The paddock now looked like a showground.

'Shall we start giving rides?' said Pat, and this proved to be an excellent idea. Everybody who was dressed for it – and heaps of people were in shorts or jodhpurs – wanted rides, and presently there was a continuous line of horses going round the paddock.

'This is a great affair!' cried Major Foster, bustling up with Alison and Alison's fond mother. 'Why, the whole neighbourhood is here. You kids ought to congratulate yourselves.'

'Yes, but we don't know what's going to happen when they get to the tea and bun stage,' said Bar. 'We only allowed for about forty and there are at least eighty.'

'Oh, don't worry about that,' said the Major, and he whispered something to Alison's mother who afterwards melted away, and about ten minutes later returned with several bags of cakes.

'Oh, thank you!' cried Bar, rushing off to the harness room to add this wealth to the buffet at which by now some people were hungrily looking.

'You'll never get everybody round that table,' said the Major. 'Why not bring it out into the yard? It will look more festive and everybody will be able to get at it.'

We thought this was a good idea, so the Major and Pat and a few others carried out the table into the middle of the yard, and just then out came Agatha with two enormous pots of tea, the pots being the ones they used at the church for Sunday school teas and harvest suppers and so on.

Mary Dangerfield came up to me and said, 'I do think this is fun. I've had a ride on Ballerina and the Walters boy told me all about you buying Pedro. Isn't Cecilia here?'

'She would have come,' I said, 'but there's a dancing display at her dancing class.'

'What weird tastes some people have!' said Mary in a very friendly woman-to-woman way, and I thought that when I got home at night and told Cecilia that Mary had been there she would be green with fury that she had stayed away for a silly dancing display.

The next minute I heard Mike ringing a bell and everybody stopped talking, and then Major Foster stood up on the old mounting block and said, 'We can hardly let this occasion go by without thanking our hosts and hostesses for this very delightful entertainment they have so kindly arranged for us. Those of us who love horses couldn't ask for any improvements in these model stables and the way the horses here are looked after, and I for one would like to move a vote of thanks to Walters and Crewe Ltd who have the welfare of horses throughout the world so much at heart.'

Everybody clapped like mad, and then Major Foster himself picked up an empty plate – they were all empty by now! – and began taking the collection. The coins simply rained in and it was obvious that everybody was giving more than a penny. (Actually the collection came to one hundred and ninety-three pounds sixty-five and when we had paid ourselves back for the buns and things we sent one hundred and seventy-five pounds seventy-five to the Blue Cross Fund for Horses and got an awfully nice letter back which we stuck up with adhesive tape on the inside of the harness room door.)

Then all of a sudden Bar said, 'Oh, help, here are some more people!'

Eleven latecomers were just coming in at the gate.

'There isn't a thing left to eat,' I said.

'Have you any money?' said Bar.

'Only about one pound sixty,' I said.

'Well, look,' said Bar, 'we can't possibly worry Major Foster with this. You nip down to the shop and get about eighteen mixed cakes as quick as you can, and tell them we'll pay them on Saturday. They ought to know us by now. Meanwhile I'll try and get round Agatha to make just one more pot of tea. We can't possibly spoil this splendiferous do by turning the hungry from our door.'

With that she rushed off to welcome the newcomers

who proved to be Diana and Brenda Prince with their father and mother and kid sister, and a boy called Bill Manners with what looked like the whole of his family.

15 I am knocked for six

I seized the nearest bike — which happened to be Pat's — and did the half-mile to the confectioner's in under two minutes, bought the cakes, and came back pedalling hard up the hill, holding the bag of cakes in one hand and coping with the peculiar steering habits of Pat's bike with the other.

As I got to the gate of the stable yard I noticed a tall, youngish clergyman with black curly hair standing looking in rather a stunned way at the notice board which said Walters and Crewe, Hacks for Hire.

I slid off the bike and said, 'Can I do anything for you?'

'Yes,' he said, 'what's the meaning of this?'

'It's a hacking stable,' I said kindly. 'Walters and Crewe. I'm one of the partners, Crewe.'

'Oh, are you?' he said in a peculiar tone. 'And what are all these people doing?' — waving his hand to the scene of bright activity in the yard where certainly a lot of people seemed to be milling about, though some had gone home by now.

'It's an open day,' I explained. 'There's a tea, and the stables are on view. You can come in if you like.'

'Oh, can I!' he said. I thought he had a very strange manner and seemed to talk in questions.

Just then Pat hove into view leading Pedro with Alison Foster up and Alison's fond mother fluttering around her.

'Patrick!' the clergyman fairly roared. 'Come here this minute!'

Pat looked round.

'Oh, hullo, Daddy,' he said in a rather wilted voice.

Well, actually you could have knocked me for six. So this was the Walters' father! Actually I had always pictured the absent vicar with a long white beard and tottering on two sticks.

Mr Walters strode into the yard and said, 'Where are Barbara and Michael?'

They detached themselves from the crowd, and quite a lot of people said, 'Hullo, Mr Walters', while his three progeny (as children are sometimes called) stood around and waited and I hovered near.

'Now what have you been up to?' said Mr Walters, looking round at all the people and the remains of the tea and horses all over the place, and not unnaturally overcome, having left everything so dead and dirty and peaceful when he went away.

'Oh, please, Daddy, let everybody get away,' said Bar, 'and then we'll explain.'

At last everybody had gone and we were left with just the six horses, and Agatha helping to clear up the cups and things.

'Really!' said the vicar. 'I don't know what the bishop would say.'

'Well, it just depends whether he's in favour of free enterprise,' said Bar, which I thought was rather good. 'We're running a stable and it's very successful and self-supporting and these people who've been here to tea are our clients and their parents and friends, and I do hope you don't mind, Daddy – '

' – because the whole idea,' went on Pat, 'was to make Ballerina earn her keep so you wouldn't sell her when you came back – '

' – and she has done, and I hope you won't,' finished Mike.

'This beats me,' said the vicar. 'Whose idea was it?'

'I'm afraid it was mine,' I said, chipping in for the first time.

'Break it gently,' said the vicar. 'Who are you? How dare you put ideas into my children's innocent minds?'

I began to giggle, and Bar said, 'Innocent minds my foot!'

'I'm Jill Crewe,' I said quite seriously, 'and I'm staying here with my aunt, and I know what it feels like to think you are going to lose your pony because you can't afford to keep him – or her – because I've had it myself, so naturally I had to think of a plan to keep Ballerina from being sold, and this was it.'

'Naturally!' said the vicar. 'Naturally!'

'It was a jolly good plan,' said Pat, 'and it worked.'

'But where on earth did you get all these horses?'

'Three of them are from Uncle Toots,' said Mike, 'and Jill bought the other two for the stable. Begorra's a hunter, isn't she smashing? And I must tell you about Pedro – ' and off he went into an absolute jumble about J. Biggs and all the rest of it.

'And what has Agatha had to say about all this?' asked the vicar.

'Oh, Agatha isn't a bit to blame,' said Bar hastily. 'She was against it from the beginning but of course she couldn't actually stop us.'

'Come in the house,' said the vicar, and we all followed him to the study.

'I've had my breath taken away,' he said, looking round at us, 'but you don't seem to have done anything very frightful. Of course you'd better go and get that board down before your mother comes home tomorrow, and this whole thing will have to stop immediately. The bishop would have a fit.'

We all looked at each other.

'It seems a bit sudden,' said Mike.

'I don't know what the clients will think,' said Pat.

'Never mind that,' said the vicar. 'This is hereby the end of Walters and Crewe, not forgetting the Ltd. I'm glad *something* was limited. This is a vicarage, not a hacking stable or any other kind of stable. Do you know you are not supposed to run commercial enterprises on vicarage property?'

'Good afternoon,' said a sudden voice, and the face and form of Major Foster appeared at the window. 'I suppose you are the vicar?'

'To my sorrow,' said the harassed parent of Bar, Pat, and Mike.

'Well, I'm Major Foster, and I just wanted to tell you that in my opinion these young people have put up a first-class show. I heard what you were saying, and I daresay the whole thing has been a little irregular and will have to come to an end, but I have nothing but praise for the way these four have worked, kept everything clean and on a business footing, and looked after their six horses.'

'Oh, thank you, Major Foster!' cried Pat. 'Did you hear that, Daddy?'

'Well, well!' said the vicar. 'You children seem to have made a good impression on *somebody*.'

'A very good impression,' said Major Foster, suddenly putting one leg over the windowsill and climbing into the room. He then introduced himself properly to Mr Walters and went on. 'If this business is to be wound up here and now, please let me be in at the winding.'

'Oh, thank you, Major Foster,' said Bar, Mike, and I simultaneously.

'You people look a bit blue,' said Major Foster. 'What's the trouble?'

'We've got an awful lot of horses on our hands,' I said, because I felt particularly blue, realising that

Begorra and Pedro were my slightly unwanted property and wondering what on earth I was going to do with them.

'I suppose Bungie and Mipsy and Dot can go back to Uncle Toots',' said Pat, 'but they will find their lives dull after having such a good time with the clients.'

'Oh, Bar,' I said, 'do you think your father will let Begorra and Pedro stay here for just a little while? I don't know what on earth to do with them. I don't really want them for myself, but I can't bear to think of sending them to some sordid auction room where they might even be bought by that foul Mr Biggs or somebody just as soulless. I mean, for the poor things just to have got away from such beastly surroundings into all this, and then to go back again – '

By now I was nearly choking, and I must have sounded frightfully eloquent because Bar snatched at her hanky and even Pat and Mike gave snorts like boys do when they would cry if they weren't boys.

'Jill!' cried the Major. 'I mean, Miss Crewe. Just put all ideas like that out of your head. I've got it all arranged. Nobody is going to ride Begorra but me. She suits me down to the ground, and if you'll sell her to me I'll be proud to have her. Will you?'

'Oh, Major Foster!' I nearly yelled. 'How absolutely terrific of you!'

'And what's more,' he went on, 'I'm going to buy Pedro too, for Alison's birthday present. The kid will love him and he's a grand little pony.'

By this time I was knocked for six, Bar and Pat and Mike were beaming with excitement, and even the vicar said, 'I'm getting interested in this in spite of myself.'

'Now then,' said Major Foster, 'I'm quite sure there isn't going to be any meal in this house tonight suitable for a family reunion and the winding up of a successful business, so I suggest you all come to the George as my guests for dinner.'

This suggestion seemed to us the last word in luxurious goings on, so Bar, Pat, and Mike flew upstairs to wash and change while I went to ring my aunt and see what sort of view she took of it. It turned out that my aunt had heard of Major Foster and he was quite an Important Person – which meant a lot more to her than it did to me because I choose my friends for their niceness and mostly they are quite Unimportant Persons – so she not only said I might go but suggested I should go straight home and change and my uncle would actually run me over to the George in the car! I felt like a film star by now. So we got to the George and the dining room was marvellous, with branching candlesticks coming out of the walls and electric candles that looked just like real ones, and pictures of country scenes hung up, and there were round tables with white cloths and vases of Dorothy Perkins, and real waiters in white coats with table napkins over their arms.

We had a sumptuous dinner and all chose different things to make it more exciting – we thought at first this might be considered a bit rude, but Major Foster said, 'Go ahead' – and finished up with coffee and milk-shakes and a silver dish full of sugared fruits and things. It was terrific.

Then Bar – who was getting a bit keen on art – said, 'Do you think we could go and look at the pictures on the walls?'

So all the Walters went to look at the pictures, but Major Foster said to me, 'Just a minute, I want a word with you, Miss Crewe.'

I stayed behind, and he said, 'Now shall you and I get down to the sordid question of cash?'

'Well, it is rather important,' I said. 'You see, the money I spent on buying Begorra who I did want and Pedro who I didn't want was what Mummy gave me to buy a show-jumper. So all that money's gone now, and Mummy might take a dim view.'

'Very well,' he said. 'Now I don't know what you gave for Begorra, but I know what she's worth to me. I'll give you eight hundred pounds for her.'

'Oh!' I said. 'But I – '

'That's settled,' he said firmly. 'Eight hundred pounds for Begorra. I know what you gave for Pedro, one hundred pounds. But Pedro now is a very different proposition from when you bought him. You've fed him, groomed him, given him some schooling, and made an attractive pony out of him. I'll give you four hundred pounds for him. That makes twelve hundred pounds altogether. Satisfied?'

'Oh, Major Foster,' I said, 'it's too much.'

'Rubbish,' he said. 'I've got two good horses. It's a fair bargain.'

So it was settled. What an evening!

16 There's a coincidence!

I went round to the stable next morning as usual, though I didn't know quite what was going to happen. After all, the horses had to be groomed and fed even if Fate was about to fling them far and wide. We turned them out to grass, and then Bar and I rang up all the clients. It must have cost a lot of money on the telephone account, and I hope the bishop helped out, as in a way it was for his benefit to save him from having a fit.

Then we wandered sort of aimlessly out into the yard where Mike was talking over the gate to Mipsy and saying, 'Oh, poor Mipsy, you're going back to grass feeding and not being groomed any more, oh, poor Mipsy'.

'Won't it seem empty when they've gone?' said Bar. 'I suppose we'll have to take them back before long. I never thought I could get really fond of Bungie and Mipsy and Dot, but I have, and we never got down to calling them Starlight and Cameron and Golden Girl, did we?'

'Do you think your father would mind if we had one last ride?' I said sadly, and Bar said she was sure he wouldn't only he was in his study and hadn't to be disturbed, so we saddled up, and Pat rode Begorra, Bar rode Ballerina, I went on Pedro and Mike on Mipsy, and we had a marvellous canter on the common with the wind streaming through our hair and that wonderful feeling that only riding can give you.

When we got back there were Mr Walters and Major Foster in the yard.

'Here they come!' cried the Major. 'Had a good ride, people? How did my two nags go?'

And as if they knew, Begorra and Pedro made straight for the Major who took lumps of sugar out of his pockets and gave it to them.

'I've got an idea,' he said, 'and that's why I came over. I thought it would wind everything up very nicely if you people came over to Woodbury Hall for tea on Saturday afternoon. My nephew and niece, Alison's parents, extend you a very hearty invitation and that includes Mr and Mrs Walters, and *your* aunt and uncle and cousin, Jill. And my niece is going to invite about twenty people she knows who have ponies and we'll get up a few open events like musical chairs and bending races, so the horses will have to come too. Two of you can ride Begorra and Pedro and then hand them over to me. How does that strike you?'

'How absolutely gorgeous!' Bar and Pat and I yelled in chorus, and Mike said, 'Wow!' and fell flat on his back.

Then he got up again and said, 'Is there going to be jumping? Oh, Major Foster, do let me help to make the jumps.'

'Don't you let him, Major Foster,' said Bar. 'Last time he made some jumps they looked so beastly edible that the ponies just stood still and munched.'

'I don't think we'll have any jumping on Saturday,' said Major Foster, 'because we haven't any jumps at Woodbury Hall, but you might be drafting out a schedule of the sort of events that anybody can go in for, regardless of age or type of pony.'

Then he took me on one side and handed me a bulgy envelope, saying, 'There's your money, in twenty-pound notes. Would you like to count it and see it's right?'

'Oh, I don't think I'll bother,' I said, and he laughed.

'Now put it carefully in your pocket,' he said, as though I were six, 'and when you get home give it to your aunt to take care of.'

What an idea!

When I got home and told Auntie P. and Cecilia about the invitation to Woodbury Hall on Saturday they were thrilled, but instead of helping me with ideas for some events in the pony show they could talk about nothing but what they would wear. As if anybody would look at them when there were ponies to watch!

Then Cecilia whispered something to Auntie P. and they both laughed mysteriously and began to whisper and giggle, and I thought they were slightly crazy but was too busy wondering how I was going to round up enough clean handkerchiefs for the handkerchief race to care about anything else.

Needless to say, everybody spent the whole of the next day, which was Friday, saying, 'Do you think it is going to be fine tomorrow?' because it looked a bit doubtful. However, the Met Office must have relented and sent the deep depression packing off to Iceland or somewhere because Saturday turned out to be a lovely day with a slight mist in the morning and the sun just breaking through.

By one o'clock it was blazing, and I was ready dressed in my clean shirt and coat and jodhpurs, my boots polished by the gentle hand of Doris and rubbed up by my own, and I had done my hair in one plait and turned it up and tied it in a rather sophisticated way that Bar had showed me.

'You had better go on ahead, Jill,' said my aunt, 'and we will come along in the car later, probably about four o'clock.'

And she looked at Cecilia and they both giggled.

'That's awfully late,' I said to Cecilia, when she came to the door to see me off, 'you'll miss most of the events, but you'll be in time for tea,' and I thought that was probably all she cared about, which was misjudging her as you will see.

Everybody was buzzing around excitedly when I got to the stables.

'Oh, isn't it splendid,' shouted Bar. 'Daddy says

we can keep Ballerina. So everything has been worth while, and it was all your idea in the first place and we're frightfully grateful, because if we had never met you we should still have been feebly moaning on a gate and Ballerina led away to the slaughter.'

'You'd have thought of something,' I said. 'How are we for money now the stable is closing down?'

'Just about evened out,' said Bar. 'There's forty pounds owing to you which I'll give you today. And actually there's quite a lot of oats and bran and hay and stuff which belongs to us jointly.'

'Oh, no,' I said. 'You keep that, Bar, please. It will give Ballerina a good start for the winter.'

'That's awfully decent of you,' said Bar. 'Now I actually haven't a care in the world. I do think the whole thing has been fun, don't you?'

'Terrific,' I agreed. 'Whatever should I have done if I hadn't met you people?'

Just then Mrs Walters – who had arrived home the day before – came out with a tray with glasses of iced lemonade which made a lovely start for the afternoon. She had on a grey skirt and blue blouse and looked much younger and prettier than vicars' wives usually look, owing to their cares. She and Mr Walters were going to bike over to Woodbury Hall while we rode the horses.

'You do look nice,' she said to us all, 'and don't a lot of horses give an exciting look to a place? I never realised it before.'

I entirely agreed with this noble sentiment and liked Mrs Walters ever after for saying it.

Then we all prepared to move off. I was riding Pedro again, as I had got used to him and wanted to be the one to try him in the pony events, and Bar had got Begorra, Pat was on Ballerina, and Mike on Mipsy. At the last minute we decided to take Bungie and Dot along too, to see the fun, so we led them.

Woodbury Hall was only about two miles away and was a lovely place with a large field at the side, just made for pony races, and a long line of what looked like stables at the side but proved to be nothing but sordid garages. Think of anybody being so soulless as to have stables and turn them into garages! But now that Alison was getting Pedro they would have to start turning them back into stables again, which was a step in the right direction.

Everything looked very jolly, only I knew there was going to be trouble when I saw Alison in a pair of new jodhpurs and a riding hat miles too big for her, and she made one wild dash for Pedro, taking it for granted she was going to ride. Of course, I had to let her, and in the end I swallowed my disappointment and got up on Dot with my feet nearly touching the ground. I had wanted to try Pedro in the events for the first time, but after all he was going to be Alison's pony. Actually as it turned out, Alison couldn't keep her seat more than five minutes and Pedro wasn't any use without a skilled rider and they were last in everything, but they enjoyed themselves so much that I didn't mind any more, and Alison's mother said, 'Don't they look a lovely little pair? I'm sure they'll be winning everything together in a year or two.'

I had my doubts, but I do think the main thing in life is letting everybody be happy in their own way.

The lawn in front of the house was dotted with tea tables, and in the show field the poles were set up for the handkerchief race, and altogether it was a thrilling scene. About twenty people had brought ponies of all types and sizes, and among them was Mary Dangerfield who came up and talked to me very chummily. She looked at Dot and laughed and said, 'You believe in keeping near the ground, don't you?' so I explained and we both laughed together.

In the end, Bar, Pat, Mike and I got together and decided to pool horses and ride the better ones in turns. But when it came to the events Dot surprised us all. Not for nothing had she been ridden at many pony shows by the vet's daughter in her palmy days. She remembered her stuff, and Mike won the egg-and-spoon race on her while I was second in the bending.

Bar was first in the bending with Ballerina, and Pat was first in the flag race on Begorra, and I was first in the blindfold rider race on Mipsy.

By half-past three everybody was breathless but happy, and though I had looked several times out of the corner of my eye I knew my aunt's party had not arrived which rather disappointed me.

'Now for the prizes,' said Major Foster. 'Everybody line up.'

It turned out that there were four prizes for each event, so everybody got at least one, even Alison who had won the Crazy Costume race, simply because everybody else had fallen off their ponies with laughter and she had stuck solemnly on and passed the post.

The prizes turned out to be very nice things. I got a silver propelling pencil that wrote red and green as well as black, and Bar got a wallet and diary all in one. Pat got a riding stick, and Mike a book called *Two Boys and a Pony in Wild Wales*. Mary Dangerfield got a yellow tie and Alison got a pair of string gloves.

'And now,' said Major Foster, 'before we have tea – for which everybody is dying – we'll have a Grand Parade. Twice round the field, please.'

So we took ten minutes to spruce up ourselves and the ponies, just like at a real show, and then we rode round in a ring carrying our prizes, and all the guests – for most people's parents were there – cheered and clapped. It was the best affair I had been to for ages.

Just as we completed the second round of the field I happened to glance towards the drive, and there drawing to a standstill was my uncle's car. It stopped, and out got my aunt, then Cecilia, and then not my uncle but somebody in a grey dress and a white hat.

My heart jumped right up in the air, turned over,

and flopped back again. I couldn't believe it. I was dreaming or else I really had gone mad.

Then somehow I had tumbled off Mipsy and was whizzing across the grass pulling the astonished Mipsy with me and shouting, 'Mummy! oh, Mummy!'

Yes, it was my mother, back from America. I still couldn't believe it.

'It's our surprise,' said Cecilia. 'We knew she was coming today, and we were going to the station to meet her at half-past three. We didn't tell you to make it more of a thrill.'

'I caught an earlier boat,' said Mummy, as we exchanged bear hugs.

'Well, if this isn't the most magnificent day of my life!' I said.

Ten minutes later we were sitting round a table on the lawn having tea, and I was doing most of the talking, telling Mummy all about the stable. Her story about America would keep till later.

Long before I got to the part about buying Begorra and Pedro she interrupted me and said, 'By the way, you haven't bought a show-jumper yet, have you, Jill?'

'No, Mummy,' I said.

'That's good,' she said. 'Because on the boat coming back I met some people who told me of a pony they have for sale. He seems just the thing for you – a show-jumper who has done well for their daughter but she is too old for the children's classes now. They would like you to go over and give him a trial. Of course they want rather a lot of money for him – twelve hundred pounds – '

She stopped and looked at me as though expecting me to say something.

'Gosh!' I said. 'Now *there's* a coincidence!'

A Complete list of the JILL SERIES by Ruby Ferguson

Read the exciting adventures of Jackie and
her pony, by Judith M. Berrisford.

These are the adventures of the famous Black
Stallion and his friend Alec that are available
in Knight

Walter Farley
The Black Stallion
The Black Stallion Revolts
The Black Stallion Returns
The Black Stallion and Satan
Son of the Black Stallion
The Black Stallion's Courage
The Black Stallion's Filly
The Black Stallion Mystery
The Black Stallion and Flame
The Black Stallion's Ghost
The Black Stallion's Challenge
The Black Stallion and the Stranger
The Black Stallion Legend
The Young Black Stallion